The Taint of Midas

ANNE ZOUROUDI was born in England and lived for some years in the Greek islands. Her attachment to Greece remains strong, and the country is the inspiration for much of her writing. She now lives in the Derbyshire Peak District with her son. She is the author of four other Mysteries of the Greek Detective: *The Messenger of Athens* (shortlisted for the ITV3 Crime Thriller Award for Breakthrough Authors and long-listed for the Desmond Elliot Prize), *The Doctor of Thessaly*, *The Lady of Sorrows* and *The Whispers of Nemesis*.

BY THE SAME AUTHOR

The Messenger of Athens
The Doctor of Thessaly
The Lady of Sorrows
The Whispers of Nemesis

The Taint of Midas

Anne Zouroudi

BLOOMSBURY

LONDON · BERLIN · NEW YORK · SYDNEY

First published in 2008

This paperback edition published 2011

Copyright © 2008 by Anne Zouroudi

Map on p. vii © John Gilkes 2008

The moral right of the author has been asserted

Bloomsbury Publishing Plc
36 Soho Square,
London W1D 3QY

Bloomsbury Publishing, London, New York, Berlin and Sydney

A CIP catalogue record for this book
is available from the British Library

ISBN 978 1 4088 2491 7
10 9 8 7 6 5 4 3 2 1

Typeset by Hewer Text UK Ltd, Edinburgh
Printed by Clays Ltd, St Ives plc

MIX
Paper from
responsible sources
FSC® C018072
FSC
www.fsc.org

For Will, with love

Dramatis Personae

Gabrilis Kaloyeros – a bee-keeper and small-holder
Maria – his wife (recently deceased)

Hermes Diaktoros – the Fat Man, known to Gabrilis as The Professor
Kokkona – the Fat Man's housekeeper
Sostis – a barber with a preference for fishing
Ilias Mentis – a lawyer with responsibility for the Fat Man's affairs

Aris Paliakis – a property developer, and owner of the Taverna Delfini
Ourania Paliakis – Aris's wife
Pandelis Paliakis – Aris's eldest son, a lawyer
Kylis Paliakis – Aris's younger son
Aris Paliakis Snr – Aris's grandfather (deceased)
Father Babis – a priest and close friend of Ourania Paliakis
Sotiris, Grigor & Sonya – staff at the Taverna Delfini
Telma Lalagi – a singer known as the Songbird
Haroula & Katina – ladies of the night
Costas & Vassilis – customers of Sostis the barber

Manolis Alfieris – a planning officer
Messrs Routsis, Horiatis & Fitrakis – employees of government departments

Thanos Gazis – a police sergeant
George Petridis – a police constable
Yorgia – Petridis's girlfriend
Dinos Karayannis – a radio news journalist
Manos Vrettos – driver of a car involved in an accident

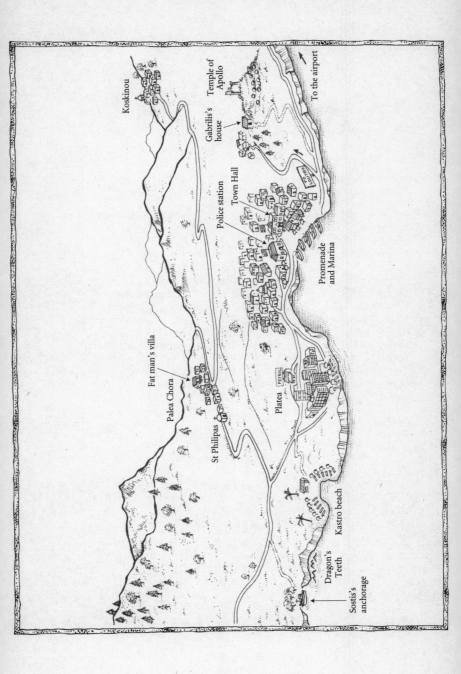

Koskinou

Temple of Apollo

To the airport

Gabrilis's house

Police station

Town Hall

Promenade and Marina

Fat man's villa

Palea Chora

St Philipas

Platea

PETROL

Kastro beach

Dragon's Teeth

Sostis's anchorage

The rich poor fool, confounded with surprise,
Starving in all his various plenty lies:
Sick of his wish, he now detests the pow'r,
For which he ask'd so earnestly before;
Amidst his gold with pinching famine curst;
And justly tortur'd with an equal thirst.
At last his shining arms to Heav'n he rears,
And in distress, for refuge, flies to pray'rs.
O father Bacchus, I have sinn'd, he cry'd,
And foolishly thy gracious gift apply'd;
Thy pity now, repenting, I implore;
Oh! may I feel the golden plague no more.
The hungry wretch, his folly thus confest,
Touch'd the kind deity's good-natur'd breast;
The gentle God annull'd his first decree,
And from the cruel compact set him free.

'The Legend of King Midas'
Ovid, *Metamorphoses, Book XI*

One

Blind eyes bear no witness.

At the hilltop, a breeze stirred the branches of the pine trees, and twenty hives were cool beneath their shade. All were painted yellow, their legs and edges picked out in red, and each bore a number on its side. And on each hive roof, a painted eye stared up towards the sky – a woman's eye, exotic like the kohl-rimmed eyes of yashmaked faces, the whites very bright, the irises brash blue. They were the eyes of hieroglyphs in Egyptian tombs – but these eyes watched the living, not the dead. They kept a vigil, warding off the Evil Eye: one for each hive, deflecting the badness of ill-wishers from the bees.

The breeze carried the scent of the summer sea – salt, wet rock, the soft decay of marine debris – and on the water far below the swell peaked in light foam. Close inshore, a speed-boat left a wake of white; far out by the distant islands, a small yacht raised its sail.

At the hill summit, amongst the stones that marked the outline of the ruin, even the turquoise-tailed lizards took shelter from the sun. The depleted spring was just a trickle, though the trough where the waters collected was always full; damp from splashing there, Manyiatis (an ageing, ugly dog) bent his head round to his flank, tugging at the burrs stuck in his coat.

Ants ran amongst the breadcrumbs on the tabletop; wasps settled on the fish bones on the plate. Gabrilis Kaloyeros had sat too long at lunch, time slipping by whilst he indulged in memories. Still, all must be in place by 5, and nothing was ready; each day he found it harder to keep moving. An ant tickled the liver-spotted skin of his hand, traversing the ridged veins and arthritic knuckles to where, above his wrist, the bruises coloured like aubergines (the bruises came from nothing, from the lightest knocks and bumps) had still not healed.

He rose unwillingly from his chair, and leaned a moment on its back until the breathlessness passed. Above his head, the vine shading the verandah was full of grapes, but with no Maria to hold the ladder steady, climbing up to cut them would be madness. So, like the fox in Aesop's fable, he told himself the grapes were sour, and made his way inside.

The house was small – a single room – but Maria was gone, and without her care nothing was as it used to be. Dead flies floated in the chamber pot he used at night, and in the heat the stale urine stank. His clothes lay rank and dirty in the corners until he put them on again unwashed. Though he'd lit no fire since spring, the fireplace was filled with wood-ash and soot-falls, and mice were nesting amongst the winter blankets stored beneath the bed.

His baseball cap lay on the tangled sheets. The cap had been a gift when the professor last visited, and when it was new, the Post Office insignia – the letters *ELTA*, and a stylised head of Hermes in his winged helmet – were bright on its blue cotton. The blue was faded now, and without Maria's washing, salt-marks from his forehead's sweat lined its inner rim. When the professor gave Gabrilis the gift, they'd had a drink from the bottles the professor had brought up from his vineyards. Laughing, he'd waved his hands over the hat: installing charms, he said, protection from the idiots on the roads. And then he became serious, and made Gabrilis promise he would wear it every time he went out on the highway. *I'm a superstitious man*, he said, *so humour me, old friend*. The promise was an easy one to keep; the cap was easy-wearing as old slippers. But the memory of that evening was from years ago – seven summers at least had come and gone – and the cap's peak had lost its stiffness, the stitching in the seams was loose and ragged. The professor had been gone too long, this time; sadly, he'd find – if he returned – that the news here in Arcadia wasn't good. Everything was changing for the worse; the olive groves they used to walk were being felled, so the land could be turned over to a new, more profitable crop: foreigners. This small place, though, remained untouched; the professor, with his interest in the ruins, would be glad, at least, of that. And the bees were doing well, the honey yield improving year by year, so if he came this summer he could judge between the orange flower and the thyme. But there'd be no Maria to serve him her *yiouvetsi*; that she'd passed on was more bad news to break.

He pulled on the cap, and hitched up his drooping trousers from hips to skinny waist. He'd lost his belt again, not noticing it slip from the chair-back under the table, and without his glasses (they, too, had disappeared, and, like so many things he lost, seemed unlikely to be found) he couldn't pick his belt out from the shadows.

Outside, he made his slow way down the path through the trees. The day's heat was at its height, filled with the shrilling of cicadas. Close to the hives, the roar of bees was loud, and he listened as he passed to check the swarms were well. The bees in turn showed their interest in him; they crawled across

3

his back and on his chest, flew gently buzzing round his head and face, and he, untroubled, wafted them away.

Below the last of the pines – where the path met the steep track up from the road – was level ground. Here, Gabrilis kept his tricycle, a heavy, antique contraption acquired for a handful of coins at the war's end. The wicker basket on its handlebars was stacked with tins of honey, the hand-built, two-wheeled trailer at its rear was emptied and ready. He wheeled the tricycle to the high wire fence put up to keep out goats, but at the gate his hands would not be steady, his eyes would not hold focus, and he struggled to fit the small key to the padlock. The lock clicked open at last, and he stepped into his garden, on to the terraces where the watermelons and cantaloupes grew.

The professor claimed the terraces were ancient, used centuries ago for vines and wheat, and when he spoke of how it was, his words were eloquent. As if he'd seen with his own eyes, he painted pictures of the temple in its glory, the hillsides cultivated and fertile, and a prosperous town where there was nothing now but scrub. Under Gabrilis's care, the level, orderly rows were flourishing again, the plants' great leaves providing shade for healthy, heavy fruit. At the terrace ends were piled the stones cleared from the soil; most were the rough rocks of the hillside, but amongst them, smooth as eggshells, fragments of marble showed the stripes of mighty pillars or the remnants of skilled carving: leaves, fruit, petals, and on one a woman's face, without a nose but still beautiful, set high up on a fence-post to watch the passing boats. Sometimes his digging turned up artefacts: terracotta beads with flakes of pretty glaze, a tiny statuette without its base, a beckoning marble finger, finely made and long as a man's hand. Everything Gabrilis found he'd shown to the professor, but at the question of museums, the professor laughed. *They*

4

are relics of this place, he said, *and here's where they should stay*, so they wrapped the pieces carefully in straw and oil-cloth, and buried them in a hole behind the spring.

The sun was blazing, and its heat was intense; the stains of sweat spread at Gabrilis's armpits, and on his bony back his shirt was damp. The watermelons lay fat amongst their foliage, their green, cream-mottled skins fresh on the powdery dirt. He bent, and rolled one side to side to gauge its weight; judging it ready, he reached down amongst the prickling leaves and, with a kitchen knife, sliced through the stem. He wrapped his arms around the melon, and heaved it to his chest, labouring with it to the tricycle and laying it carefully in the trailer.

But as he went to cut a second melon, Manyiatis struggled barking to his feet.

Listening, Gabrilis heard what had disturbed Manyiatis: the pop and snap of stones beneath a vehicle's tyres. As the sound grew louder, Manyiatis's bark grew bolder, and he limped a few arthritic steps towards the track; but Gabrilis whistled, and ordered silence, and Manyiatis, wearied by barking, was glad to sit.

Around the bend in the track, navigating with care around the pits and potholes, a sleek new car appeared, its silver gloss dull with chalky dust. To maintain its air-conditioned cool-ness, the car's grey-tinted windows were tightly closed; an orchestra playing Skalkatos on the sound system was muted behind the windows' seal. The car stopped; the engine and the music were switched off. With the noise gone, the cicadas' rhythmic shrilling seemed intense.

A young man stepped from the car. He smiled, but his eyes were hidden behind dark glasses, and Gabrilis thought of flies' eyes, which seemed sightless but saw everything, from every angle. The young man's shirtsleeves were rolled above his wrists, his collar was open at the neck, his buff-coloured trousers held a knife-pleat even in the heat. He seemed a handsome man, but as he drew close to Gabrilis his flaws became clear. With not a touch of tan, his skin was pale as an invalid's, and where a man his age should be muscled there was flaccidity and fat, so his chin – which could have been noble – appeared weak, and an older man's soft stomach spilled over his trouser-belt.

Attempting another challenge, Manyiatis gave a single bark and trotted growling after the young man. But the young man's stride was quick, and Manyiatis, noticing the coolness of the tricycle's shadow, gave up and lay down there instead.

The young man reached the fence, and shouted a greeting through the wire.

'*Kali spera, kyrie!* How are you, Mr Kaloyeros?'

Gabrilis squinted, and focusing his cloudy, red-rimmed eyes, recognised his visitor. He bent to a watermelon, searching amongst its drying leaves for the umbilical length of stalk and slicing it through. As he lifted the melon, heavy as a small child, into his arms, a bee resting on an opening flower took flight. Gabrilis made his struggling way towards the gate, where Pandelis Paliakis waited.

Pandelis spoke through the fence, as though the old man was imprisoned.

'That's hot work,' he said. Sweat was beginning to glaze his forehead. 'Perhaps you'd like to talk in my car. It's cooler there.' As he spoke, on the breeze he caught the old man's smell, intense and musky sweat strong as a billy goat's, and his smile faded.

But Gabrilis shook his head.

'I don't have time, sir,' he said with regret. 'Unfortunately. Hot or not, I've work to do.'

He passed through the gate, and dropped the melon into the trailer with the first.

'Then I'll be brief,' said Pandelis. 'There's bad news, and there's good. The bad news is, as we expected, a compulsory purchase order is to be issued on your land. The good news is my father's agreed that, as our family's affected by a similar proposal, we should file a joint action to fight the town council. I'll be handling the case, as I explained the other day. So I'll just need your signature to say I have the power to act for you – I have the papers in the car – and I'll get on to it straight away.'

'It's a bad business,' said Gabrilis, 'when land you've lived on a lifetime can't be called your own. I built that house myself, over fifty years ago. I built it with these hands, every last brick and every plank of wood.' He offered his palms to Pandelis; their lines were dark with dirt, the nails were black and broken. 'I haven't a daughter to leave it to, that's the pity. A daughter would take care of me, now I'm old. You'll have daughters, I'm sure.'

'I'm not married.'

'You should be. You're old enough. Your mother should arrange it. I'm not so old I don't remember how it goes. There'll be some young lady you've got your eye on, isn't there?'

But Pandelis seemed not to hear the question.

'I'm confident the council's case is flawed,' he said. 'Please don't worry. I have every confidence we'll win.'

Gabrilis looked up at him with tearful eyes.

'What I don't understand is why they want my land. It's only good for farmland – you can see that – and it's hard work, even then. What do they want it for? It's not much use to anyone but me.'

A bee landed on Pandelis's forearm. His face creased with worry, and he swiped it away.

'I believe,' he said evasively, 'they want to build a phone mast. It's the elevation.'

7

'But I don't have a phone,' said Gabrilis. 'Never thought I needed one. Maria always wanted a phone. I don't know who she thought she was going to be ringing up.'

In Pandelis's trouser pocket a mobile phone trilled. He took it out and glanced at its tiny screen, then flipped it open.

'Yes? . . . Not now . . . Tomorrow. I said tomorrow . . . No . . . No, I haven't forgotten . . . I'll call you later, OK?' He slipped the phone back into his pocket. 'Lawyers,' he said. 'They drive you crazy. Look, my father says you're not to worry about the money. There'll be nothing for you to pay. He tells me we have a family connection. Your sister's husband was my father's second cousin, I believe.'

In puzzlement, Gabrilis frowned.

'Which sister does he mean, sir? I had three sisters. They were all younger than me, and I've outlived them all. Now is that a blessing or a curse? Diana was the last of them alive. What was her husband called?' He couldn't remember, but Pandelis was in any case walking away. At his car, he took a sheet of paper from the glovebox, and a silver fountain pen from his calfskin briefcase.

Gabrilis leaned on the handlebars of his tricycle. His breathing was laboured, his colour was high. Pandelis came to his side, uncapping the pen and pointing to the line where Gabrilis should sign.

'I'll be all right in a minute,' said Gabrilis. 'It's the heat that takes it out of you.'

'Just there,' said Pandelis. 'I'll date it for you later.'

Gabrilis didn't read the document, because he couldn't; his eyes were bad, and anyway, he wasn't a reading man. He held the paper on his palm and made his mark: not quite a signature, but a scribble he had perfected for such times as these.

Pandelis took the paper, blew on the ink to dry it and recapped the pen.

'Don't worry,' he said. 'Everything will turn out in our favour. If nothing else, we'll stretch it in the courts. Four years, my record is so far. Let's see if we can beat it.'

'Four years,' echoed Gabrilis. 'That's a long time, at my age. God may not grant me another four years.'

'I'll let you know when there's news.'

Pandelis turned away, but Gabrilis touched his arm.

'A moment before you go. Would you mind just helping me with one small thing? Will you cut me a few grapes off that vine? Just a few. They're lovely fruits, and the wasps are getting the best of them. You're welcome to cut some for yourself, of course. Take some for your father, with my compliments. It'll only take a minute of your time.'

Pandelis looked up towards the house, where the vine spread wide over the verandah, and glanced anxiously at his watch. He hesitated. Then, removing his sunglasses, he smiled.

'I'm late already, and my father will in any case be angry,' he said, 'so I suppose five minutes more will make no difference. And – who knows? – a few grapes might sweeten his temper.' He laid a hand on the old man's shoulder. 'We must be quick, but show me the way, and I'll cut them for you. But I warn you, I'm not much of a climber, so promise me you'll hold the ladder steady.'

Gabrilis watched until Pandelis's car was out of sight. Picking out a third melon, he wondered if he should have said that there were papers. Whether they'd help the case or not, he wasn't sure; he could produce them if it seemed that they were needed.

9

In the meantime, he'd keep them safe, in their hiding place with its formidable guardians.

Down on the coast road, the horizon was unstable as a mirage, rippling in the super-heated air. At the edges of the softening blacktop, the surplus tar was sticky liquid; here and there along the carriageway, the hot tarmac swelled in domes like buboes. Before the road improvements, this journey smelled of thyme and sage-brush. Now the stink was chemical, of melting pitch, burned diesel and the fumes of car exhausts. When the road was poor, the traffic travelled slowly. There was no need for caution now; the way was smooth, and from airport to resort took only half the time.

Gabrilis's journey-time had not decreased. He cycled carefully, straining to keep the gearless tricycle moving on the uphill gradients, squeezing on the brakes to prevent his heavy cargo from carrying him away on the downhill stretches. He kept close to the road's edge, though on the town-bound journey the drop down to the sea was treacherously close. And, siren-like, the sea drew him; the lure of cool, blue water was strong, and if his eyes strayed there, he found his wheels directed to the steep, rocky slopes down to the bay.

The landmarks of his route had changed. These days, he measured his progress by the building sites, counting off the barely begun, never-to-be-finished ruins: grey-rendered, prison-block walls, empty window openings and the iron spikes ready for the upper storeys bent and rusty. The builders were long gone, but their rubble and their rubbish was still here, in roadside mounds of beer bottles and empty cans, of hardened cement and cigarette packets, of hamburger cartons and the paper wraps of sandwiches.

At the two-mile mark, opposite a Vespa with deflated, perished tyres, the wires from its electrics dangling loose, its saddle ripped with yellow foam exposed, there was a chapel. Gabrilis made the triple cross over his heart, and cycled on. A car swerved round him, its driver showing a hand out of the window, maybe a greeting, maybe a curse. Another car passed, and another. A motorbike roared by. He wiped away the sweat that stung his eyes and pedalled on.

A navy-blue liveried taxi was travelling towards him, airport-bound, and a the taxi drew close, the blast of a horn came from behind, and a coach pulled out wide to overtake the tricycle, encroaching on the taxi's share of the carriageway. The taxi-driver hit his horn; the coach moved back towards Gabrilis, so close its great flank blocked out the light as it slid by him, and as it pulled away its slipstream carried off his precious cap, dropping it in the caper bushes at the roadside.

Gabrilis cycled slowly to where his hat lay, and stopped. The road was, for the moment, quiet; as he climbed off his tricycle, there was just a single vehicle coming over the hill's brow. He took his cap from the caper bush, and with the backs of his fingers knocked the dust from it. Far below, the heat had laid its calming hand on the sea, so the limpid water seemed still and soothing, and he thought of home, of his bed and sleep.

The approaching vehicle was growing close. There was dust on his shoes too, and he bent to wipe it off. When the vehicle changed course, he was busy with his shoes, and didn't see it.

It hit him hard, and took the tricycle and trailer with him. The melons bounced down the hillside until they burst, spattering their red flesh on the sharp stones. The tricycle rolled twice, and then was caught and held amongst the largest rocks.

Gabrilis himself didn't go far: just far enough to be unseen by passing traffic. He was on his back, his broken arm bent painfully beneath him. A little blood trickled from his nose.

Time passed; the pain diminished. Above him on the road, a refuse truck was followed by a moped, whilst, down amongst the thorny capers and thyme bushes, Gabrilis lay unmoving, his eyes staring blindly at the brilliant sun.

Two

The evening was slipping into twilight, the day's heat was mellowing into the humidity of a breezeless summer night. As they sped down the coast road, Sergeant Thanos Gazis watched the sunset's red fanfare in sideways glances; scarlet and orange lit the black of the still-warm asphalt, its chemical miasma obscuring the scent of herbs he remembered on this road as a boy.

Traffic was light, but PC Petridis switched on the blue lights and the siren anyway; he claimed it was a good way to impress the girls. Gazis rested his arm on the sill of his open window, but there was no coolness in the through-draught, and inevitably the starched crispness of his pale-blue uniform shirt was softening into creases.

'For God's sake, Petridis,' he said. 'Put the air con on.'

'I'd rather not, sir, if you don't mind,' said Petridis. His accent was from the islands: dropped syllables, incorrect vowels. 'My grandmother says air conditioning gives you dry spots on your lungs. That's what causes TB. And pneumonia.'

Gazis slowed for a light that was against them. Petridis reached for the soundbox and switched the siren to double time, halting the traffic. Gazis manoeuvred them through the junction, and Petridis switched the siren back to its normal wail.

'Does your grandmother have a medical qualification, then?' asked Gazis.

'In what way, sir?'

'If she's such an expert on lung disease, presumably she's a qualified medical practitioner?'

Petridis considered.

'Not an official one, sir. She delivers a lot of babies, though. We should be getting close now, shouldn't we? That was the turn for Loutro we just passed.'

On the seaward edge of the road, a car was angled towards the water. Gazis signalled and crossed over the carriageway to pull up in front of a red Namco Pony, nosing up close so there'd be no easy getaway.

'Namco,' said Petridis. There was respect and admiration in his voice. 'Did you know these are the only Greek cars still in production, sir? Good cars, they are. Real workhorses, go through anything. My uncle's got one he's had twenty years; never had a thing wrong with it.'

'Poor man's Jeep,' said Gazis, 'good for nothing except export to our country cousins. Only Romanians and Bulgarians'll buy them. Look at it. It's a cross-breed, can't even decide whether it's a saloon or a pick-up.'

Gazis switched off the siren, killed the engine and turned the rear-view mirror to check his close-cut hair. Petridis, already out of the car, approached the Pony. Of its owner, there was no sign. Executing a slow circle of the car, he peered inside and bent to inspect the tyres. By the time he reached the driver's door, Gazis, straightening his collar, was waiting for him.

'Save your pennies, one day you could have a runabout like that,' said Gazis, sarcastically. 'Personally, I'd rather take a

14

bus. It's in good nick, though. Clean. Usually these things are all goat shit and muck. Where's it registered?'

A slight pinkness travelled up Petridis's cheeks.

'I didn't notice, sir,' he said.

Without glancing at the plates, Gazis recited the Athens licence number.

'Basic rule of policing, to make a mental note of the registration. If he'd taken off when he saw us and we didn't have the number, we might have looked pretty incompetent, don't you think? Though God help us if we couldn't run down this heap of junk.'

'He might have shot out our tyres,' said Petridis.

'You watch too much TV, son,' said Gazis. 'And it'd be a poor criminal who'd use a Namco Pony to make a getaway.'

'Looks like he's made his getaway without it,' said Petridis. 'No sign of any driver.'

'He won't be far away,' said Gazis. 'We passed no pedestrians on the road. As you'll no doubt have observed.'

Petridis looked up and down the highway. Despite the fading light, the carriageway both towards the airport and back towards town was still visible to the horizon. As far as they could see, there was no one.

Gazis moved to where the rubble left by the road-builders joined the rough hillside terrain. Over the water, a single seabird was silhouetted against the flaming-red sky. Below his feet, he saw what they had come to find.

An old man lay on his back amongst the mountain shrubs. The crookedness of his limbs, the trickle of dried blood under his nose, his wide and vacant eyes left Gazis in no doubt he was looking at a corpse.

On a rock by the old man's head sat a second man, head bowed, hand covering his eyes. His curly hair was greying and in need of a cut; he wore a well-tailored suit in cream linen which did much to conceal his corpulence, but the effect of the elegant suit was ruined, in Gazis's eyes, by the old-fashioned white-canvas tennis shoes on the fat man's feet. On one broad thigh, tortoiseshell-framed glasses were straddled, reflecting the sunset in their lenses. And here and there, on the slope down to the sea, were the splattered green and pink remains of several watermelons, and the wreckage of what Gazis assumed to be a bicycle.

From behind Gazis, Petridis moved forward for a better view.

'What's happened here?' he asked. There was excitement in his voice; here was a story for his family when he got off shift. But Gazis sighed with the weariness of experience; it was clear there was going to be an awful lot of paperwork before the night was through.

'I have no idea,' he said, 'but it doesn't look good. Go and check what the status is on the ambulance.'

Petridis left Gazis at a run, whilst Gazis himself scrambled down to where the fat man sat, disturbing as he did so a rattling shower of stones and earth. The fat man lifted his head showing cheeks wet with tears. Seeing Gazis, he wiped his eyes on the back of his hand and put on his glasses; they gave him an owlish look, an academic innocence which in no way fitted the sophistication of his clothes.

Gazis crouched beside the old man's body and put two fingers on his neck. There was no pulse; he had expected none. He ran his eyes over the corpse, looking for obvious injuries. The old man's clothes were worn and dirty; there were buttons missing on the cheap cotton shirt, stains on his trousers. There was, too, a stink about him which wasn't the first whiff of decay; though that was present, it was only slight, and Gazis guessed the old man hadn't been dead too long: hours rather than days. But the presence of any decay at all surprised him. He had taken this to be straightforward, a traffic collision and a remorseful culprit. Now, it seemed, if that were the case, the fat man had sat with the body for hours – two or three at least – before calling the police. And given the day's heat, that seemed unlikely.

Gazis addressed the fat man.

'Move away from the body, please, sir,' he said. 'Without touching it, just step away.'

The fat man stood. He was tall, and his height seemed to diminish his weight, so he seemed not fat, but big.

'How did this happen?' asked Gazis. 'Are you injured at all?'

'You're making the wrong assumption,' said the fat man. His speech was beautifully enunciated, clear and perfect as the Greek of TV newscasters. 'I was not involved in this accident. It was I who found the body. I stopped someone on the road and asked him to call 100 on his mobile phone. I do not own a mobile phone myself. But I am in no way responsible for Gabrilis's death.'

'Gabrilis? You know this man, then?'

'He is Gabrilis Kaloyeros, one of my oldest friends. He has a smallholding at the site of the ancient Temple of Apollo at Mavrovouni. He has – had – a stall selling watermelons on the harbour promenade in town.'

Gazis looked closely at the corpse's face. The fat man's identification was correct. Gazis knew the old man well, by sight: on off-duty summer evenings, he had often bought his boys melon from Gabrilis's stall, as his father had for him, in years gone by.

'And you're saying this death has nothing to do with you?' he asked.

'I found the body. That is the whole extent of my involvement,' said the fat man.

Petridis appeared at the hilltop.

'Five minutes,' he called, and Gazis nodded his acknowledgement.

'Wait here,' he said to the fat man. He made his way up to where Petridis was standing and spoke quietly in his ear.

'Go over every inch of that car,' he said. 'I want to know about every scratch, every dent. If there's an impact point, find it.'

'What's his story?' asked Petridis.

'Nothing whatsoever to do with him.'

'Do you believe him?'

'In my considerable experience, son,' said Gazis, 'the obvious solution is usually the right one. He's saying what anyone would say in his position. He knows the victim; that's as much as he's prepared to say at the moment. But he might soften up, with a bit of careful handling. Give him some mitigating circumstances – poor light, no lights on the bike – and there's a good possibility he'll admit to it. Now, go and check on the car.'

Gazis scrambled back down to where the fat man stood patiently a few feet from Gabrilis's body.

'If you look back up towards the road, sir,' said Gazis, 'you'll notice you can't see your car from here. Which means that, conversely, you couldn't have seen the body from the road.'

The fat man's expression changed from melancholic to an unmistakable astuteness.

'Was that a question, Sergeant?' he asked.

'Indeed it was, sir. I'm asking how, if this accident was nothing to do with you, you came to find the body.'

The fat man's hand went to his pocket, and he took out an old baseball cap, faded blue with the remnants of a yellow logo, stained with sweat and pale with dust.

'This,' he said. 'I saw this at the roadside.'

'And you stop, do you, for every piece of rubbish that you pass?'

'I gave Gabrilis this hat,' said the fat man. 'He wore it always. I saw it on the ground here, so I stopped.'

'There's more than one blue cap in town. What made you think it was his?'

'I was looking for him. I know his routine. I wanted to surprise him. I expected to find him on the road.'

'And the Pony up there, is it registered to you?'

'Yes.'

'Let's go up, then, and I'll take some details from you.'

Gazis allowed the fat man to go ahead, expecting a man of his bulk to struggle on the incline; but the fat man moved swiftly, reaching the road much faster than Gazis himself. From the direction of town, the ambulance siren's wail was coming into earshot; Petridis had forgotten to tell them it was a morgue job only, no need for the blue lights after all.

Petridis waited by the Pony, feet apart and hands behind his back in the 'at ease' stance they'd taught him at police college. When he saw Gazis, he gave a small shrug, signalling he'd found no damage on the car.

Gazis took out his notebook and, ignoring the fat man, clicked on his pen and began, slowly, to write. He wrote down the date, time and location; he noted the nature of the incident as 'road-traffic fatality', and the deceased's name the fat man had given. He wrote down the details of the fat man's car – make, model, colour, registration – and the weather and road conditions.

Patiently, the fat man waited.

When he could think of nothing more to write, Gazis looked the fat man in the eye.

'OK,' he said. 'Name.'

'Diaktoros. Hermes Diaktoros.'

The ambulance siren was very close. Gazis took down the addresses the fat man gave – one local, one in Athens – and a date of birth.

'Right,' he said. 'I want to see your licence and insurance papers. Find them, please, and wait for me in your car.'

The fat man left them, and Gazis turned to Petridis.

'What did you find?' he asked.

'There's not a scratch on the car. Clean as a whistle.'

Gazis frowned.

'Maybe he didn't actually hit the old man,' said Petridis. 'Maybe he just ran him off the road. Has he said any more?'

Gazis told Petridis about the cap. Petridis looked sceptical.

'Doesn't sound very likely to me,' he said.

'It sounds so unlikely it might even be true,' said Gazis. 'We'll let him go for now, tell him to come in and make a statement tomorrow, after they've done the autopsy. Put a call in for CID, tell them we need them to take a look. Then we'll have facts to throw at him. And tell the ambulance crew not to touch anything until CID have had a good look round. There'll be something to nail someone with, for sure.'

'Won't CID want to look at his car?'

'You've already looked, haven't you?'

'And if he absconds tonight?'

'If he absconds, we'll know he's guilty, and we'll fetch him back.'

Petridis seemed uncertain. The ambulance pulled up behind the police car, lights flashing, the siren slowly dying. Petridis asked the crew to wait, and they, indifferent, climbed down from their cab, opened up the back doors and sat on the wheelchair ramp, lighting cigarettes.

Over Gazis's shoulder, Petridis watched a small, white car approaching fast; on its roof a long antenna flailed. A short distance from the ambulance, it braked hard and crossed the carriageway without signalling, cutting across a moped carrying two Scandinavian tourists in visored helmets. The moped swerved and wobbled; the blonde girl riding pillion clutched the driver tighter around the waist.

The white car pulled up behind the ambulance, skidding on loose stones, parking at an angle to the road to show off the pink logo painted on its side: *FM107*. When the driver cut the engine, it silenced the thudding beat of American rock music.

A young man in cut-offs and a white T-shirt stepped from the car. His long hair was gathered in a ponytail down his back, the leather sandals on his feet were stained with seawater, and Gazis, noticing the young man's unshaved stubble, rubbed at his own smooth jaw with satisfaction.

Approaching the policemen, the young man held out his hand; drawing close, he caught his foot in a hole in the tarmac, and stumbled. As he looked back to see what had tripped him, Gazis gave a small, slow smile.

'Watch your step there, Dinos,' he said.

'Hey, Sergeant Gazis.' Gazis didn't take the proffered hand, but the young man, unperturbed, slipped it casually into his shorts pocket.

'Ambulance-chasing again, Dinos?'

'Picked it up on the airwaves, Sergeant. Sounds like there might be a story here for me.'

'You bet.' Gazis's smile broadened. 'Call the press office tomorrow morning; they'll let you have the details.'

'But since I'm here, now, in person,' said the young man, 'how about you giving them to me? Who died?'

'What makes you think anyone's died?'

'An ambulance going nowhere and you guys? It's like two and two. Anything to see?' He took a step towards the sea, but Gazis gripped his upper arm.

21

'You ever heard of next of kin, Dinos? They get to know before you do. It's just how it works. Like I said, press office, tomorrow morning.'

Gazis turned and walked away; the young man made a mock salute to his back. Then, as if seeing him for the first time, he turned to Petridis.

'How's it going?' he said. He held out his hand. 'Don't think we've met. Dinos Karayannis, FM107 news. You'll be Sergeant . . .?'

'Constable,' said Petridis, shaking his hand. 'George Petridis.'

'New recruit? You'll be seeing a lot of me. We have a lot in common. Wherever there's bad news, we're always there – that's right, isn't it?'

'I suppose it is.'

'And if I'm not there, I always appreciate a call. I look after my sources, you know what I'm saying? Anything you give me, no names are ever mentioned. That's the key to good journalism, see – respect your sources. Never name your sources. Here.' From his pocket he took a business card and pressed it into Petridis's hand, closing Petridis's fingers firmly over it. 'You got anything for me, any time, day or night, you call me, I'll see you right. Any time.'

He jumped back into his car, and with a casual wave was gone, heading back towards town.

Petridis opened his hand. The neon-pink business card bore Dinos's details in sixties script – an office address, fax and phone, a mobile number. Beneath the card was something else, a piece of paper folded small.

Petridis knew what he was looking at. He spread the banknote, and held it out between the thumb and forefingers of both hands. Gazis stood by the Pony, bending to speak to the fat man. Petridis shrugged, and slipped the money into his trouser pocket.

'We'll need you to come into the Central Police Station tomorrow,' Gazis was saying as Petridis reached him. 'We'll be wanting a statement.'

'You're welcome to a statement,' said the fat man. 'In the meantime, I trust you'll be taking all possible steps to find the person responsible for my friend's death. Perhaps tomorrow you'll be good enough to update me on your progress. *Kali spera sas.*'

The policemen watched the fat man drive away.

'What do you think?' asked Petridis.

Gazis bent to brush dust from the hems of his trousers.

'Prime suspect, circumstantially,' he said. 'He's at the scene, he finds the body. There's no one else here. Seems cut and dried.'

'We could have arrested him.'

'Indeed we could,' said Gazis thoughtfully, 'but when you've got as many years as I have under your belt, you'll find you know in your gut when they'll run and when they'll stick around. We'll be seeing him tomorrow. And he could be our man, quite easily; but you and I are going to take our time, so when we make an arrest – and I fully intend we will make an arrest – we'll be absolutely sure we've got it right.'

Three

Mid-August, high season, and nights at the Delfini restaurant were far too quiet. Beneath the sign of the
smiling blue dolphin, the foreigners, sun-scorched and under-
dressed, might pause to read through the menu; but not
tempted by over-bright amateur photographs of meatballs
and kebabs, most moved on down the flagstoned street to the
shops selling T-shirts and sandals, where they admired re-
productions of ancient ceramics and fingered handwoven
rugs, spinning the postcard stands – *Four cards a euro, stamps
on sale inside* – and sniffing like dogs at the dusty bags of
herbs. Few were buying. Times were lean, and Aris Paliakis's
sales strategy – a sharp decrease in prices, clawing back what
was lost in drinks and cover charges – was delivering poor
results.

There was a time – when Despina was still cook, when the
tablecloths were plastic and the wine in the jugs came from
local barrels, when the old men drank ouzo in the kitchen,
raising their glasses to everyone who walked in the door – that
Germans and Italians would wait half an hour for a table. The
street was quiet then. There was no club with pounding
music, no cheering, jeering, chanting English football fans
in the sports bar. The Taverna Delfini stood between Janis's

kafenion and the little grocery store where Fortini sold rice from hessian sacks and incense and charcoal for cemetery shrines. On Saturday nights, Short Tolis the electrician played accordion for the diners, singing travellers' songs in his cigarette-damaged baritone. Short Tolis was dead now; Fortini's shop became the sports bar. In the neighbourhood, a transformation; in time, less than a decade.

Aris Paliakis saw no faults in his business. He laid the blame for reduced takings on the foreigners' palates, on their choice of pizza over moussaka, of hot dogs and hamburgers over vine leaves and stuffed peppers. He laid blame, too, on his countrymen; like crows settling on fresh carrion, they'd left the villages and the mountains to join him in his killing on the coast. In this square mile, the battle for the cash from foreign wallets was fought with many weapons: silver rings and gold necklaces, pistachio nuts and cruet sets, oil-painted views and plastic donkeys, books of traditional recipes and icons made in China.

Competition was fierce.

The English family – mother, father and children, grand-father and grandmother – were good-natured and compli-ant, believing the words of welcome and the genuine-seeming smiles.

Sotiris the waiter took leather-backed menus from the stack and led the family through the empty restaurant to a terrace table clearly visible from the street. (Paliakis had taught Sotiris the trade's tricks. *Every night needs its Judas goats*, he said, *so stake them out. Foreigners are like sheep. Where one goes, the others always follow*.) Fawning, Sotiris made a show of pulling out the ladies' chairs, leaning in close as he lit the candle-lamps, holding their eyes a moment too long as he handed out the menus. He fetched a basket of bread (just half

25

a loaf, sliced thinly) and a dish of the cow's milk butter the English always required, then left the floor to Paliakis.

Paliakis did not dress for the seasons, but for business; he rarely made concessions to the heat. His navy-blue suit and black dress shoes (hidden in the heel were lifts, which gave him the extra inch he'd always craved) were the same he would wear in winter; but tonight the heat was bad, and his white shirt was unbuttoned at the neck.

He stood behind the children's chairs and smiled, hands on their shoulders like an affectionate uncle, his bald, damp head shining, his cologne not quite masking the smell of his sweat. So short he barely had to bend, he spoke into the children's ears of the delights he planned to serve them.

'Best spaghetti Bolognese in all Greece,' he said. His English was heavily accented; catching garlic on Paliakis's breath, the boy grimaced at his father. 'My wife make specially for you.'

To the kitchen staff, the speech was familiar, the once amusing lies now tedious with repetition. Mrs Paliakis had never worked in this kitchen. This season's chef was Grigor – a hirsute Albanian with little skill whom Paliakis hired only for his cheapness.

Paliakis turned his charm on the adults. His smile grew wider, his gold canine glinted in the candlelight.

'Ladies and gentlemen,' he said, 'I hope you will allow me to present you this evening with the very best Greece has to offer.'

Sotiris raised his eyebrows at the chef. Both knew what would come next. In the fridge, three kilos of expensive fish was going stale. Every time the fridge was opened, the stink was nauseating.

'I have some sea bream my cousin caught today,' said Paliakis. 'Freshest on this coast. Grilled on the barbecue

. . .' He kissed his thumb and forefinger in the Italian gesture of perfection. Grigor looked doubtfully at Sotiris: the fish was good for nothing but the cats. But the English dupes were smiling in anticipation of a feast. 'Some Greek salad, perhaps, with feta cheese from my own goats' – Paliakis owned no goats – 'and to drink, may I suggest a local wine, one of the best wines in all Greece.'

'Lovely,' said the father.

Sotiris took the litre bottle of sour, factory-made white wine from the fridge, unscrewed the cap and filled a terracotta jug. The olives sunk in the mouldy brine of a gallon can were small and hard with little flesh, fit only for pressing. With the ladle, he fished for an even dozen and tipped them on to a dish.

Paliakis was closing his speech.

'And something a little special,' he was saying. 'A gift from me, to my most special customers. I bring you a plate of olives from my own orchard, special for you.'

In the kitchen, his smile was gone.

'Two spaghetti, four bream,' he shouted. 'Half a litre of white and a salad. Two Coca-Colas. And make it fast.'

Grigor was not a particular man, but even he balked at the fish.

'Is too old,' he said in his hesitant Greek. 'Make them sick.'

'Crap,' said Paliakis. 'Put plenty of oregano on it and give it an extra five minutes on the grill. The English know nothing about fish.' Bothered by runnels of sweat, he ran a cotton handkerchief over his forehead and his upper lip. 'Get that wine out there,' he said to Sotiris. 'By the time they've drunk that, they won't know what they're eating anyway.'

Sotiris carried out the olives and the wine, filling the glasses with a smile and a flourish, pouring a little extra for the ladies.

Back in the kitchen, Paliakis was on the phone.

27

'Those bricks should have been delivered five days ago,' he shouted. 'You're holding up my builders! Time's money, for Christ's sake.' His face was red; on his neck, dark veins were taut beneath the skin. He shook his forefinger in admonishment, as if the merchant on the other end of the line stood before him. 'Tomorrow,' he yelled, 'tomorrow, or you'll hear from Pandelis.'

As he said his son's name, Pandelis himself came into the kitchen from the street.

Behind his hand, Sotiris whispered to Grigor.

'Here's the devil's servant,' he said.

Pandelis Paliakis wished Grigor and Sotiris *kali spera*. Sonya, the Russian girl, was scrubbing pans; when she raised her eyes to his, he looked away, though a blush rose from his neck up to his cheeks. Sonya smiled to herself. Pandelis approached his father, who ended his call, and scowled at his son.

'What do you want?' he asked.

Pandelis's brow, like his father's, was beaded with sweat. He took a paper napkin from a holder and dabbed it on his face.

'We need to talk,' he said.

Sensing something of interest, Sotiris replaced the English family's salad on the counter, and taking up the bread-knife and a loaf of yesterday's bread, began to slice.

'So talk,' said Paliakis. 'I'm busy.'

'Here?'

'Why not here?'

Pandelis looked doubtfully around the kitchen. Grigor was chopping onions, Sonya was rinsing glasses. For a moment, he watched Sotiris, but Sotiris seemed absorbed in cutting bread.

Pandelis kept his voice low.

'The old man's dead,' he said.

'What old man?' Paliakis's phone rang. He glanced at the number display and switched it off.

'Kaloyeros. The melon man.' Grigor stopped chopping onions, Sonya turned off the running tap. Sotiris laid down the bread-knife and turned, arms folded, to listen to Pandelis. 'It was on the radio news.'

'Poor old thing,' said Sonya. She made the Orthodox triple cross over her breast. Paliakis glared at her; Sonya bent back over the sink.

'He was old,' said Sotiris. 'Eighty-five if he was a day.'

Now Paliakis glared at Sotiris, but Sotiris just stood waiting for the details. Paliakis grabbed Pandelis by his elbow, and, like a naughty child, marched him outside.

In the street, Paliakis and Pandelis talked below an open window half obscured by the fridge that held cold drinks. Leaving the bread table, Sotiris moved across to the fridge, and began to shift around the water and the beers, from the third shelf to the second, from the second to the third. Above the chatter of foreign voices and the beat of music from the bars, he could hear the two men clearly.

'How can he be dead?' asked Paliakis. 'You told me you saw him this afternoon.'

'Hit-and-run. The police are involved.'

Paliakis swore. For a moment, both were silent.

Then Paliakis said, 'This isn't anything to do with Kylis, is it? Because I said no short cuts, didn't I?'

'Don't be ridiculous,' said Pandelis. 'Even Kylis wouldn't be that stupid. The old guy had signed, for God's sake. I told him what you told me to say, all that crap about compulsory purchases and phone masts. He believed me, of course. I could see his heart breaking. I won't keep lying to people like that, Papa. It isn't right. It isn't necessary. And as it turns out, it was all for nothing, anyway.'

'Is there a will?'

'How the hell should I know?'

Now Paliakis spoke angrily.

'You don't know if there's a will, and you're standing here talking to me? Go, for Christ's sake, go!'

Sotiris left the window. When Paliakis came back through the door, Grigor was chopping onions, Sonya was drying cutlery on the chef's discarded apron. Sotiris was slicing more unwanted bread.

Paliakis kicked at a cat under a chair, and reached to his breast pocket for his cigarettes. There were none there. In silence, he went through the kitchen door into the street. From the doorway, Sotiris watched until Paliakis reached the *periptero* by the ceramics shop, then folded his arms and leaned back on the bread table to be comfortable.

'That's bad news,' he said. 'I remember the melon man from being a boy. Hot nights like this, my grandpa used to take me to that stall he had on the promenade. He bought me watermelon, then left me on a bench to eat it whilst he and his cronies chewed the fat. And I'd get in a mess, red juice and seeds all over my Sunday best. Pappou never noticed. Never noticed and never cared. My mother used to give him hell, when we got home.'

'A hit-and-run,' said Sonya, drying her hands. 'An old man like that. Who would have thought it?'

'The English wait their salad, Sotiris,' said Grigor. 'If he was old man, what difference how die?'

'But who would do that terrible thing?' asked Sonya. Putting the clean knives in the drawer, she began to dry the glasses.

'That's not the mystery, though, is it?' asked Sotiris. Across the street, Paliakis was walking back towards the restaurant,

30

peeling the Cellophane from a pack of Marlboros. 'The big mystery is, what have the devil and his children to do with the melon man? And why on earth should they be interested in the old man's will?'

Four

The way the fat man remembered was not there: that road was gone. Where he used to take the country lane leading inland from the coast, where a dilapidated sign had carried the name of a single village, everything was changed.

Now, there were traffic lights, and a lane to filter right. The barren dunes and flatlands had disappeared, so in daylight the sea view would be no more; instead, there was a supermarket, and a vast car park marked out in grids.

He recognised nothing, and yet he knew that this must be the way: the village – Palea Chora – was named with others on the new sign spanning the road. The traffic light gave him a green arrow, and he made the turn, expecting the winding lane he knew and a slow, meandering drive through wooded hills up to the village. Instead, he found a four-lane highway built in a man-made chasm, a fast, straight road which ignored the natural contours of the land, and cut through everything geology and ecology put in its way.

In the near dark, he followed the tail-lights of the car ahead of him at a careful distance. Vehicles flashed by him in the outside lane. Disoriented, he drove slowly, until a sign showed Palea Chora to his right where the fat man expected it to his left. Half-blind in the bad light, with the strange road lit only by his headlamps, he pressed on, until at last he felt the landscape was familiar: in silhouette, he recognised a stand of trees, then a rock formation, and finally the little church of St Philipas, its dome and white walls ancient and unchanging, marking the southern limit of the village boundary.

And the village itself seemed the same. Lights shone in the windows, and, on the front steps and the balconies, women talked and fanned themselves against the heat. Children ran shouting down the dark alleys, the old men were drinking in the *kafenion* on the square, and, as the fat man passed, every one of them – men, women and children – noticed him pass.

Beyond the square, he took the road following a summer-dry riverbed, where rushes flourished on water hidden below ground. Around the second bend, the gate in a high stone wall stood open; with the ease of familiarity, the fat man drove between the gateposts, and pulled up beneath the trees of his villa's garden.

The scent of the jasmine was sweet, the garden still but for the rustling of a cat hunting amongst the roses. Though night was obscuring the last vivid reds of sunset, the house was lit in welcome. The windows were open to the evening air (though mesh-screened – as he insisted – against flying insects), and on the verandah, candles burned with the lemon scent of citronella, and the flame of an oil lamp was turned high over a table laid for one.

In the verandah's shadows, a woman rose from a wicker chair and stretched out her arms to him.

'Welcome,' she said, 'welcome.'

'Thank you.'

For a moment longer than appropriate, they embraced; she held her face up to him, and he kissed her on both cheeks, close to the mouth. Then, stepping back, his hands still on her shoulders, he looked at her. The hair that he recalled as long and black was short, and almost grey; her once-slender figure was, undeniably, stout. The last time he had seen her, she wore a pretty blouse and skirt; now, the unforgiving black of mourning made her plain.

Affectionately, he smiled.

'How do you do it?' he said. 'They'll burn you for a witch. You haven't changed at all.'

Kokkona laughed.

'Liar,' she said. 'You're still the same, at least.' And it was true: he hadn't changed. As always, the years washed over him and touched him little, like water over granite. In others, time did its work, the changes subtle in youth more pronounced as each year passed, but he seemed always immune. 'Except you've put on a pound or two. And you're wearing glasses. So perhaps you are getting older, like the rest of us.'

He took the glasses from his face.

'The glasses are a disguise,' he said, 'to make people think I'm clever.'

'That will never work,' she smiled. 'You'll never take anyone in. Will you change before dinner? You're later than I expected.'

The good humour left his face, replaced by a weariness he had never shown before; and suddenly, he did seem aged, so she asked herself how she could have missed the change so obvious in him now.

'You're right,' he said, 'I'm late indeed. The question is, am I too late?'

He waved away her question as to his meaning.

'Let me bathe and change,' he said, 'and I'll tell you the bad news whilst I eat. Will you open me a bottle of last year's

34

vintage? It was an excellent year, and I've been looking forward to seeing what they made of it. And perhaps a glass or two will make the news a little easier to bear.'

In the kitchen, she dressed the salad and plated up his food. A bottle of Australian Chardonnay stood on the table. She knew, of course, he wouldn't be fooled, and then she'd have to give him some bad news of her own: that no one could be found, these past two years, to pick the grapes and make the wine he loved.

The fat man took linen trousers and a cotton shirt from the wardrobe. They were clothes he recalled wearing, classic in style but, acquired almost a decade ago, dated in their cut. They had been beautifully cared for, laundered and pressed each year, with the moths kept at bay by the sachets of herbs that hung amongst them – herbs sent by the fat man from the north, and unknown to Kokkona. There were dried buds scented like almond and rose together, and leaves smelling strongly of bergamot; and amongst these were bear-brown pods like laburnum, which split and scattered hard round seeds on the wardrobe floor. In the hand, the seeds had no odour at all, but when Kokkona, in curiosity, had crushed several in a pestle and mortar, their stink was foul as dog faeces, and she had understood at once why they might repel the moths.

He laid the clothes over the bedstead carved with barley sugar twists, and sat down on the mattress covered with cool white cotton sheets. Beneath the bed, where no rug covered them, the black-stained floorboards shone with the beeswax Kokkona applied and buffed by hand. He bent to find his espadrilles – ochre-yellow Turkish leather, embroidered in gold and red – and picking up the slippers, ran his eye over several boxes and packets stored there, hidden away. Their sizes varied, from a ring box to a carton; most were wrapped in plain brown paper and carried the stamps and marks of post-office delivery. One was in pink tissue, another was in striped paper for a birthday. He made a count of them, and satisfied himself that – apart from Kokkona's careful dusting – they were untouched.

On the ornate dressing table where the mirror was spotted with age, two bottles – one of cologne, one of hair oil – stood on a cloth of handmade lace. Taking the stopper from the cologne, he sniffed at the bottle. The exotic scents so expertly combined by the perfumier – the bitter orange of Tunisian neroli, the sweet honey smell of immortelle, the earthy tang of vetiver – were tainted by age.

His bag lay on the bed. The style of bag he favoured never changed – a leather holdall of the kind that others used for sport. The colour, however, varied, and normally his choice was bright: red, blue, green, purple. But this one was sombre: black, with a distinctive picture on its base, a silver sun half-risen, emanating silver rays.

From the holdall he took a fresh bottle of the dressing-table cologne, and, splashing a little into his hands, patted it on his cheeks. From a small jar, he took a fingerful of sweet pomade and stroked it through his damp curls. He ran the tip of a steel file behind his fingernails, and polished each one with a chamois buffer; he cleaned his teeth with powder freshened with cloves and wintergreen. He slipped the espadrilles on his feet, and sat down to daub his tennis shoes with a full coat of whitener. In the treads of the left shoe, a watermelon seed was lodged. With the point of his nail file he removed it, held it up to the lamplight, then placed it on the lace cloth on the dressing table.

He pulled on the linen trousers, slipped on the cotton shirt taken from the wardrobe, but the trousers were tight around

36

his belly, and the shirt's buttons gaped open on his chest. His reflection in the mirror showed a man not at his best.

From the holdall he took a polo shirt in lemon-yellow, and Italian slacks in navy-blue, and changed his clothes again. Hanging the clothes he had outgrown back on the rail, he closed the wardrobe door.

In a drawer of the bedside table was a small aluminium tin embossed with a flying bee. Twisting off the lid, he sniffed at the waxy ointment it contained; it smelled of pollen, with a faint tang of citrus. Replacing the lid, he slipped the tin into his pocket, and went to join Kokkona on the verandah.

Kokkona served him food he would enjoy: a home-reared rooster stuffed with rice and its own liver and broiled in giblet broth, a dish of artichoke hearts dressed with olive oil and lemon, a fresh loaf to dip in the juices.

As he took his seat at the verandah table, the night's heat drew beads of sweat on his upper lip. Around the oil lamp overhead, a helpless moth danced.

The cold wine was decanted into a ceramic jug painted with lemons. She moved to fill his glass; he held it to the lamplight, which shone through the golden, glistening wine and the condensation forming on the glass. He sniffed at the wine, sipped it, and placed the glass back on the table.

'A miracle has occurred,' he said. For a moment she was hopeful, but the look he fixed on her was shrewd, and she turned her eyes from him on to the fluttering moth. 'My vines, which have always, in the decades since they were planted, produced Roditis grapes, have this past year produced Chardonnay. I wonder what the explanation could be, Kokkona.'

She spread her hands before her.

'I didn't know what to do,' she said. 'I didn't know how to tell you, knowing how disappointed you'd be.'

'Disappoint me, then,' he said. 'A little disappointment can do no more to spoil the day.'

'There's no wine,' she said. 'The past two years, there's been no one to pick the grapes, no one to make the vintage or bottle it. No one wants that work now.'

He held out his glass to her.

'Taste this wine, Kokkona.'

She shook her head.

'No wine for me,' she said.

He sighed.

'In the old days,' he said, 'women didn't deny themselves small pleasures. This new morality our Orthodox friends all foster, this making virtue of denial, seems pompous and cheerless to me. Of course they don't allow you wine. You might become giddy and wanton.' Smiling, he winked at her, and pushed his glass away. 'So you'll have to take my word for what I say. The wine's not bad. Pour it back in to the bottle and recork it, and give it, if you wish, to someone who'll enjoy it. But to me, its taste is strange; it tastes of foreign soils and rains. It lacks the taste of home – of these hills, our sun, our soil and stones, our vines. And that, to me, is everything that makes drinking wine a pleasure. I'll have a jug of water, if you please. If there's still water in the well.'

She fetched water and filled his glass.

He drank, and inclined his head in satisfaction. 'I'm sorry,' he said. 'I didn't mean to give offence. You're not to blame, I know. And you don't drink wine, and so you may not understand me when I say that in our wine I taste the sky: every sunrise, every sunset that the vines have seen have given flavour, given spirit to the grapes. Every drop of rain, every molecule of earth at the vine roots, every stone, even the goat dung that washes down the hillside is held within it. Our wine distils the flavours of this land, the very essence of this countryside. The wine you served tastes of another country, a place of deserts and muddy rivers. What joy can that bring to a Greek soul? Believe me, Kokkona – there is no pleasure like the song your heart sings to the accompaniment of a glass of your own wine.'

For a few moments he was silent, looking out into the night, contemplating, as if considering the truth of his own words.

'At least,' he said at last, 'I used to think so. It seems I'd struggle now to find anyone of like mind.'

From the wicker chair, she watched him eat a little of the chicken. With the edge of his fork, he sliced an artichoke in two and speared one half of it, chewing on it for a long time without swallowing. He took no bread. Before long, he laid down his fork.

'I find I have little appetite tonight, Kokkona,' he said. Removing his glasses, he pinched his nose as if against a headache.

'I expect you're tired. It's a long journey.'

'It's more than that,' he said. 'It's because the news is bad. Gabrilis Kaloyeros is dead.'

'*Panayia mou!*' She crossed herself, and sat back in the chair with both hands clasped on her chest. 'When? How?'

'I found him on the coast road,' said the fat man. 'A hit-and-run.'

'*Panayia mou!*' She crossed herself again. 'But who would do such a thing?'

'Who indeed? Who would leave an old man dying at the roadside?' He rose from the table and crossed to the balcony railing; leaning there, he stared up at the stars. 'He had a noble heart, and deserved a better end.'

'He wasn't the same, you know, after Maria went. He wasn't well. Perhaps it was his own fault: a fall, or his old

39

heart giving up. He was too frail to be making that journey in this heat, but he was a stubborn man. No one could tell him.'

'It wasn't his fault,' said the fat man. 'Gabrilis was hit by some vehicle, and the driver left him there to die alone. Of course the police suspect I'm responsible, because I found him. Their habit is to look for the obvious.' He turned to face her. 'But I shall look further afield.'

'Where is he now?'

'The mortuary, I assume.'

'He must be fetched home. Who'll make the arrangements?'

'Are there no suitable relatives?'

'I'm a third cousin myself. There're other cousins, but no one else, I don't believe.'

'Will you take charge, then? I'll pay the bills, of course. Make sure all is done correctly. Spare no expense.'

'I must call my sister to organise the vigil. We'll have to speak to the carpenter and the priest. There's so much to do.'

'Do you have a telephone at home?'

'We all have telephones now. Except you.'

'Except me,' he agreed. 'I'll drive you there.'

'But you've barely eaten.'

He crossed to where she sat, and placed a hand on her shoulder.

'As always, Kokkona,' he said, 'your food is of the best. But Gabrilis's death has made me very angry, and when anger fills the stomach there's no room for food. So put this feast away, and bring it out again tomorrow when I might do it justice. Then get your things. You've arrangements to make, and I have matters to attend to myself, before the night is over.'

The wine cellar was reached through a wooden trapdoor in the flagstones of the kitchen floor. The staircase down was short, six steps, the treads spotted with the holes of old woodworm. The ceiling was a vault of stone, which at its high point cleared his head, but, over the wine racks, its curved line dropped low, and to choose a bottle he had to stoop, or crouch.

As he turned up the gas on the lamp to its fullest, the soft light fell on bottles thick with dust, whose labels were fading into illegibility. At the cellar's end, where the racks disappeared into darkness, the remains of the oldest and greatest vintages were stored – a little left from before the forties war, and some very special bottles from Macedonia. Close to where he stood were the wines from the most recent decades, in better quantities.

But in the racks allocated for the last two years, where several dozen bottles should be stored, there was no wine.

In the past, there had been tastings that went on long into the night, prolonged by good-natured arguments over the merits of the '63 or '75. There had been times they drank so much they couldn't tell whether they were drinking red or white. But there was no argument here tonight, nor any laughter; and the friends themselves, where were they? The cellar lay in silence, a reproach on his neglect both of this place and of his friends. Gabrilis had been amongst the last of these. The fat man had returned too late, and found only the echoes of a more cheerful past. The cellar he used to enter with such anticipation was a mausoleum now, and as the lamplight showed him the dusty bottles, he heard the whispers of happier times, and was sad.

No one to make the wine, this year or last: the news here in Arcadia was bad indeed. But some good might be salvaged still. He searched amongst the racks, and found a single bottle: the last of a wonderful vintage, the '68. It was an appropriate tribute to his friend.

As best he could, he brushed the dust and sandy dirt from the dark-green bottle and, tucking it beneath his arm, climbed up the cellar steps.

Five

Late at night, the Namco Pony pulled off the highway on to the track leading to Gabrilis's house. In the fat man's long absence, no repairs had been made, and every pothole was more treacherous than he remembered.

The fat man was a cautious driver. For fifty metres, he persuaded the Pony slowly forward; but, when the exhaust pipe scraped on stone a second time, he stopped the car, and in the dim light from the dashboard dials opened the glove-box. A national route map (so well used the creases were deteriorating into holes) covered a rubber-cased torch, large and heavy as a cudgel. He switched it on; its response was poor, a weak, dull-yellow glow. The fat man shook it, and whacked the torch once on his thigh; it leapt to life, giving out a well-charged beam of light.

In these small hours, no traffic was passing on the coast road, and as he walked up the track the night was quiet. Above him, the pine trees were black against the glorious stars, the temple ruins dark behind them. A breeze fresh with the tang of resin and pine bark ruffled the fat man's hair. From amongst the trees, a silent owl rose and glided away.

In his left hand was his holdall; his right hand held the torch to light the way. Through the soft soles of his tennis shoes, the stones were sharp; the torch's range was short, making the way to the house seem longer than in the past. When the track began to level, he knew he was close to the house, and that ahead of him, in daylight, he'd see the melon patch. But things were not as they had been. Tonight, there was no Manyiatis, barking, jumping, sniffing at his hands for treats.

He shone the torch beam straight ahead, and the light picked out a section of green foliage, framing a small piece of the garden as if in a camera's viewfinder. And something was intruding in the picture. By the fence, a white transit van was parked. The fat man, it seemed, was not alone here after all.

He approached the van with caution, and touched its bonnet with the back of his hand, finding the engine warm but cooling. The licence plate was local. In the rear window, a sticker advertised Valvoline motor oil. He shone the torch beam through the driver's window, showing, on the passenger seat, waxed-paper wrappers of takeaway souvlakia amongst empty cans of beer and iced coffee. A pair of charms – a blue glass eye and a ceramic bulb of garlic – hung from the rear-view mirror.

He turned off the torch, and waited for his eyes to adapt to the darkness. Through the trees, the unsteady light of a flame burned in Gabrilis's window.

Avoiding the path, the fat man made his way up to the verandah. There, on the table where he had sat so many hours with his friend, was a plate littered with the bones of small fish, the end of a stale loaf, an empty glass, and a bowl filled with grapes cut from the overhead vine.

Concealing himself behind the house wall, the fat man looked in at the window. At the centre of the floor an oil lamp burned; by its light, a man was ransacking the room. The bed had been stripped of its dirty sheets, the mattress overturned; the cheap icons had been taken from the walls and lay face down on the rug, their cardboard backing ripped from their frames. Glass and china lay broken on the tiles. The clothes from the chest of drawers were flung about the room, little white balls of moth-deterring camphor scattered amongst them, and the empty drawers upturned by the stove. The shotgun Gabrilis had kept hidden under the bed stood on its stock beside the door.

Dark as a shadow, the intruder riffled through a sheaf of papers discovered amongst Maria's elastic stockings and flowered housecoats. The gaslight was poor for reading, and the intruder bent close to the lamp, but the words, apparently, remained unclear. In impatience, he roughly folded the papers, and stuffed them in the pocket of his shorts.

Now the intruder looked about him, as if for hiding places he might have missed, and his eyes settled on the shelf above the fireplace. Here, Gabrilis kept the treasures the fat man brought him, a gift each time he visited. *The professor's curiosities*, Gabrilis had called them; and many were curious indeed, intriguing trinkets of obscure origin.

The intruder took the oil lamp, and moved with it towards the fireplace, holding it up to view the collection. Some pieces, it seemed, held his attention: an ivory chessman, shaped like the crowned king of a Norse tribe; a small finger bone sealed in an ebony reliquary; a carved box, which when opened played Slavic tunes; a terracotta horse in the naive style of ancient Troy; a two-handled cup painted with dancing satyrs. It was the cup that tempted him most, and he reached out his hand to take it from the shelf, but as he did so the fat man opened his own hand, and let his torch fall clattering to the verandah's wooden boards.

The intruder stood rigid, and listened for a moment, then set down the lamp, and, moving quickly across the room, opened the door. Peering out into the night, again he listened. Hearing nothing, he turned to go back inside the house, but the fat man picked up a stone and tossed it behind him, where it landed with a thump and a trickling of dirt beneath the trees.

With no further hesitation, the intruder crossed the verandah and slipped away into the darkness. His footfall faded; a few moments more, and the van's engine roared. The fat man stepped on to the verandah, and watched the van's headlamps light its way down to the coast road, and away towards the town.

He picked up his torch. Laying his holdall on the single chair at the table, he carried the plate and the stale bread into the house, stepping carefully over the possessions littered on the floor. The corkscrew was easy to find, but the glasses by the sink weren't clean; so he took the bucket Maria always used for water, and made his way downhill towards the spring.

The fat man laid his torch on the edge of the stone trough and dipped the bucket into the water. Lowering the full bucket to the ground, he crouched to cup his hands and drink, and there, by his knees, the torchlight showed the body of poor Manyiatis.

Manyiatis lay as he used to when stretched out in the sun, but plainly he was not simply asleep. Drying blood marked a fracture line along his skull. The socket of one eye was crushed and misshapen.

The fat man stroked the dog's injured head and tickled the fur of his still-warm belly. His memory of Manyiatis was of a young dog, lively, fast and keen to play; could this fat, grey-whiskered animal be the same creature? The fat man's absence had truly been too long. He'd been away a lifetime for the dog.

'Poor old Manyiatis,' the fat man said aloud. 'If you could have kept your mouth shut, just this once, he'd never have known you were here, and you'd have lived to fight another day.' He sighed. 'Come on, old man. We'll find a place for you to sleep tonight.'

The dog was heavy, but the fat man made light work of carrying him to the house. He laid the dog beneath the verandah table and, returning to the spring for the water, washed himself a glass.

From his holdall, he took the wine he had chosen, and an object wrapped in pale-green velvet. He drew the cork from the bottle, filling Gabrilis's empty glass before his own. Sitting, he sniffed the bouquet. The wine smelled good; age had given it richness, and great depth.

The fat man raised his glass to the stars.

'Good journey, old friend,' he said, and drank the mellow wine, thick with fruit and must. 'Like us,' he said, 'greatly improved with age. And I have brought you one last curio, the final piece, it seems, for your collection.' Unfolding the velvet, he laid Gabrilis's gift beside the bottle. It was, in appearance, a flintlock, but deformed. The stock was overlaid in silver and finely engraved, and the trigger was quite usual; but, in place of a firearm's barrel, the stock held a foreshortened, complex mechanism cast in iron. 'It's an odd-looking thing, you'll agree,' said the fat man to the night. 'You'd never guess the use, unless you fired it.' He held it out in the palm of his hand, as if inviting scrutiny from above. 'A wealthy man's pistol tinderbox. A nice example: English, eighteenth century. I meant it to be useful, a standby for when your matches were all damp. But now . . .'

He carried the tinderbox inside and, moving the Trojan horse along the shelf, placed the tinderbox amongst the other curios.

He drank the wine slowly, until the first pink line of dawn showed over the sea. With daylight enough to see by, he walked down to the melon terraces and found a shovel to dig a grave for old Manyiatis. As he worked, the sun's warmth increased; by the time the hole was deep enough, the flies crawling on the old dog's eyes were plentiful. Wrapping Manyiatis in a sheet, the fat man carried him to his grave, and, weighting the sheet with stones to deter the rats, buried him deep beneath the dry earth.

When the work was finished, he stood awhile at the grave-side, remembering Manyiatis as a puppy, his trick of stealing shoes, his love of chasing rabbits, the pride he took in guarding home and family.

'Run fast after your master, old man,' he said. 'He's not so far ahead. Run fast as you did as a youngster, and you'll catch him up in no time.'

He made his way downhill. Amongst the hives the bees were waking, making their first journeys of the day. By hive number nine, the fat man stopped. From his pocket he took the bee-embossed tin of ointment and, dipping into it with his fingers, smeared the lemon-scented balm over his forearms, dabbed a little on his face, his nose, his neck. Clearly, the bees disliked the smell; those settled on his clothing flew away, those airborne and flying near increased their distance from him.

The painted eye on the hive roof stared up at him; he felt the watching of the other eyes around him. As he lifted the lid of number nine, no bees rose to fight off his intrusion. The smells of sweet honey and of wax were intense, the noise inside the hive like a powerful engine muted. The frames were almost filled with honeycomb. The fat man tugged at the right-most frame, loosening it enough to be removed, whilst the agitated bees dared not trouble him, as if the ointment put a shield of glass between him and them. On this frame, sealed beneath the honeycomb, was an irregularity, a swelling. Using a knife brought from the kitchen, the fat man cut away the comb, letting it fall to the ground, offering in his mind an apology to Gabrilis for the waste. Then, with thumb and forefinger, he extracted the cause of the swelling: a polythene-wrapped parcel thickly bound with tape, sticky with wax and honey. Carefully, he replaced the frame and the hive lid, and pushed the honeycomb he had removed under the hive. Except for a little stickiness on the ground, there was no trace of the bees having been disturbed.

At the spring, he washed the wax and honey from his hands, and from the parcel. When cleaned, it showed no signs of tampering, of deterioration or damage. Satisfied all was intact, he thanked the bees for their good care of the documents and, wishing them *kali mera*, strode purposefully away.

Six

The village of Koskinou lay three miles further inland, where flat, dry fields of olive trees spread around modest houses with views to the distant hills. Chickens scratched in the dirt of well-tended vegetable gardens, goats were tethered on the roadside verges; a vintage tractor rusted by a woodpile, and a hobbled donkey waited, head bowed, by an open chapel gate.

The few small businesses on the square – a haberdashery with fly-spotted windows, an insanitary butcher's, a bric-à-brac shop displaying artificial flowers and cheap cut-glass, a *kafenion* advertising Fanta and pizza – were closed. A wooden bench circled the trunk of a spreading plane tree, and in the summer the old men liked to sit here in its shade, littering the ground with cigarette butts, enjoying the coffee and ouzo they fetched from the *kafenion*; but this morning the old men were all absent.

The fat man parked the Pony outside the baker's where, he remembered, they used to make an excellent bougatsa, the sweet custard pastry he was so fond of. But the bakery wasn't baking any more; a chain and padlock on the door were showing signs of rust, the paint on the shutters was dull and flaking.

Behind the square, the single bell of St Lefteris's began to toll.

The fat man followed the lane on the square's south side. In the silences between the bell's tolling, the side-streets were quiet; even in the shade of the house walls, the morning's heat was strong. A cat with one blind eye cowered in a doorway; a naked infant sat crying on the flagstones of a courtyard.

When he found the house, the gathering was small. Outside, a handful of old men waited; inside, Kokkona led the wailing, and her chorus – five elderly women only – made up for lack of numbers with their volume. A seventh woman, too old to raise her voice, moved her lips as if gurning and signed the triple cross over her sagging breasts; all gums and wrinkles amongst her widow's black, she stared up at the fat man with bewildered eyes.

A priest, obese and malodorous, wafted a censer back and forth, chanting as it rattled and billowed smoke perfumed with frankincense and roses.

Gabrilis lay in his coffin on the table. The fat man greeted the women – '*May his memory be eternal*' – and looked into the casket. They had prepared him as if for a celebration – the bristles had been shaved from his chin, his old clothes replaced with a suit – so he seemed a parody of the young bridegroom he had once been, a melancholy reminder of time's cruelty. His skin was the tired colour of old newspapers; beneath the scents of bergamot and starch, the heat promoted a subtle note of decay. Above his right eye, there was bruising; his arthritic hands, folded across his chest, were grazed across the knuckles.

The fat man laid his hands over Gabrilis's, and squeezed them in a final clasp before placing a kiss on the corpse's forehead. Giving a full bow to the coffin, he made no cross over it, but simply turned away.

The women pursed their lips in disapproval.

The cemetery at the hilltop was sheltered from the worst of winter's storms, and in spring white lilies bloomed. But in summer the heat must be borne. They laid him in his place beside Maria, and the women left in silence, clutching their bags of *koliva*, grave food of boiled wheat and almonds.

The priest removed his hat and scratched at the bald spot on his head, then took cigarettes from his cassock and offered them to the fat man.

For a while, they smoked in silence, listening to the cicadas in the cypress trees.

'It was a pitiful attendance for such a long and honourable life,' said the fat man as he finished his cigarette. He dropped the butt to the stony earth and ground it out with the toe of his tennis shoe, then bent to pick it up and slipped it into his pocket for later, more careful disposal.

The priest shook his head sadly.

'It's a misfortune, these days, to die in summer,' he said. 'He'd have done better waiting till November. You could be the Archbishop himself and die in August, and you'd only get the old to see you off. The rest are all working, milking the tourist cow – the bars are busy, the shops never close, the nightclub workers sleep all day to be ready for the next night's shift. Death comes only once to us all, but business is business. They've no time for goodbyes when there's money to be made.'

'There were no close relatives remaining?' asked the fat man.

The priest ground out his own cigarette, watching the dusty toe of his black shoe as he did so.

'No,' he said. 'There was no one.' He glanced at a watch whose strap was tight around his plump wrist. 'I must be going,' he said. 'If you could see your way . . . my fee . . .'

The fat man drew three large-denomination notes from his wallet and handed them to the sweating priest, who bowed his head in acknowledgement and stuffed them in his cassock.

'God bless you,' he said. 'You're most generous. Most kind.'

'The payment's generous, as you say,' said the fat man. 'So do well by him. Say Mass for him as it's prescribed; he was a great believer in your faith. All the prayers and rituals, make sure you attend to them. If more cash is required, inform Kokkona and she will contact me. Do you understand?'

As the priest followed the women down the hill, the fat man stood beside the open grave, staring at the handfuls of dry dirt thrown on the coffin lid. After a while, he took out a small gold coin and tossed it into the grave.

'Something for the ferryman, old friend,' he said. 'More than enough to pay your fare. The best of journeys to you.'

Gathering up a handful of dusty soil, he scattered it over the coin to cover it. Beside the ossuary, the sexton waited with his shovel. The fat man called out to him to begin his work, and followed the other mourners back to the village.

Seven

In the police cafeteria, Gazis and Petridis were the only customers. Gazis led the way to a table with a view across the square to the town hall's grand façade: high windows, classical pillars and a balcony where, on public holidays, the Mayor's entourage invited visiting dignitaries to watch the military parades. On the stone steps, red-legged pigeons strutted and fluttered; the blue-and-white Greek flag hung flaccid from its rooftop pole.

Petridis took a bite of his cheese-and-spinach pie. The filo was greasy with oil, and scorched with reheating. He leaned over his plate to catch the falling flakes of pastry; still crumbs dropped on to the tabletop, on to his uniform shirt and trousers. The table, Gazis noticed, had not been wiped after its previous occupants' breakfast; they'd left sugar crystals and milk stains, a smear of peach jam. Petridis chewed. A crumb of white feta stuck at the corner of his mouth.

Gazis's coffee was just as he expected: bulked out with chicory, and bitter. He ripped open another envelope of sugar – the packet showed a scene he recognised, the antelopes guarding the harbour entrance at Rhodes – and stirred it into his cup. When he tasted it again, the coffee was not improved, just too sweet to be enjoyed.

'For thirty years I've been drinking coffee in this cafeteria,' he said, 'and for thirty years, I've been expecting some improvement. Would you say that makes me an optimist, or a fool?'

On the square below, the Mayor's black Mercedes pulled into the *No Parking* zone by the town hall steps. The Mayor's regular driver – a lean man with an opulent moustache – climbed out and stood by the car's wing, turning the pages of this morning's *Ethniki*.

'This cheese pie's not bad,' said Petridis.

'Cheese pies aren't what they used to be. That's factory-made junk. Eat too many of them and you'll fatten up like a pig.'

'My *yiayia* makes the best cheese pies. When I go home, I'll bring you some.'

'But does your grandmother make her own pastry? Factory pastry gives me bellyache. I remember when I was your age I could eat anything. A lifetime of this coffee has rotted my gut.'

Behind the counter, a sullen girl laid out film-wrapped sandwiches: processed ham and cheese on sliced bread, salami and tomato on French rolls. In the kitchen, a metal pan clattered on to the tiled floor, and a woman shouted a foul curse.

Gazis raised his eyebrows.

'In my day,' he said, 'women didn't know such words existed. Now they shout them in public.'

Across the square, the Mayor's driver turned the pages of his newspaper.

'Let me tell you a story,' went on Gazis. 'When I was a rookie like you, I ticketed the Mayor for parking in that zone. Not this young mayor we've got now, obviously. He was an older man. Before your time, no doubt; before you were born, possibly. I wrote out the ticket in front of the Mayor himself, whilst he just stood there smiling. Every morning his car was parked there, and that didn't seem right to me. So I wrote him a ticket. Next morning, I was summoned to the third floor, to the Inspector's office. I'd never met the man before. My knees shook as I walked through his door. And the first thing I saw was my ticket on his desk, ripped right in half. *We don't write tickets for the Mayor*, he said, and I said, *Surely we do, if he's parked illegally. It's our job to apply the law to every citizen impartially*. He thought I was being cocky. He told me to get out.

'Next day, the Mayor parked in the same place – right there, where that Mercedes is now. So I wrote him another ticket. This time, there was no call to the third floor. This time, I got a letter slapped in my hand by some clerk from personnel as I went off shift. First disciplinary warning – failure to follow orders. I've got the letter still. But I had a wife to support, and our oldest was still in nappies. When my wife started to cry, I gave it up.' He fixed his eyes on the black Mercedes. 'What do you think, Petridis? Are you going to write that guy a ticket?'

Petridis wetted his fingertip, and dipped it in the pastry flakes on his plate.

'Not much point, is there?' he said, licking off the crumbs. 'Waste of time and paper. And anyway, the Mayor's someone you want to stay on the right side of, surely? You'd never make Chief Constable if the Mayor stirred it for you, would you?'

'I, personally, shall never even make Inspector,' said Gazis, 'though you might. Chief Constable's another matter. Is that where you want to be? That's a job you have to arse-lick your way into: no other way. Me, I never had the taste for other men's backsides. But maybe you're different.'

'Maybe not Chief Constable, then. But Inspector . . . I'd love to see my parents' faces, if I could make Inspector.'

'I expect they're very proud of you, in that uniform.'

'Every time my mother sees me in it, she gets all weepy. She's driving the neighbours crazy, my father says. Every conversation she has – and she talks a lot, my mother – she gets it in, somehow – *my son the policeman*. She should take care: they'll be cursing us, if she's not careful. There's a lot of jealousy on our island. And when they're jealous, they put bad eyes on you.' He pointed to the centre of his forehead.

'Didn't your father want you to go into his trade?'

'There's no money in building boats.'

'But it's a craftsman's job. I always thought I'd try my hand at boat-building, if the police career didn't suit me. It's a job with a long-term future: there'll be work for boat-builders until the seas run dry.'

'Work, maybe. But money, no. My father's never been ambitious, but I'm going to make something of myself. You can't do that in the islands. There's nothing there but goats and church-going.'

'I'll take the vacancy you've left, then,' said Gazis. 'I've always thought the island life'd suit me very well. A little place by the sea, a boat to putter about in, a few hands of cards in the evenings. What more could a man need?'

'You'd die of boredom,' said Petridis. 'Winter and summer, the same people, the same places. Nothing happens. Every day's the same.'

'A life of variety like this one makes the ordinary attractive. A few years of every day being the same would be a blessing to me. That's what my retirement savings will buy me: a place somewhere nothing ever changes.'

Across the square, the heavy doors of the town hall swung open.

'Here he is,' said Gazis quietly. 'The man of the moment.'

Three men in French-tailored trousers and pastel, well-pressed shirts ran down to the Mercedes. Behind dark glasses, their eyes were hidden. The driver folded his paper and tossed it through the open window on to his seat, then opened the rear door for one of the men. The car cut into the traffic, making the turn towards the centre of town.

'Like Mafia,' said Gazis. He took his beret from the chair beside him, brushing pastry flakes from its crown and smoothing his hair before he put it on. 'I'm still proud to wear this uniform. I've been proud since the day I buttoned up my first blue shirt. And you know the easiest way to stay proud, son? The rule is very simple.' Petridis looked expectant as Gazis leaned forward to advise him. 'Never do anything you wouldn't want your mother to know about.'

Along the ground-floor corridor, officers were gathering for the day shift. On the rear door, a new sign had been posted, large red letters laminated on card: *Staff use only. This door to be kept closed at all times.*

But the air conditioning had failed again.

'If it's like last year,' said Gazis, as he and Petridis descended the metal-banistered staircase, 'they'll get it fixed some time in November. We'll have air-cooled offices right through the winter, colder than you can imagine. And come May, it'll be on the blink again. Every year the same. Better tell your grandma to start knitting you some vests.'

The rear door was wedged open, as always – today, by a pencil-stub shoved under its edge. Outside, amongst the police cars and prisoner-transport vans, policemen talked, smoking and sipping iced coffee. To promote a through-draught, the public entrance at the corridor's far end was propped open, too, giving a view of the promenade and its squat, fat-trunked palm trees. On the water, the tour boats were lined up stern-on, gangplanks lowered, placards at their ends advertising the day's excursions – beaches, islands, ruins – and the boatmen were competing for the business of the dithering tourists. Already, the day was hot.

At the curve in the stairs, Gazis stopped beneath the Chief Constable's portrait.

'Here you are,' he said. 'Something to aspire to.'

Petridis looked up at the photograph, seeing a corpulent man in martial uniform, who smiled severely, as if smiling was an indulgence he did not often permit himself.

'They've touched up his hair,' said Gazis. 'He's balder than that when you meet him. Greyer, too.'

In the picture, the Chief Constable sat rigidly beneath a coat of arms Gazis recognised.

'They borrowed that from the Law Courts,' he said. 'Someone must have thought it would give the right tone. That's the motto we're supposed to work by.'

Petridis squinted at the coat of arms, unable to make out the wording on the scroll at the lion's feet.

'Equality in justice,' Gazis told him. 'Unless you're the Mayor, of course.'

Near the public entrance, the Desk Sergeant in his glass booth pressed a phone to his ear; as he listened, he watched a woman weeping on a bench, a small girl all in pink silent and solemn at her side. Close by, two constables listened to a joke told by a third; at the obscene punchline, the officers all laughed, and the weeping woman turned away her face.

Gazis sent Petridis to sign out their car. Gazis checked his watch by the clock on the wall, finding the clock one hour and eleven minutes slow. Down the corridor in the dispatcher's office, Petridis laughed, and a young girl's voice scolded him for his flirtatiousness. Intending to hurry Petridis, Gazis moved down the hall, but outside Interview Room 1, he stopped.

The interview-room door was opening; inside the room, two men were speaking.

'Thank you for coming in,' said one, 'and for all your assistance. We appreciate your taking the time.'

The second man spoke in a remarkable accent: clean, perfect Greek, a TV announcer's voice.

'No trouble at all,' he said. 'If I can be of further help, please let me know.'

The door opened wide, and the fat man stepped into the corridor. His eyes were bloodshot and swollen beneath, as if he had passed a sleepless night.

Neither Gazis nor the fat man smiled.

'Good morning, Sergeant,' said the fat man. 'As you requested, I've come to give my statement.'

'I'm pleased to hear it,' said Gazis. 'It would have caused you some embarrassment, no doubt, if we'd had to come and fetch you.'

'I'm not easily embarrassed,' said the fat man, 'and as you see, I came quite voluntarily. As I told you yesterday, my involvement begins and ends with finding the body of my poor friend. I suspect you doubt my version of events; but I think you'll find Detective Belesis here will confirm that it wasn't my car involved in this tragedy.'

Gazis looked at Belesis, who shrugged indifferently.

'He's right, Thanos,' said Belesis. 'The vehicle that hit the old man was white, no doubt about it. But, as I've explained to the gentleman, in cases like this, with nothing to go on, it's unlikely we'll identify the culprit.'

'Culprit?' queried the fat man. 'The word is killer, surely?'

Belesis seemed uncomfortable.

'Killer, I suppose so, yes. Paint samples have gone to the lab, of course. And we'll be in touch if there's any news.'

The detective waited for the fat man to walk away, but the fat man showed no intention of leaving. Instead, he frowned, as if considering putting a question. Belesis, having no answers, looked up at the inaccurate clock.

'Christ,' he said, 'is that the time? I've a meeting in five minutes. Thanks again for coming in.'

He left them, taking the stairs two at a time. Petridis emerged from the dispatcher's office, jangling a set of keys.

'Well,' said Gazis to the fat man, 'Detective Belesis doesn't sound too hopeful for your friend. You'll be disappointed, if there's little hope of a conviction.'

'In my experience, there's always hope of a conviction,' said the fat man. 'And that hope, unsurprisingly, increases in direct proportion to the amount of effort expended to resolve the case. This is manslaughter at best, Sergeant, and possibly something worse. As I said to Detective Belesis, I would not expect the constabulary to abandon so serious a matter as a "no-hoper".' He waved a hand towards the portrait of the Chief Constable. 'I draw your attention to the motto beneath which your leader sits. *Equality in Justice*. My friend is entitled to justice, as is every man. Elderly though he may have been, his time had not yet come. The case is no less serious because the culprit, as Detective Belesis terms him, pre-empted death by only weeks, or months.'

Gazis's expression was apologetic.

'You're right, of course,' he said. 'But the question remains, where does one start?'

'Clearly,' said the fat man, 'Detective Belesis would like to avoid starting at all. I hope I find a better ally in you, Sergeant. And if I were investigating, I'd start in the obvious place – the local garages. Someone's got a vehicle with damage on it they'd prefer no one to see. The likelihood is, they'll move quickly to get it repaired. A visit to a few garages whilst you're out and about will soon spread the word.'

'We could contact the press,' put in Petridis, 'get it in the town newspaper and on the radio. That way, the garage proprietors would come to us.'

Gazis and the fat man looked at him.

'You're learning,' said Gazis. 'We'll make a policeman of you yet. We'll have to clear it with CID, but they won't stand in our way. They're not likely to object to us taking on their workload.'

'I want to offer you my services, if you need them,' said the fat man. 'Please contact me if I can help in any way. I know sometimes your hands are tied by protocol and regulations. In those circumstances, a civilian's greater freedom can be useful.'

He held out his hand, and Gazis took it.

'I'll stay in touch,' said Gazis.

'Is he off our list, then?' asked Petridis, as the fat man passed through the public entrance. 'He was our prime suspect.'

'He was our only suspect,' said Gazis. 'Be glad we didn't take that, yesterday, as definite guilt. Mr Diaktoros isn't a man to overlook a night down in the cells. If we'd made that mistake, we'd be on our way to the third floor now, pleading for our jobs. So, there's the second rule of policing for the day, and it's an important one. Never be afraid, Constable, to doubt your first conclusions. Of course, having no suspect is not the best place to begin any case. But our man's out there, and our job's straightforward. We have to name him.'

Forty minutes into their shift, Gazis and Petridis responded to an 'all units' call. Gazis drove fast through the town traffic;

Petridis switched on the blue lights and played with the soundbox, switching the siren to double time at every junction, or when he saw a pretty girl.

Their colleagues had already closed Apostoli Pavlou Street. Blue-and-white tape criss-crossed the road between two lamp posts. An unmanned police car was angled across the intersection, blocking access. Gazis parked on the pavement of 25th March Street and, telling Petridis to leave the lights flashing, led him at a run to where the crowd had gathered.

On the building site, the rubble of a collapsed wall lay scattered with poles of scaffolding. Three walls still standing had shifted from the perpendicular, and loomed, threatening, over a scene of chaos. Amongst fallen bricks and planks, three men lay unmoving. Others crouched grim-faced beside them, clasping their hands. Stripped to the waist, four men had grabbed a length of scaffolding, and rammed its end beneath a block of still-cemented bricks crushing another's legs; piling all their weight on to the pole's end, they shouted to the gathering crowd to join them as their lever failed to work. The man whose legs were buried was silent, and pallid; his head slipped to one side as he lost consciousness.

Bewildered, Petridis looked about him. The sound of approaching sirens merged with crackling VHF transmissions; the thick dust in the still, hot air soon changed his clean, black hair to old man's grey. A red-faced inspector yelled to Gazis to clear the onlookers, and he and Petridis spread their arms to herd them from the scene.

'Get back!' ordered Gazis. 'Get out of here, get back!'

'Go!' shouted Petridis. 'Go, all of you!'

But the people, stubborn and fascinated, ignored them; they stood together in the road, watching the first ambulances arrive, staring as the paramedics ran with stretchers to the labourers on the ground.

A crying girl, no more than twenty, tugged at Gazis's sleeve, pleading with him in a language he didn't know; but her distress was evident and, taking her gently by the arm, Gazis led her on to the site. Petridis watched as he led the girl between the injured men, and saw her shake her head at the first two victims.

But at the last, where the men still strained to lift the crushing bricks, she found her man; and, whispering his name, she turned his dirty face towards her own, and kissed the lids that covered his closed eyes.

Eight

There was a cove where, in years gone by, the fat man liked to swim – a stretch of fine sand shelving gently into clear turquoise water.

But the road to the beach was hard to recognise. What had been a pitted, rarely used dirt track was paved, and smooth, and the overlook where the first clear view of the sea appeared was now a car park where thirty, forty vehicles – cars, motorbikes and mopeds – were lined up in the midday heat.

With difficulty, the fat man found a small space for the Pony, then made his way to the edge of the dunes above the beach. At the horizon, the view as he had known it – the dark-blue water merging with the paler sky, the distant headlands and a hazy run of mountains – was still the same.

But the beach was not as he remembered. The soft sand was filled with rows of sunbeds, where near-naked bodies stretched out beneath the sun or curled up in the shade of striped umbrellas. In the shallow water at the sea's edge, crowds of young children played, and on the water, more of them floated, splashing and shouting, on every kind of inflatable. Bikinied girls shrieked as they tossed a ball between them. A motorboat prepared to tow a giant rubber banana out to sea.

In the past, there was a wooden shack, where in the hottest months they served chilled beer, fresh sardines grilled on a driftwood fire, and cool slices of watermelon running with juice. There was no shack now. Where it had stood was a slick and canopied beach bar, manned by young men with wide smiles and tattoos who dispensed vodka cocktails and bobbed their heads to throbbing Euro-pop. There was a queue for hamburgers and hot dogs; there was another queue for ice-cream.

At the fat man's feet was rubbish: plastic bottles and empty drinks cans, fast-food wrappers and cigarette ends, the smashed green glass of an empty wine bottle, the torn pages of a magazine, ice-cream sticks. Every possible sign of growing prosperity lay there amongst the dune grasses, tickled by the breeze like flowers in spring, and in the background the music thumped on, its intense, aggressive beat marking, in rapid time, timelessness passing.

There was another place he knew where only a footpath led to the sea. The beach was small and rocky, with no temptations for developers. By his car, he changed his shoes; his pristine white tennis shoes were unlaced, and zipped away, face to face, in the front pocket of his holdall; his white sports socks were folded carefully beside them. From the same holdall pocket he took a pair of black diving shoes. Before he pulled them on, he flexed his feet. His toes were long and elegant, his ankles beautifully shaped; his calves were strong and muscled, their skin golden from the sun.

The day's heat was at its height, and the cicadas hidden in the ferny branches of the tamarisk trees were singing loudly. A tiny jetty, its base a natural outcrop of rock levelled by cement fissured by salt water, jutted into the sea. At the jetty, a small fishing boat – painted blue, with fine details added in red and yellow – was tied in close.

The fat man found a place of shade beneath the tamarisk trees and laid his holdall by their roots. Removing his shirt, he hung it from a low branch. His naked chest was firm and strong, but swelled into a well-fed belly; his chest hair was thick, but greying. He removed his watch and glasses and tucked them in the pocket of his shorts; then he removed the shorts too, and hung them in the branches with his shirt. He stood now in a pair of yellow bathing shorts and his diving shoes. Without his clothes, he appeared not fat, but imposing. From his holdall he took a snorkel mask and pipe of professional quality and, picking his way across the rocky beach to the water's edge, waded in up to his knees.

The sea was clear, and cooling. Small, silver fish darted in the shallows; black urchins formed deep blotches on the rocks. He rinsed his mask and pulled it on, placing the pipe in his mouth. Smoothly, he entered the water, swimming out in an expert crawl to where, from land, the water changed from turquoise to ultramarine, where the sea floor dropped away from almost touchable to the blank, mysterious depths, and the view beneath the surface was a blue infinity, like space.

For several minutes the fat man lay face down, watching the blueness where nothing moved but the shafts of broken sunlight, savouring the sun's heat on his back and the gentle rocking of the water's undulations.

As he sculled slowly back to shore he made for the jetty, and for a while puttered back and forwards there, watching the quickness of the fish, the slow, steady marching of the sea centipedes, the reflection of light on the weed-covered rocks, the gentle waving of the pink and peach fronds of the anemones.

He surfaced by the fishing boat, blew water from his pipe, then dived deep to touch the pebbles on the sea floor, resurfacing at the boat's stern. He dived again, resurfaced, and pushing his mask from his face, wiped the stinging salt from his eyes and trod water, peering down at the bottom of the sea.

'*Kali mera*.' The fisherman in his boat was brewing coffee. A small butane stove roared on the wooden engine housing; a long-handled *kafebriko* filled with water and ground coffee was rising to the boil.

'*Kali mera*,' responded the fat man.

'How's the water?'

'Perfect. Warm as a bath.'

'May I offer you coffee?'

The fat man smiled.

'I'd be much obliged to you,' he said and, wading from the water, he made his way down the jetty to the boat.

'Climb aboard,' said the fisherman. 'Take a seat beneath the canopy. It's a hot one today. Forty degrees, they're saying in the town.'

The boat was stacked, rear and prow, with the fishing paraphernalia of an opportunist: lobster traps, wicker baskets with coiled long-lines for tuna, hand-lines with fine hooks for inshore fishing, heavier lines with vicious barbs for calamari, nets for casting, a harpoon gun for spearing, and an old red bucket with no handle, which held a small catch of whitebait deteriorating in the heat. There was no order on board, but the boat appeared well cared for: the paintwork was fresh and bright, the glass on the instruments was free of salt stains, and above the wheel, the brass bell – engraved with the boat's name, *Agatha* – was recently polished.

Beneath the awning, the fat man sat on the wooden bench that ran inside the stern, and slid his hand along the tiller's hand-hewn length as if it were a temptation.

'She's a lovely craft,' he said. 'Well put together. Made to last.'

Wiping it first on his oil-stained shorts, the fisherman offered his own hand.

'They call me Sostis,' he said. 'Well, my wife calls me many things, but Sostis is my name.'

He gave a cautious smile. He was a man whose face and body youth had left; there were flashes of silver in his black hair, and many lines around his eyes from squinting into the sun. He wore no shoes, so the skin on his feet was hard with calluses and his toenails were disfigured and hard as horn. His T-shirt was spotted with the blood of his catches, and his skin showed through a rip at its shoulder seam. In his face was the weariness of a man who was losing life's battles, and a perplexity in his eyes that seemed habitual.

'Hermes Diaktoros,' said the fat man. 'My pleasure.'

'The boat was my father's,' said Sostis. 'Man and boy, he's been a companion to me. We've had some adventures together, me and *Agatha*.' The coffee was boiling, its fragrant foam rising to the pot's rim. He took the pot off the flame and turned off the gas, then lifted a section of the wooden bench to reveal neatly packed storage beneath. The fat man saw life jackets and a blanket, a ball of twine, spanners and a mallet. There was a large aluminium saucepan holding plates and cups, knives and forks, and from it Sostis chose two demitasse cups painted with Japanese ladies in kimonos. He ran his finger around their insides to remove the worst of their stains, then poured the coffee, handing the cleanest cup to the fat man.

'No sugar, I'm afraid,' he said. 'No biscuits, either. We're low on niceties.'

'I don't take sugar,' said the fat man. He tasted the coffee, finding it excellent. Beneath the canopy, the day seemed cool.

In lines of white crystals, the salt water was drying on his body, the salt powdery in the hairs of his forearms and calves.

'There's fresh water under your seat,' said Sostis. 'It's not cold, but it's cool. You'll be thirsty after swimming.'

The fat man stood and, lifting his seat, took out a cooler and two beakers. He filled the beakers and drank deep from his own. The water was fresh and sweet, well water collected from winter rain. He sipped again at his coffee, then peered into the red bucket near his feet.

'Forgive me,' he said, 'but your catch is poor.'

'Maybe so,' said Sostis, 'but I enjoyed not catching what I didn't catch. A boat, a line, and the quiet of the sea – what more could a man ask for?'

'Indeed.'

'Though my wife doesn't see it like that. She curses the day she married a lazy dog like me.'

'This isn't your trade, then?'

'Sadly not. I'm a barber by profession. I have a shop in town.'

The fat man raised his eyes to the sky, ascertaining the position of the sun.

'You've closed early today, then.'

'What time is it? Noon, one? I don't wear a watch. I close when I've done my quota for the day. A dozen heads, morning and evening, puts bread on the table. When I've done my dozen, I'm out the door. Today I was lucky, I got a few regulars in early. I'll be back there tonight, when it's cooler. My wife curses me, tells me how rich we'd be if I put in proper hours. We could have two shops, she says, hire people to work under me. But look at me! I'm an unlikely boss for anyone. And there's nothing we need that money can buy. I was blessed with one son – no daughters' dowries to find. He curses me, too, sometimes, for the electronic gadgetry I don't buy him and the designer shoes he doesn't have. I say to him, go barefoot, like me, then you won't need shoes. And if he's bored, he can take a line and fish. Poor beggar. Can there be a worse curse than a lazy father?'

'The wisdom to know you have enough is a blessing, surely, not a curse?'

Sostis laughed.

'Well said, friend, well said! Come and say it to my wife sometime, wipe some of the sourness from her face. You see this place? Could any man not recognise its beauty? I brought her here once, but she was bored. No company, she said, and the stones too hard to sit on. She has no love of solitude. Not like me.'

'Then I've intruded on you. My apologies.'

'None needed. I smell a kindred spirit in you. And not many folks find this place. How come you did?'

'I was here last some years ago. I lost something of value then. I had a vague hope of recovering my property.'

'What did you lose?'

'A ring, a gold ring. It was of sentimental value, a gift from my mother. There was less of me then – the ring slipped from my finger whilst I swam. It's a slim, slim chance, of course, after all this time. But I am by nature optimistic.'

For a moment, Sostis was silent.

'This ring,' he said, 'what was it like?'

'A plain band set with a small gold coin, an unusual coin. It had a rising sun on one face, a young man in profile on the other.'

Without speaking, Sostis rose and slid back the wooden door to the inner cabin. Stooping inside, he took a plastic tub with the fading imprint of a margarine brand on its side. The tub was filled with oddments – screws and washers, a key tied on a length of twine, fuses and fuse wire, assorted buttons, a pencil stub, a rusting lighter, the cork from a wine bottle. He rummaged until beneath it all he found the glint of gold, and took out a ring. Its shine was dulled by dirt, but unmistakably it was a ring such as the fat man had described.

Sostis held the ring out to the fat man.

'Like this?' he said. 'Looks like your luck is in.'

The fat man's smile was broad.

'Where did you find it?' he asked.

'I found it in the shallows, here,' said Sostis. 'It caught my eye amongst the rocks. I thought it was my lucky day then, too. But I only wore it once. Here, take your ring. You're welcome to it.'

He placed the ring in the fat man's hand, and the fat man, pleased, held it up to catch the light.

'You didn't like my ring,' he said. 'How come?'

Sostis closed the cabin door and returned to his seat.

'It's a strange story,' he said. 'I've told no one.'

'You'll find me discreet,' said the fat man, 'and a good listener.' He tried the ring on the third finger of his left hand, but it was too small. He placed it instead on his little finger, where it fitted very well, and he admired it there.

Sostis took a drink of water.

'How many years ago would it have been? You'll know better than me, perhaps, the date you lost it. I came here to fish on a day the weather wasn't good. It was late in the season, the wind was picking up and it was threatening rain. But I didn't want to be at home, listening to the same cracked record of my wife's complaints. Because of the weather, I'd stayed longer in the shop than usual, but it did me no good: the weather kept everyone close to home, and the takings were poor. All fuel to her fire. So I came to take the boat out, even though it was against my better judgement. And as I prepared to cast off, your ring there was winking up at me amongst the rocks. I fished it out and put it on my finger, pleased as punch at my good fortune. Something, I thought, to keep the harridan quiet. Forgive me, but my first thought was of selling it. It's a beautiful ring, antique it seemed to me, and I knew a jeweller who'd be glad to buy it. I put it on my finger, and it looked very well there; it made me cheerful, because I thought if I caught no fish – and the way the weather was, I expected nothing – I still had this precious thing to justify my trip.

'I didn't plan to go far. I thought I'd tow a line for tuna – you'll know they like the windy weather – make a tour or two around the bay and then head back. Well, I certainly had no more luck that day. A kilometre from shore, the engine died. No warning – it just spluttered and cut out. So there was I, alone and drifting – but I wasn't drifting back towards the beach. I was being blown towards the headland over there.' He pointed to the east, where the shore ascended steeply in rocky cliffs. 'And believe me, you don't want to be drifting over there. They call it the Dragon's Teeth – shallow water and sharp rocks that'll slice through your hull like paper. Now I'm not a bad swimmer: that wasn't my worry. But I've no insurance, and if I lost my *Agatha* . . .' He patted the engine housing as one might caress a dog. 'Well, there'd be a lot of haircuts needed to replace her, and a lot of time to be spent with my dear, gloating wife whilst I was boatless. But there was nothing I could do. I was drifting with no other boat in sight. So I decided to wait until I was in shallower water to drop an anchor off the prow, then swim a line from her stern to the rocks. That would hold her fast whilst I tried to fix the engine. So we drifted and drifted until we were getting into shallower water and I could see those rocks coming into clear view. But the water was still too deep to drop the anchor, so I waited some more until I saw a spot I thought would do OK.

And I was just about to drop the anchor when . . .' He shuddered, and crossed himself over his heart. 'I thought I saw a face looking up at me through the water, a foot or so beneath the surface. A man's face, I was sure, pale as death, eyes wide open and staring, and beneath the waves his mouth moving, as if he was speaking to me. Well, in that moment, friend, I learned what folks mean when they talk of your blood running cold. But the boat was still moving, and we passed over this face, so I crossed to starboard and looked down into the water – and damn me, something was still there, so I knew I didn't dream it. Part of me thought it couldn't be real and part of me thought I must get him out. I was scared, and I couldn't think. I ran for the boat-hook, but by the time I'd fetched it we were amongst the Dragon's Teeth, and everywhere I looked there was no sign of any man.

'So I went to drop anchor, and dropped it willy-nilly hoping it'd catch and hold us before damage was done, and in a minute I felt it hit bottom and I tied it off. So now all I had to do was swim to the rocks and tie a stern line, and we'd be secure. *But I did not want to get into that water*. Not because it was cold and choppy, but because I didn't want to be bumping into any dead man. In my mind I was persuaded, see, that's what I'd seen – a dead man talking. So I talked myself into it, and from somewhere I found the courage to strip naked, and in I went. By God, it was the coldest sea I've ever known – unnatural cold. I carried the line to the nearest rocks and tied *Agatha* secure – and all the time I was in the water, I was looking over my shoulder and down at my feet, thinking he was behind me or below me, I didn't know which. But I believed he was there somewhere in that cold, cold water, and that he'd like my company permanently if he could catch me. I swam out and I swam back as fast as if the devil were at my heels.

'I dried and dressed myself, and then set off a flare. I might have fixed the engine, but my need for company out there was strong. I knew the flare would be quickly seen – there're always craft in the channel beyond the bay – but there was no knowing how long before the coastguard would get to me, since I was pretty well hidden amongst those rocks. Well, for a while I sat in silence. The sea was dark and agitated, and the wind was making strange noises in the awning. And after a while my imagination started playing tricks – first I heard a knocking on the boat side, then I heard a slithering on the prow. And then, merciful God! An engine, and the coastguard comes roaring round the bay.

'Of course I told them I'd seen a body in the water. They launched a dinghy and took a look around – and it wasn't long before they found the body.' He laughed. 'I felt a fool. It was a billy goat fallen from the cliffs, a week at least in the water, hairless and rotting and stinking all to hell. Imagination, they said, and shadows; the water causes distortion, changes shapes. I suppose they're right. But as they towed me back to shore, I took off your ring and put it away inside the cabin. I couldn't tell you why, but it seemed to me no coincidence that the wearing of it led me to see a dead man's face. I haven't worn it since, and I never showed it to my wife. It wouldn't have been to her taste, anyway. She likes the modern style, in everything; but, thinking she'd appreciate the cash, I offered it to a jeweller in the market. Happily for you, he wouldn't take it. More than his job was worth, he said, to touch antiquities. So I brought it back here, and kept it. I thought, in any case, it would be wrong of me to pass on to someone else something that troubled me. Maybe, I thought, it was no accident that it was in the water. Maybe someone else saw what I saw and wanted to be rid of it. But I've no business saying so, have I? It doesn't trouble you, I see.

Forgive me. It's a beautiful ring. I'm sure you're glad to have it back.'

'My mother will be delighted,' said the fat man. 'It's an old family piece. Of course I must give you something for your trouble.'

Sostis held up both his hands.

'I want nothing,' he said.

'Well,' said the fat man, 'it may be, in any case, I'll come across in my travels something that would be a suitable token of my thanks.'

'Travels?' asked Sostis. 'Are you a traveller, then?'

'Throughout this country and our islands, yes. My business makes it necessary. Sometimes I have been beyond our existing borders, though still within the limits of our ancient boundaries – mostly to parts of what is now Turkey, what was claimed by the Ottomans. Our boundaries have moved so often, no man could ever hope to keep track of them.'

'I spent some time in Turkey,' said Sostis. 'The Turks are the finest barbers in the world. I took a boat to Marmaris, and apprenticed myself there to a man who spoke very little Greek. And I spoke less Turkish, so the process was slow; but for a fee he taught me all he knew. When I returned, I told no one where I'd been. They appreciate my skills, but I would never call myself a Turkish barber. Or even a barber in the Turkish style. They'd rather die here than give business to a Turk.'

'The prejudice runs deep.'

'So what brings you here? It'll be family, no doubt.'

'Not family, no. I have a house near by, where I am staying for now. A good friend of mine has died suddenly, and his affairs demand my attention.'

'What friend?'

'Gabrilis Kaloyeros was his name.'

'My condolences. I knew him, by sight only. The melon man. He was very old. I suppose his time had come.'

The fat man's face darkened.

'Indeed it had not,' he said. 'His end was brutal and untimely. A hit-and-run. A cowardly, despicable crime, especially when such an elderly man is involved.'

'The police are looking into it, then?'

'They had me at the head of their list of suspects, as the finder of the body. Though I think they have reconsidered now.'

'Their minds are simple. They look always for the obvious.'

'You have a good head on your shoulders, barber. Yes, the obvious is their usual domain; but the obvious is very often not the truth. I specialise in hidden truths, and the truth is hidden here.'

'You're a detective, then?'

'A sometime investigator, shall we say?'

Sostis was thoughtful for a moment.

'It troubles me you say the old man's death was not natural,' he said, 'because I know of someone for whom his death might be very convenient.'

'Who?'

'A client of mine. Paliakis is his name. Aris Paliakis.'

'I see.' The fat man nodded. 'And why would Gabrilis's death be convenient for Mr Paliakis?'

But Sostis was reluctant to say more.

'You'd be surprised what people tell me when they're sitting in my chair,' he said. 'Some treat it like the confessional, treat me as if I have a priest's obligation to keep silence. I'm not a gossiping man – most I keep to myself – but the things they say! Mistresses and misdeeds, dirty deals and malice . . .'

'But, as you say, you have no obligation to keep silent. Do you know the story of King Midas? King Midas had a secret only his barber knew – that Midas had been cursed by the god Apollo with a pair of ass's ears. The barber told no one, but the secret burned inside him. So to unburden himself, he dug himself a hole and whispered what he knew into the ground. Regard me as your hole in the ground, and tell me what you know of Aris Paliakis.'

'You know him, then?'

'I seem to remember our families have had dealings in the past. But this Aris, I have not yet met.'

'Well, Aris Paliakis has fingers in many, many pies. He fishes the rising tide of tourists – the mosquitoes that plague us in their thousands. He hires them cars, he feeds them in his restaurant, they sleep in his hotel, they buy their souvenirs in his shops. They call him – what's the word? – an entrepreneur. A crook, to you or me. He started in a small way, and now he's built a fortune. He's a man whose lust for money can't be satisfied. His greed is like a thirst that can't be slaked.' He drank deeply from his water beaker. 'Every Friday, he sits down in my chair to get his hair cut, and every Friday, he talks to me about his plans. In the past, those plans were small, though the whole has added up, bit by bit, to an empire. Now he has his sights on bigger things. What, exactly, I don't yet know, but the site he has in mind is the hillside at the Temple of Apollo.'

The fat man laughed.

'He'll have to look elsewhere, then. The temple's an ancient monument. He'll never get the necessary permissions.'

'Never say never, friend. He has a son, Pandelis – a lawyer and a very clever one, unmarried and his father's right-hand man, with nothing to do in life but to bend the law whichever way his father wants it. Money changes hands, no doubt of it. And where the palm-greasing doesn't work, he sends his second son, Kylis – his delivery boy, his debt collector, who might apply a little pressure where it's needed. Pandelis the brains, and Kylis the muscle. With poor old Gabrilis out of the way, you can't help but think Paliakis's way is clear. The temple's no Parthenon, is it? When all's said and done, who'll stand up for a few old stones? You wait, friend. There'll be blind eyes turned, permissions'll be issued, and the bulldozers'll move in before you know it. Who's to stop it? Old Kaloyeros had no children; who'll inherit his land? If there's no one to object, the way is open.'

For a while, the fat man was silent. Sostis threw his coffee grounds over the side, then leaned out of the boat to rinse his cup in the sea.

The fat man rose.

'I must go,' he said. 'Thank you for your hospitality. And my ring.' He laid a hand on Sostis's shoulder. 'Take my word for it, friend. There'll be no construction at the Temple of Apollo. The game is far from lost. In fact, it hasn't yet begun.' He pulled a long curl of his damp, salt-matted hair to its full length. 'I need a haircut. Tell me where to find your shop, and one day soon I'll be one of your twelve heads. And tell me where to find this Aris Paliakis and his sons, too. I'm thinking perhaps it's time for me to go visiting.'

As they travelled back to the police station, Petridis was quiet; Gazis suspected the memories of a difficult day were troubling him. According to the ambulance crews, one of the builder's labourers was likely to lose his legs.

Locking the patrol car, he tossed Petridis the keys.

'Take these back to dispatch,' he said. 'Tell them the car needs cleaning up. Then meet me upstairs. I've a job for you before you go.'

In the office, he dropped the Yellow Pages on Petridis's desk. Petridis frowned; his thoughts were on a cold beer, and a plate of his aunt's pastitsio.

'A little task to take your mind off things,' he said. 'Call the local radio stations, and ask them to put a bulletin out on the Kaloyeros case. Tell them what we're looking for: a white vehicle with damage on it. It was your idea, and it was a good one. Now follow through on it.'

Petridis's last call was to FM107. He didn't use the directory, but dialled the mobile number on the card Dinos had given him.

'Sergeant Petridis, *kali spera*!' Dinos's voice was bright. 'How are you doing this evening?'

'Constable,' said Petridis. 'It's Constable Petridis.'

'What can I do for you? It's George, right? May I call you George? Do you have something for me?'

Knowing Gazis would never permit such a liberty, Petridis was uncomfortable with Dinos's use of his first name. But Dinos was a media man; compared to his old company in the islands, Dinos seemed cool, urbane. Petridis allowed the liberty to pass.

'We'd like you to put out a request for information on your news bulletins.'

'Absolutely, no problem at all. Always glad to help the constabulary; Mr Gazis will tell you that. Space permitting, obviously. We've a big story running. A wall collapsed on a building site.'

'I was there,' said Petridis.

'I heard some of those guys aren't too good. Great story. We don't get many big stories round here, believe me. Those we do, we capitalise on, keep them running as long as we can. I wired some of our pictures through to Athens, and I'm doing an illegal-immigrant follow-up tomorrow. What are they, Albanians, Russians? You work for nothing, cut corners, you've got to expect consequences.'

'I've heard it was the site owner who cut the corners.'

'Maybe so. But bad news for Albanians is good news for us. That's the way it is in this business.'

'I'm calling about another matter, actually – the old man's death. The hit-and-run on the airport road. You were there.'

'*I* was there? I don't think so, George.'

'You were there,' insisted Petridis. 'You gave me your card.'

There was silence on the line, then a shuffling of papers, the snap of the glovebox.

'Hello?' said Petridis. 'Are you still there?'

'Sorry,' said Dinos. 'This car makes a lousy office. I can't find a pen that writes. OK. Fire away.'

'The airport road,' repeated Petridis. 'The hit-and-run.'

'I'm with you now,' said Dinos. 'You know how it is – I'm here, there and everywhere. I lose track. It goes with the territory, occupational hazard. I can't remember where I was an hour ago, never mind yesterday. What have you got on it?'

'We want to issue an appeal to all garages. Anyone who's worked on a damaged vehicle brought in within the last forty-eight hours, anything that comes in, in the next week or so.'

'You're looking for a car with new damage on it.'

'Exactly.'

'Make, model, colour?'

'White.'

'That's it, white?'

'That's it.'

'Manufacturer?'

'We've no idea. But we don't want you to say that, obviously.'

'It's a long shot, then, isn't it?'

'We're exploring every avenue.'

'But if the guilty party hasn't taken the car in for repair yet, won't knowing you're looking for it stop them from doing so?'

'Probably. That leaves the evidence for us to find.'

'And if they have taken it in, you'll get the call.'

'That's the plan.'

'Clever. OK, I'll see what I can do. Can't promise, though. With this building site thing, the bulletins are full. What's the old guy's name?'

'Kaloyeros. Gabrilis Kaloyeros.'

'Leave it with me.'

'We appreciate it.'

Petridis was about to hang up, but Dinos stopped him.

'Listen, George,' he said, 'are you a fan of the Songbird?'

The Songbird – Telma Lalagi. Petridis had her poster on his bedroom wall at home. She was beautiful, sexy; her voice was like caramel, smooth and warm.

'No man alive who isn't,' he said.

'Did you know she's in town tonight?'

'My brother tried to get tickets. All sold out.'

'I got tickets. Freebies. Press box. You want to go, be my guest? There'll be some hospitality thrown in. It'd give you a chance to meet some people, hang out. What do you say?'

Petridis hesitated. He was expected home for his day off, had promised to catch the boat at the end of his shift. His mother missed him; it had been a while since he'd seen Yorgia.

He could go early the next morning. His mother wouldn't mind, and Yorgia could be persuaded to understand.

'I'll have to clear it with Gazis,' he said.

'Gazis? What's it got to do with Gazis? This is your private life we're talking about. Even policemen are off duty sometimes, George.'

'It's the hospitality thing. We're not supposed to accept hospitality.'

'So don't. Bring yourself a cup of coffee, if that's what you want to do.'

Petridis remembered the lecture Gazis had given him on his very first day on the job, his number one rule of policing, as he had called it. *You're never off duty*, Gazis had said. *From now until the day you resign, retire or get shot in the street, you're a policeman. People expect a lot from policemen. They've a right to. Remember that, and you won't go far wrong.*

Gazis had a lot of rules; every day there was a new number one. And this was Telma Lalagi. His brother would be mad with jealousy. It was a concert, nothing more.

'OK,' he said. 'That would be great.'

Dinos pressed the button on his phone to end the call. On the piece of paper in his hand, he'd written only two words. *Gabrilis Kaloyeros.*

His phone rang again. As he put the handset to his ear, he dropped the paper on to the passenger seat.

'*Yassou, koukla mou.* How's the prettiest girl I know?' With the phone still to his ear, he moved the car forward, pulling out into the narrow side-street. Parked vehicles lining its kerbs left passage for only one car, one way. The draught from the open window wafted the paper he had written in to the footwell, where it lay amongst the rubbish: cigarette packets, last Friday's newspaper, three empty water bottles.

In the tourist restaurants, the waiters were laying the tables for dinner. Outside the bars, the touts were in position, hands full of *First drink free* vouchers. Dinos drove slowly past Bolero's, where Marie (a Scottish girl, a redhead with good legs) worked. But she wasn't there; a brunette in heavy make-up and whore's clothing had taken her place.

'I'm on my way back now,' he said into the phone. 'There's nothing new out here.'

As he braked at the T-junction, traffic on the main road was light. He checked the rear-view mirror. No one was behind him.

'Not tonight, *koukla*,' he said. 'Unfortunately. I promised to go to my mother's. It's been days since I was there.'

He glanced to left and right. A moped ran by on the main road, then a small Fiat.

'I can't,' he said. 'She'll want me to stay the night. My aunt's visiting this week. You know how it will be.'

A red Namco Pony passed along the main road, travelling from east to west. A silver Toyota followed a tiny Smartcar and, a little distance behind, a streamlined black German saloon.

'Gotta go,' said Dinos. 'I'll call you tomorrow. Be good. *Ciao*.'

He ended the call, tossed the phone aside and fastened his seat belt.

The black saloon was close, approaching from his left.

Dinos looked right, and pulled out into the main road.

There was a horn blast, and a screeching of tyres; his car was jolted by the impact as the black car hit his wing. Then came a short silence as Dinos shook his head to stop the dizziness; and then the silence was broken as the driver of the saloon began to yell.

By the black car's front end, the two men considered the damage. The glass from a broken headlamp glittered in the road; the car's bonnet rose to an angle at its centre, and the silvered radiator grille was bent.

'I'm sorry, friend,' said Dinos, 'truly sorry. I just wasn't thinking straight. And such a beautiful car. I always wanted one of these. Is it drivable?'

The man looked at him with weary eyes.

'Does it look drivable, to you?' he asked. 'I hope you've got good insurance, because I'm coming to you for every cent. In the meantime, I'll take your name and address.'

Behind Dinos's car, a motorcyclist revved his engine with impatience; behind the damaged BMW, a young woman in a small Opel peeped her horn.

'I'll get you a card,' said Dinos.

'You do that,' said the BMW's driver. 'And make a note of my name, too, for your insurers; they'll be needing to know where to send the cheque. They call me Vrettos, Manos Vrettos. I can lend you a pen, if you want to write it down.'

Nine

Beneath the spotlights, Telma Lalagi's face shone with sweat and melting greasepaint. On the giant video screen, her face was magnified in close-up, and Petridis was surprised to see the lines of middle age running from her upper lip to her nostrils, and crow's feet around her heavily made-up eyes. But she was still lovely, and still adored, and as she raised her naked arms to the night sky, the shouts and whistles of the crowd broadened her carmine-painted smile over those tiny, perfect, pearly teeth.

The lights dimmed suddenly, blacking out the band and the backing singers like a magician's trick, so the Songbird seemed to stand alone at the centre of the vast stage, a single spotlight reflecting off the sequins of her sculpted dress. In a pose of abject grief, she closed her eyes and dropped her head, allowing her dark, glossy curls to fall over her face. The crowd grew quiet.

With a pure and soulful beauty, a single bouzouki rang out in a trembling melody. Recognising the first notes of Telma's greatest hit, the crowd roared its appreciation, and the Songbird threw back her head as if in an ecstasy of pain, and the whole band took up the dramatic theme of a thousand heartaches.

In the press box, Petridis was bewitched. Under Telma Lalagi's influence, his guilt over the girl he'd left behind turned to nostalgia. He remembered how Yorgia had cried when he had left her; he recalled all the promises he'd made – to call, to visit – that he had failed to keep. He'd told himself there was no formal arrangement between them; she and her family had mistaken his intentions. He'd thought his ties to her were fading, that she mattered less; but now this powerful anthem of tragedy and abandonment made him doubt himself. The mainland girls all seemed so sophisticated, and quite beyond him. He found he missed Yorgia's innocent smile, and the comfort of her fingers wrapped around his.

The stage lights took on the colours of heartbreak – indigo, violet, red – as the Songbird slowly turned, slender hips writhing in a sensual Turkish dance. She held her hands out to the crowd as if she would embrace them all.

'Come on, my children!' she cried. 'Help me!'

Together, the Songbird and the crowd took up the song:

> *The blame, my faithless love, lies all with you,*
> *I gave you everything a woman can,*
> *Heart, body, soul, the very best of me,*
> *We lay together, you were my only man,*
> *But now you've gone, the season's changed, grown cold,*
> *Our star which glittered bright no longer shines,*
> *My faithful, aching heart was always true,*
> *The blame, my faithless love, lies all with you.*

Below the press box, the flames of hundreds of lighters flickered like candles in the dark, and the Songbird's plaintive voice soared above the tuneless singing of the crowd. On the video screen, the despair on her face seemed agony. With the edge of a long, red-lacquered nail, she wiped away a tear that left no mark.

He could call Yorgia now. It wasn't too late. Though she'd be cool at first over his prolonged neglect, he knew, once the recriminations were past, she'd welcome him back. Petridis had learned that the grass here wasn't greener; far worse than that, he had found no grass at all.

But as the audience moved haltingly into the second verse, the neck of a bottle chinked against the rim of his glass. Splashing in more Scotch, Dinos clapped a hand on Petridis's shoulder, and shouted into his ear.

'She's something, isn't she?'

Petridis smiled his agreement.

'There's some people I want you to meet.'

The press box was small, and the dozen people gathered there made it crowded. When Dinos had introduced him – to producers and announcers, to advertising salesmen, to a nightclub owner, to a couple of hangers-on – he hadn't mentioned Petridis's occupation, nor given any reason for his being there. Now there were two women he hadn't met, leaning on the broadcast console. The stage lights dimmed again, pulling shadows across their faces.

Dinos grasped one of the women around the waist. Petridis smelled the floral sweetness of her perfume.

'Meet the girls,' said Dinos. He pulled the woman close, nuzzling her ear until she smiled. She gave his cheek a pouty kiss, leaving a mark of burgundy lipstick.

'The lovely Katina,' he said. 'And this is Haroula. Haroula, say hello to George.' His hand slid to a skinny buttock barely covered by her miniskirt.

Haroula drew unsmilingly on a half-smoked cigarette. Her eyes held Petridis's; as she exhaled smoke, they narrowed as if to bring him into clearer focus.

'*Yassou*, George,' she said.

Leaning back on the broadcast console, she crossed one naked, oil-sheened leg over the other, giving Petridis a glimpse of the intriguing darkness beneath her skirt. Her blouse was tight, the neck unbuttoned and showing a chain of white gold which fell into her rounded cleavage. The chain held a scarab beetle worked in the same white gold, its back a glittering stone too large to be a genuine ruby.

Dinos held up the half-empty bottle.

'Another drink, girls?'

The women held out their glasses to be filled, then drank. Haroula's lips were wet with whisky, and now she smiled widely at Petridis.

Beyond the press box, the tempo of the music became upbeat. Haroula leaned forward; her breasts touched Petridis's shoulder. Before she spoke into his ear, he felt the tickling of her breath.

'I love this song,' she said. 'It's good to make love to.'

Her breath smelled of whisky and smoke; Yorgia had breathed nothing on him but lemons, and fish. Haroula leaned away from him, smiling expectantly, waiting for his response.

For a moment, he hesitated, unsure of what to say, or do. The scarab's fake ruby caught the light, putting sparks in her wide and welcoming eyes.

'I like your necklace,' he said, and putting out his hand, gently lifting the beetle from her neck, he leaned in close to study it, brushing her soft, exposed skin with the tips of his fingers.

Pandelis Paliakis was careful in his undressing, folding his trousers along the leg-pleats and slipping them on to a wooden hanger, folding the shirt, too, and placing it in the calico sack provided by the laundry service. Stripped to his socks and underwear, he turned from the dresser mirror, disheartened by his soft, boy's belly plump with an over-indulged taste for ice-cream. He pinched a roll of fat, and shook his head; what other grown man, he asked himself, had vanilla ice-cream as a vice?

He lay down on the bed where only he had ever slept. The night was hot, and still. Through the open window, the music from the concert in the stadium came to him with the whistles and cheering of the crowd. Kylis was there, on cheap tickets from some tout. He'd gone with friends. Pandelis was not invited.

He might have offered his mother a game of draughts, but her room along the hall was dark, and silent; the tablets she took for migraine were potent, and made her sleep for hours. There was work to do, of course (he hadn't even opened up his briefcase, and the papers his father was screaming for were still unchecked), but the pricking of his conscience was over-ridden by a feeling unfamiliar to him: restlessness, or bore-dom, or ennui.

His mobile phone began to ring. Taking it from the bedside table, he knew before he looked who would be calling and, sure enough, his father's office number was on the screen. Pandelis let the call go to the messaging service. In the stadium, the crowd was applauding as a woman's voice boomed through the speakers, too distorted by echo to understand.

His phone rang again. He dropped it on the sheet beside him, ignoring it until it was silent.

He placed his hands behind his head, and thought: of sleep, of his brother, of a cooling shower. He thought of Sonya in the restaurant – her smile, her eyes, the shape of her breasts beneath her T-shirt – and the restless feeling grew. She'd be there now; in the next hour or so, she'd be getting off work. He could call and ask if she'd like coffee, or a cocktail, if he could walk her home . . .

He grabbed his phone and dialled the restaurant number; but as the phone rang out, he cut the call, and dropped the phone back on the bed.

'*Malaka*,' he said hopelessly. 'What would she want with you, *malaka*?'

Music rang out again from the stadium, a song he knew of love, anger and passion, and the crowd began to sing, thousands of voices sharing the emotion. Pandelis left his bed, and closed the window to shut them out. Lying down once more, he turned out the light, and closed his eyes to try and sleep away the lonely night.

Ten

Outside the Hotel Sparta, the departing tourists dragged their bags and cases to the waiting bus. The bus was old, its exhaust system was illegal; engine running, it pumped smoke and hot fumes over the dry-mouthed, queasy passengers as they boarded. Last night had been a night for making memories – drinking, eating, dancing into the small hours – but the memories, this morning, were blurred behind red eyes, nausea and headaches, behind the stale garlic from the last dishes of tzatziki and the lingering aniseed taste of too much ouzo.

From the *kafenion* next door to his shop, Sostis the barber watched the foreigners climb the steep steps into the bus. He pitied them; he pitied them their grim and cheerless journey, and their return to the damp, dour climate of their homeland. His own plan for the day was the same as almost all others: one dozen customers, close the shop, and fish. His Greek coffee was sweet and reviving, and he had chosen this morning a sticky pastry scattered with toasted almonds and filled with creamy marzipan.

The street ran downhill to the promenade, where the masts of chartered yachts rocked gently in the swell. A ferry bound for the islands steered between the high walls at the harbour mouth. A plane passed low overhead, the linked coloured rings of Olympic Airlines on its white fuselage. Like men condemned, the departing tourists gazed up at the plane.

Sostis raised his cup to them.

'*Kalo taxidi*,' he said aloud. 'Don't worry, my friends. In twelve months' time, you'll pass this way again.'

Inside his shop, the phone rang. He glanced at his watch: 8:35. He took a bite of his pastry, savouring its sweetness and the light crunch of the almonds; but the ringing phone persisted, intruding on his pleasure. So, leaving his coffee half-drunk and his pastry unfinished, he went inside the shop to take the call.

'Yes?'

'Is that you, barber?'

'It's me.'

'Are you free?'

Sostis thought of his coffee and pastry.

'Five minutes,' he said. 'No, make it ten. Just to be sure.'

'I'm on my way.'

There was no goodbye, no pleasantries. On his way back to his table, he switched on the air conditioning and turned over the sign in the shop doorway so that it read, from the street, *Open*. He took his seat in the *kafenion*, and gave his full attention to his breakfast. If Aris Paliakis arrived promptly, he would simply have to wait.

'Cappuccino,' said the fat man, 'and a panino with ham, cheese and tomato. No mustard.'

The café was chic and Continental, furnished with soft chairs in modern prints and low, smoked-glass tables, all occupied by breakfasting Greeks, and tourists. The gritty-voiced singer on the music system sang in Italian; behind the counter, huge chrome machines hissed and steamed as the scowling woman wrote down his order.

93

'Cappuccino,' she said with disapproval. 'Panino. I'll bring it out.'

She ran a hand through her limp hair, then turned to one of the machines and, pulling out a scoop with a deft twist of her hand, knocked out the wet coffee grounds.

The fat man watched her slop milk into a metal jug.

'How interesting to find an Italian café on this coast,' he said. 'Are you Italian by birth?'

'Italian?' She banged the milk jug on to the counter. 'You insult me, *kyrie*. I was born not ten kilometres from here. My family were shepherds; my family have always been shepherds. It was a good life, peaceful. Now you see me here making *collo*-cappuccinos and panini. Sit. I'll bring it out.'

'Forgive me. I meant no offence.'

'This . . .' She wafted a hand at the chrome machinery, at the coloured boxes of biscotti and the Italian wines and liqueurs on the shelves, at the freezer filled with gelati – peppermint-green, delicate pink, the yellow of butter – where flies hovered by the wafer cones. 'This is all my son's idea. But do you see my son here? No. My son is sleeping after staying up too late, here till 4 a.m. drinking with his customers. So I am here. Pay someone, I say. It's not a mother's job to be making Italian coffee, serving Italian food.'

'But this place is charming,' said the fat man. Beyond the café's boundary was a harbour view, where the crews of rich men's cruisers prepared to sail. 'Your son has vision.'

'My son has debts. For authenticity, everything, he says, must be imported. Even the ice-cream. Buy Greek ice-cream, I say, who'll know the difference? But he knows best. So there'll be two more seasons at least, till he breaks even.'

'The business looks very successful.'

'If successful means never a moment to sit. You sit. I'll bring it out.'

'You're very kind,' he said. 'By the way, I'm told you have a regular customer here. One Kylis Paliakis.'

Before she turned back to the machinery, she jerked a thumb towards a table close to the sea, where three men sat together, laughing.

'On the right,' she said. 'Now there's a man of leisure, if you like.'

The tables to both left and right of Kylis Paliakis were occupied. On one side, a Scandinavian family sat with beach bags and blonde children; on the other were two Greek women of a certain age, dressed in much younger women's clothes. One of the women talked into a phone; the other, chewing gum, looked around in boredom.

Smiling, the fat man approached their table and spoke to the woman chewing gum.

'*Kali mera, koritsi*,' he said. At the compliment implied in the word *koritsi* – young lady – she looked up sharply. The fat man smiled on, watching her assess him – *too old, too fat, but nonetheless a man* – until she, still chewing, gave a small smile. 'I was wondering if you would let me buy you coffee.'

The woman on the phone was watching, listening. As the fat man, receiving no rebuff, moved to take a seat, she spoke into her phone.

'I'll call you back,' she said, and, lips tight in jealous disapproval, snapped the phone shut. 'We're just leaving,' she said to the fat man. From a pink handbag, she counted out the exact change for their bill, and stood. 'My sister and I don't accept drinks from strangers. Eleni, let's go.'

The fat man winked, and made a face at Eleni which meant, *Let her go, you stay*.

But her sister saw it.

'Hurry, Eleni,' she said. 'We've business to attend to.'

'What business?'

'Let's go.'

With reluctance, Eleni rose from her seat.

'It seems I must go,' she said. Her shoulders rose in a small shrug of resignation.

'Another time, perhaps,' said the fat man.

'Another time.' She smiled more openly, her face showing a remnant of past prettiness. As she followed her hurrying sister along the harbour-front, Eleni turned her head in hope the fat man was watching.

But the fat man's true interest lay elsewhere. Already in her vacated seat, his holdall at his feet, he laid this morning's local paper on the table, put on his sunglasses and, seeming to be gazing at the view, observed Kylis Paliakis from behind dark lenses.

Kylis was several days unshaven, his hair had grown out of its cut, his shirt and shorts were rumpled as if picked up off a floor. Slumped indolently in his chair, he had too much weight on his belly, too much flesh around his neck. But Kylis Paliakis had been, no doubt, handsome in youth. His looks were not all gone; but he looked a man who'd be unkind, to a certain kind of woman.

He laughed, and, as if responding to a prompt, one of his companions joined in the laughter. But Kylis's laugh was loud, intruding on the quiet conversations at other tables, and his second companion – whose curling beard gave him the appearance of an artist, or musician – frowned disapproval. Kylis said a few more words, and two of the three laughed again.

'Cappuccino,' said the woman, placing a foaming cup in front of the fat man. Coffee had overflowed into the saucer. 'Panino.'

'Thank you,' said the fat man; but she was busy with the

Scandinavians, removing their empty plates, tutting at a spilled pool of fresh orange juice.

As the fat man lifted his cup, coffee dripped from its base on to his shoes. He frowned, then sipped at the milky froth, took a bite of his sandwich and unfolded his newspaper. A black-and-white photograph covered the front page: a collapsed building, a man on a stretcher being rushed to an ambulance, and in the foreground a shouting policeman, his arm pointing to something out of shot. The headline was a single word – *Catastrophe!* – with a subheading: *10 injured, 2 serious, in site disaster*.

The fat man turned to the report on page two, then held up the paper as he began, seemingly, to read.

The laughter at Kylis's table became silence.

Beside his coffee cup, Kylis had a small glass of Metaxa. He picked up the glass, drank the liquor in one swallow, and slammed it back down on the table.

'Page one,' he said. 'Father's famous.'

His bearded companion asked, 'What's the news from the hospital?'

'One of them's lost his legs,' said Kylis. 'The other's still unconscious. And Father's raging. We've no insurance. I've told him to get Mama's priest to start praying for their deliverance. If either of the bastards dies, it's going to get expensive.'

He laughed, but this time neither of his companions joined him.

'Even for you, that's cold,' said the bearded man.

Abruptly, Kylis stopped laughing. He looked the bearded man straight in the eye.

'Not cold,' he said, 'pragmatic. They screwed the job up. You give them a chance, a straightforward job, and they do nothing right. Now it's us who'll pay the price for their incompetence.'

'You gave them a chance because they're cheap,' said the bearded man. 'No training, no licences, no safety procedures, no inspections. Don't tell us your father didn't know that when he hired them.'

Kylis turned away his face, and ran his tongue around his mouth as if preparing to spit. Instead, he swallowed.

'You're prejudiced,' he said. 'You're prejudiced against Albanians, Russians, whatever the hell they are.'

'I'm not prejudiced against anyone who pays their taxes. And I pay my taxes, so why shouldn't they? But they're as happy to cut corners as your father, and now it's all gone wrong, they'll expect their hospital treatment for free. Though of course they can't pay anyway, poor bastards, because your father pays them nothing in the first place. So who'll pay?' Angrily, he stabbed his finger into his own chest. 'I will. Me, the taxpayer. I'll foot the bill. Your father's got what he deserved, and I truly hope, my friend, they throw the book at him. And the least you can do is to get off your arse and go and pay your respects, ask how they are. Take flowers. Or fruit. For God's sake, Kylis. This is a serious matter!'

Kylis picked up his empty glass and stared into the bottom.

'I'm not going to the hospital,' he said. 'Those people never wash. I might catch something.'

The bearded man shook his head.

'Sometimes,' he said, 'I don't know why I talk to you.' Standing abruptly, he picked up his cigarettes, tossed ten euros on to the table, then nodded at the third man. 'Takis, *kali mera.*'

As he walked away, Kylis called after him.

'Prick! *Malaka!*' He held up his glass, and called to the woman behind the counter. 'Toula! Another Metaxa!'

In objection, Takis raised his hand; the hand trembled, as if affected by some palsy.

'For Christ's sake, Kylis,' he said. 'It's 9 o'clock in the morning. Go home, get some sleep.'

Angrily, Kylis turned to him.

'And who the fuck are you?' he asked. 'The morality police? Toula, forget it! I'm leaving.'

Standing, he was unsteady on his feet. Staring for a moment at the bearded man's money, he fumbled in his pockets and drew out a fifty, dropping it over the ten-euro note.

'Wait for your change,' suggested his companion.

But Kylis was already walking away.

'Keep it,' he called over his shoulder. 'Cocksucker.'

The fat man lowered his newspaper. He watched as Kylis crossed the street, stopping the traffic by ignoring it. He climbed into a white transit van, and without signalling pulled out in front of an approaching bus, making an obscene gesture in response to the bus driver's horn blast. In the rear window was a sticker: a red-and-blue *V*, the logo of Valvoline motor oil.

Toula approached the table Kylis had left. With shaking hand, his companion held out the large banknote.

'He throwing his father's money around again?' she asked. 'You'd better credit it to his account.'

She gave a bitter laugh.

'His account's already in credit,' she said. 'He's in credit for coffee and brandy for the rest of his life. His credit's what's keeping this business afloat!'

As the fat man finished his coffee, he read the report of the accident with care, then folded the newspaper and laid it down. From the open sea, a hydrofoil was coming into port, its wash rocking the vessels moored at the harbour wall.

The fat man bent down to his holdall, unzipped it and, fumbling inside, pulled out a bottle of shoe-whitener. Removing the plastic cap, he stretched out his left foot and dabbed whitener on two spots where coffee had stained the canvas.

He inspected his right foot and, finding a scuff mark on the rubber toe, blotted it out. Satisfied, he replaced the bottle cap, and zipped the whitener back into the holdall.

From the counter, Toula watched him curiously. The fat man approached her with money in his hand.

'You're admiring my winged sandals, as I call them,' he said. 'It's a life's work, almost, taking care of them. I'll pay my bill, if I may. And if you've a moment, I'll try some of your Italian ice-cream. Is that, by any chance, pistachio?'

The ice-cream was excellent, well flavoured and sweet, but in the morning's warmth it melted quickly. Heading into town, the fat man chose the path along the harbour-front, where the palm trees gave some shade; and, being in no hurry, he took a leisurely pace, licking ice-cream dribbles off his wafer cone as he walked.

Aris Paliakis was late.

Sostis sat on outside the café, enjoying at first the warmth of the early-morning sun; then, when the heat grew too strong, he called for the waiter to roll out the canvas canopy.

He was considering a second pastry when Paliakis turned the corner, heading up the street from the harbour. In white trousers and a holiday-maker's Hawaiian shirt, he held his phone to his ear; he walked quickly, frowning, scattering the pigeons pecking for crumbs in the gutter and around the municipal bins.

Sostis called goodbye to the waiter and went into his shop. Behind the washbasins, the towels were neatly folded on the shelf; the floor was swept clean of cut hair and still damp with mopping. By the cash desk, a glass dish held breath-freshening cachous scented with violets and rose water; the bottles of toilet water – lemon, sandalwood, eau de Cologne – had been refilled and dusted.

Taking comb and scissors from the sterilising solution, Sostis dried them on a hand-towel and laid them on the shelf before the mirror. A selection of men's magazines – *Four Wheels*, *Drive*, raunchy-covered *Klik* – was stacked beside the empty chairs; now Sostis added two of this morning's national newspapers – the left-leaning *Eleftherotypia*, the right-wing *Kathimerini*.

The shop bell rang, and Aris Paliakis stepped in from the street, turning off his phone and slipping it into his pocket. In invitation, Sostis spread his hands over the back of the black leatherette barber's chair.

'*Kali mera*,' he said. 'How are you today, Mr Paliakis?'

He knew the answer he would get; but with Sostis, the habit of good manners was ingrained.

'Don't *kali mera* me, barber,' said Paliakis. He slipped into the chair, glowering at both his own mirrored reflection and at Sostis's. His shirt was bright with pattern and colour: emerald-green parrots, orange hibiscus flowers on a background of poster-paint blue. As he sat back in his seat, his feet barely touched the floor. 'I pay you to cut my hair, not to bore me with idle chat.'

Sostis threw a plastic cape over both customer and chair, and tied the cape's ribbons in a bow. Taking a soft towel from the shelf, he tucked it firmly into the cape; goaded, perhaps, by rudeness, his tucking was a little rougher than it needed to be. Without either of them noticing, he caught the delicate chain that hung around Paliakis's neck. The chain was broken; both the chain and the object it held slipped down inside Paliakis's gaudy shirt.

Sostis faced Paliakis in the mirror.

'The usual?' he asked.

'Of course the usual, man!'

Paliakis closed his eyes, but the muscles of his jaw did not relax. Sostis dipped the bristles of the shaving brush into the soap, and applied a thick lather to Paliakis's face; as he worked the brush into the skin, Paliakis's grip on the chair arms seemed to grow tighter. When cheeks to collar-line were covered with soap, Sostis opened a cut-throat razor and sharpened it on the strop. Cutting swathes across Paliakis's face, he shaved the skin clean, wiping foam and short whiskers on the towel at Paliakis's neck; then, whisking away the towel and wringing out a flannel soaked in warm water, he wiped Paliakis's face. Choosing the sandalwood, he splashed cologne into the palm of his hands, and patted it gently on to Paliakis's clean-shaven cheeks.

Paliakis winced.

'By Christ,' he said, 'that's got some bite to it. What have you diluted it with, vinegar?'

As Sostis picked up the comb and scissors, Paliakis ran his fingers over his face, searching for stray whiskers. He found none. His eyes – empty as a goat's – watched in the mirror as Sostis passed the comb through the ring of thin grey hair around Paliakis's scalp. The cut he had administered one week ago had barely grown; the lightest trim would do the job. Lifting the first ends of short hair with the comb, he snipped them off; the bristles, no length at all, fell like dust-motes, settling silver on Paliakis's black-caped shoulders.

Believing the cold, shrewd eyes were watching him, Sostis kept his own eyes on his work. But Paliakis had no interest in the barber. Something in the street held his attention, an image in the mirror he was watching.

'You know,' he said slowly, 'that is one thing I cannot bear to see. Waste. I cannot bear to see waste.'

Sostis paused in his cutting and glanced through the window at the street, where there seemed to be nothing remarkable. Outside the Hotel Sparta, the tourist bus was almost full. A street cleaner was spearing rubbish with a spike, dropping it into the sack he carried with him; as Paliakis spoke, he picked up a half-eaten, paper-wrapped doughnut, and the pigeon pecking at it fluttered away.

'These days,' said Sostis, thinking he had understood Paliakis's meaning, 'people throw away more food than they eat.'

'No, no, no,' said Paliakis impatiently. 'Not food. Them.' He pointed towards the bus, where Northern European faces stared out at the sunshine. 'They come for a week, two weeks, and then they're gone. The season's short – how many months? Five at the outside, and only July and August really profitable. It's not long enough. The investment for such a poor return isn't justified. They come and go, and there's the problem. To get a decent return, we need to make them stay.'

Around Paliakis's ears, the half-circles of hair cut so perfectly last week were a little ragged. Sostis bent in close, and with the scissor tips trimmed them back into perfection.

'Not *holidays*,' went on Paliakis. '*Holidays* are crippling us. No sooner have you built some customer loyalty – and that loyalty is never guaranteed . . .' He raised his head quite suddenly, and held Sostis's eyes in the mirror, smiling an unkind smile that showed the glint of his gold canine. 'We all value loyalty, barber; but in my experience, loyalty must be earned. Do you agree?'

Sostis did not reply; in his experience, Paliakis expected no answer. Indeed, he left no room for one, saying immediately, 'I'll tell you how it is with them.' He nodded towards the coach, where the uniformed company representative was climbing aboard. 'You spoil them for a night or two – a drink on the house, a dish of ice-cream for the children, and many of them are yours. But like fickle women, their loyalty doesn't last. How can it? Seven days, and they are gone. In come the next lot, and you must start again. Always *kamaki*, always charming, always tempting in the new ones, getting a firm grip where we can. But only for seven days. Like Sisyphus's, the task is never done. Do you know the myth of Sisyphus, barber?'

Sostis took a soft-bristled brush and flicked hair snippets from Paliakis's neck.

'He had a rock, if I remember,' said Sostis. 'He pushed it uphill every day. And every night, it rolled downhill, and he had to start again. A punishment from the gods. But not as bad as having your liver torn out and eaten on a daily basis. Who was the poor bastard who suffered that fate?'

'Prometheus,' said Paliakis. 'His liver regrew every night. At least he had no work to do. I am a modern-day Sisyphus. And there they go . . .' The coach pulled away from the kerb, disappearing around the corner. 'A waste, you see, a terrible waste of potential income. There's so much of their money they don't spend here. How much can they spend, in just a week? I must be charitable, and acknowledge it's not their fault. But there is a better way, a much better way, which I intend to exploit. No more wasting time on charm and niceties. It's the waste that gets me, here.' With his fist, he banged himself on the chest.

Sostis took a pair of surgeon's tongs from the shelf, and used them to pull a ball of cotton wool from a wooden box.

'You can't stop them going home,' he said. 'If they kept on coming and never left, we'd have real problems. We'd be overrun within a month.'

Paliakis laughed.

'You have no vision,' he said. 'You need to look at things differently. The trick would be to import the richest pickings on a full-time basis, cut down on the rest. Like Spain. The Spanish have the right idea. They've made good use of their resources – and remember, their resources are the same as ours: sun, sea, sand. Nothing more. They've still got hotels and short-timers, as we have, but they've got far more investment in the long-term market. Villas. That's where the money is – villas. A whole new town of full-time, long-term imports. Then you've got them every which way – not only your bars and restaurants, but your supermarkets, bakers, doctors and dentists, plumbers, gardeners – not forgetting barbers, barber! Everyone gets a bite at the cherry – and not just one bite! Everybody benefits, everybody!'

From a plastic bottle, Sostis squirted blue rubbing alcohol on to the cotton wool. For a moment, the shop held the sweet, medicinal smell of a doctor's surgery. With a plastic lighter, Sostis set the alcohol-soaked cotton wool alight. Covering the tip of Paliakis's ear with one hand, he held the flame to the hairs that grew around the orifice, singeing and withering them to nothing. As he passed the flame over the other ear, the medicinal smell was replaced by the smell of scorching. Sostis singed the hairs in Paliakis's nostrils, a few on the back of his neck. At every touch of the flame, Paliakis winced, but he did not complain.

'It's a great plan, barber,' he said, as Sostis dropped the burnt cotton wool to the floor and laid down the tongs. 'It'd be like keeping goats, or cattle. Milk them at regular intervals. What do you think?'

'I think there's a flaw in it.'

'A flaw?'

'Because they're not cattle, are they? They're people, with lives to live. Jobs, schools, houses. They have families. If they were refugees, that might be different. But people won't just abandon everything and come and join us here in paradise. How could they afford it?'

'But that's the true genius of my plan,' said Paliakis. 'You've got to target a certain market. Because there are people who have time and money and no responsibilities – the old ones. They'd sell their houses in Denmark or Holland or Germany and come and live here, in my development. They all have pensions, and they'll have spare capital too, property here being so much cheaper. All they have to do is start spending money. They're happy, we're happy. What could be simpler?'

The shop bell rang, and a man entered; of middle age and middle height, he had nothing remarkable about him but his hair, which seemed too uniformly black for a man of his years.

'*Kali mera sas*,' he said, smiling. 'How are things today, barber?'

'Welcome, Costas, welcome,' said the barber. 'I'm doing well, now you're here. With any luck, I'll be out of here and fishing before one.'

Costas picked up the right-wing *Kathimerini* and sat, crossing his right foot over his left knee. Reading the headline – *Farmers' subsidies increase again* – he frowned.

'*Malakes!*' he said. 'What in God's name are the clowns up to now? Have you seen this?' He held up the front page. Sostis read the headline, and smiled. Paliakis's eyes remained fixed on his own in the mirror. 'You know who'll pay for this madness,' said Costas, hitting the newspaper with the back of his hand. 'The man in the street, as always. It'll be out of our wallets, boys, put money on it.'

Sostis untied the bow at the back of Paliakis's neck and lifted the black cape from his shoulders.

Tiny clippings floated down to the chequered floor. Paliakis stood and brushed off hair he imagined on his shoulders; as he did so, the chain Sostis had broken slipped down inside his shirt and to the floor, where it fell unnoticed beneath the barber's chair.

The shop bell rang again, and another man entered; of middle age and middle height, he had nothing remarkable about him but his hair, which seemed prematurely silver for a man of his years.

'*Kali mera sas*,' he said. 'Are you well, barber?' Then, seeing Costas, he grinned. '*Yassou*, cousin!' he said. 'Hard at work, as usual?'

Costas leaned forward and offered a hearty handshake.

'Eh, Vassilis,' he said. 'How are you, how's everybody?'

'Well,' said Vassilis. 'Everyone's well.'

Vassilis sat down next to his cousin. Their physical similarity was marked; both had inherited the family nose, large, bulbous as a potato. He picked up the left-wing *Eleftherotypia*, and, crossing his left foot over his right knee, read the headline – *Farmers win fair prices*.

'And about time too,' he said, smacking the newspaper with the back of his hand. He showed the headline to Costas, and held it up to the barber, who smiled. 'They should have done it years ago.'

'And who's going to pay for it?' asked Costas. 'It'll be the man in the street, as usual. You'll not be very keen to put your hand in your pocket, I'm sure. I'm right, barber, aren't I? It'll be the working man who pays.'

'Not you, then,' said his cousin.

'Leave me out of it,' said Sostis. 'I've no interest in politics. And the fact is, what they decide today they'll change their minds about tomorrow.'

At the cash register, Paliakis counted out eight euros in coins.

'It's nine euros now,' said Sostis. 'It's gone up.'

'Gone up?' asked Paliakis. 'Why?'

'It's the air conditioning,' said Sostis. 'It's expensive.'

Paliakis pocketed his coins, and offered a ten-euro note in

their place. From the till, Sostis counted out one euro in five- and ten-cent coins, and placed them in Paliakis's hand. Ignoring both the tip jar and the slight insult implied by such small change, Paliakis pocketed these coins, too.

'It'll be going down again then, will it, in September, when you turn the air conditioning off?' he asked.

Offering no reply, Sostis slid the till drawer shut. Paliakis dipped his fingers into the bowl of Turkish cachous, and took a fistful. Popping three into his mouth, he chewed; Sostis heard the delicate sweets crack between his teeth. The rest of the cachous Paliakis slipped into his pocket with his money. As he closed the door behind him, he offered neither thank you nor goodbye.

Sostis took a long-handled broom to sweep around the chair, brushing the clippings from Paliakis's hair into a yellow dustpan. The broom's bristles caught the links of the broken chain, pulling it into view, and, picking it up, Sostis held both key and chain to the light. Much older than the chain, the key seemed delicate, antique, and so small it must belong not to a door, but to a casket, box or drawer; the silver chain glinted in the light, but the dangling key was dull and worn, dark like old iron. Sostis placed both key and chain on the counter before the mirror, and leaned the broom against the wall.

Costas folded his newspaper, and moved to the barber's chair. As Sostis threw a gown around his neck, Costas watched Paliakis turn the corner at the end of the street.

'His wall collapse made the front page of the local paper,' he said, 'though I don't see anything in the nationals. It's a bad business. One man with his legs crushed who'll never walk again, another in a coma. And here he is, cool as you like, getting his hair cut.'

'Not just crushed, amputated,' said Vassilis. 'That lawyer

son of Paliakis's was on the radio. An unfortunate accident, is what he's saying.'

Sostis tied the cape at the back of Costas's neck.

'Just a trim?' he asked.

'Never mind the trim, barber. Cut it short. I want my money's worth.'

His cousin laughed.

'Always the same,' he said, 'from a little boy. Always must have his money's worth. You'll be turning into a Paliakis yourself if you're not careful.'

'God help me if that day ever comes,' said Costas. 'You know the truth, of course.'

'Meaning?'

'Old Paliakis is short of money. He's overstretched. He owes the bank a fortune, and they're ready to foreclose for lack of payment.'

'Don't be ridiculous,' said Vassilis. 'The man's rich as Onassis.'

'Business has been no better for him than for the rest of us,' said Costas. 'The all-inclusives are hitting him hard, in the hotel and in the restaurant. Now they've got cheap fares to places you've never heard of. Forget Greece, they're off to Timbuktu and Bangkok.'

'So why's he building more, if the hotel he's got is losing money?'

'He doesn't see it that way. In his eyes, the maths are simple: more rooms, more money. Except he's doing it on the cheap. The scaffolding was put up by Albanians. Unlicensed, and no overheads, no tax or National Insurance. There'll be all hell to pay now, wait and see. The families'll sue him, if they've sense.'

'If they've sense, they won't go anywhere near Aris Paliakis with a lawsuit. That son of his is sharp as any razor. He'll eat them for breakfast, chew them up and spit them out.'

'Maybe he'll offer to settle out of court.'

'More likely he'll choose to forget the whole business. If he's allowed to.'

With his comb, Sostis lifted the shaggy layers of Costas's hair; the underside was silver as his cousin's.

'He's got a new plan,' said Sostis, making the first cuts. Black and silver hair fell to the floor. 'No more hotels and restaurants. He's going into villas, a whole town of them. He says that's where the money is, these days.'

'And where's he going to build villas, along this coast?'

'He didn't say. No doubt he's got somewhere in mind.'

'There's nowhere they'll let him do it. Not round here.'

'They might, if he has friends in the right places.'

Costas laughed.

'Now that,' he said, 'is very unlikely. You know the man as well as I do, cousin. There might be men in his pocket, but there're no friends involved. Aris Paliakis has never had a true friend in his life.'

Eleven

Petridis lay below an open window. The sky was bright with morning; the coolness of the air told him he must be near the sea. His head ached, his mouth was dry, his stomach heaved with nausea. Somewhere beyond the window, an outboard engine fired, and an unseen boat buzzed out across the water.

Beside him in the bed, Haroula muttered in her sleep.

She lay covered with a sheet, the line of her back and buttocks outlined in white cotton, her hair matted and wild. There were smears of lipstick on the pillows, and an empty wine bottle lay on the floor; a dark stain on the carpet showed where its dregs had spilt. On the bedside table were two glasses, one still full of wine, and an ashtray filled with half-smoked, ground-out butts.

Slowly, Petridis sat up. He had no memory of arriving in this place, and he didn't know this room (a hotel room, for sure: the TV mounted on the wall, the map of fire exits on the door gave it away). In the bathroom, as he emptied his bladder, he noticed the bloody marks of swatted mosquitoes on the tiles. The towels were small and thin; the porcelain basin was cracked, and the cold tap dribbled constantly.

He glanced at his watch: 9:05. Thank God it was his day off.

On the back of the door, he read the room rates, glad to find it was the cheapest of hotels; it would be down to him, he knew, to pay the bill.

But he had no cash.

His shirt was thrown on a chair, his trousers were crumpled on the floor; as he picked them up, the jangling of his belt buckle made Haroula stir. His wallet was in his pocket; as he pulled it out, something fell from there to the floor.

The banknotes were rolled tight, secured with a rubber band. Head throbbing, hands shaking, Petridis removed the band, and counted the notes. There was more than enough to pay for the room; there was more than he'd get paid in a month. He had a memory of some bar, of four of them laughing, of Haroula kissing him, her tongue pushed in his mouth, and of Dinos saying, *You're a policeman, look after this for me*. The money, then, was Dinos's. So problem solved: he'd borrow what he needed, and stop off at the bank on his way home. Dinos need never know he'd taken a short-term loan.

He'd made promises to his family for today, and the hour was still early. He should go home, shower, and change; he could catch the mid-morning ferry to see his mother.

But he needed sleep. The hour was early, and there was plenty of time. There might be a later boat, if he was lucky.

On the bed, Haroula opened her eyes. With eye make-up smeared and her lipstick kissed away, she wasn't pretty. Without the cosmetic tricks, she had aged, and she looked, through sober eyes, a whore. She was someone he'd deny knowing, if he were asked.

He thought of Yorgia, fresh-skinned and innocent.

Haroula looked up at him, and smiled a smile of welcome.

He peeled a twenty from Dinos's money, and dropped it on the bed.

'Get yourself a taxi,' he said. 'I have to go.'

'So soon?' she said. She peeled back the sheet, showing her naked breasts. 'They'll let us stay till noon. Come back to bed, *kukle.*'

Petridis hesitated.

'I have to go,' he said, after a moment. 'See you around, maybe.'

Her smile faded.

'That's all you've got?' she asked. 'Twenty?'

He left her another ten; she turned her back on him, and pulled the sheet over her head. At the lobby desk, in his hurry to be gone, Petridis let the cashier keep the change. As he stepped into the street, he kept his face turned from the traffic, and prayed no one who knew him would see him there.

'I'll see to it immediately.'

Ilias Mentis replaced the papers the fat man had given him in their brown envelope. In places, the envelope showed staining, and Ilias rubbed at one of the stains with his thumb.

'Honey,' said the fat man, in explanation. 'Gabrilis's hiding place was ingenious, but the wrapping was not entirely watertight. All things considered, the documents have survived very well.'

Through the lawyer's office door, a telephone rang, and the clatter of a keyboard stopped as his secretary answered the call. The secretary was the same efficient woman the fat man remembered – though she had aged a little – and he found it comforting so many things about this office were still unchanged: the same leather-bound volumes on civil law were on the bookshelves, the graduation certificates hung in the same places on the walls. But the photograph on Ilias's desk was different; the picture of him with his arm around his mother's shoulders had gone, replaced by a family group –

Ilias with a pretty woman and two attractive children, a boy and a girl. Ilias himself was different, too: older, stouter, better dressed. The well-trimmed sideburns he had retained were showing grey; his smile spread lines of some depth around his eyes.

Ilias glanced at the old-fashioned clock on the wall.

'I could file the papers this morning,' he said. 'The government offices don't close for a couple of hours.'

'The sooner, the better,' said the fat man. 'There are people involved who will not want to wait.'

He stood, and offered the younger man his hand.

'I'm sorry about your father, by the way. May his memory be eternal. He did excellent work for me in years gone by.'

'We had your wreath. I didn't know where to get in touch with you to thank you.'

'I've been travelling, as always. The practice seems to be flourishing, in your hands. Your mother, is she well?'

'As one would expect. She misses him.'

'Time heals,' said the fat man. 'Though often not quickly enough.'

'I'll be in touch,' said Ilias, 'as soon as there's news.'

At the door, the fat man hesitated.

'A question, if I may,' he said, 'before I go. Do you perhaps know of a lawyer by the name of Paliakis? Pandelis Paliakis?'

Ilias's face showed curiosity, and a little amusement.

'What's your interest there, if I may ask?'

'It's a name I've taken an interest in, just recently.'

'Don't ask me to stand against him in court,' said Ilias, 'because we'd be unlikely to win. The man hasn't lost a case in – four, five years. Some say he keeps a judge or two in his pocket, but I don't think so. I think his success is due entirely to the brilliance of his mind, and to his dedication. He's made the law his life. He had a reputation, in his student years, as a radical. He used to do a lot of work for free, for political causes. Fighting the system on behalf of workers' rights, that kind of thing. An idealist, or perhaps just a little naïve. Rumour has it he was a staunch supporter of the Communist Party for a while, but I'm sure he's not with them now; his father wouldn't let him waste his time. His specialities are property, and tax. If you want an off-shore company in Liberia, he's your man. But I doubt he'd work for you. He's employed almost exclusively, these days, by his father; he works hard to keep the Paliakis empire within the law. Or if not within it, not so far outside it can be touched. If there's a legal loophole anywhere, Pandelis is the one to find it.'

'I find the Paliakis family more and more intriguing,' said the fat man.

Ilias laughed.

'Then they'd better watch out,' he said. 'Your interest is something I suspect the Paliakis family would do better to avoid.'

The town hall clock struck noon, ringing out over streets wretched with heat. At the traffic lights, a bus driver wiped his forehead on the napkin from his sandwich; a motorcyclist lifted the visor on his helmet and fanned air into his sweating face. On the promenade, the gypsy children – dark-skinned, barefoot, flamboyantly dressed – had given up pressing cheap necklaces on the tourists, and lay drowsy under the palm trees. The stallholders selling dried fruit and pistachios, postcards and ceramics, sat on stools beneath their canopies, sipping at water from coolers hidden in the shade, watching the quiet sea and the comings and goings of boats.

Sostis turned the shop-door sign from *Open* to *Closed*. From tin boxes ordered from Turkey, he replenished the glass dishes of scented cachous and, taking a long-handled broom, began to sweep the fluff of cut hair into a yellow dustpan. Passing the switch for the air conditioning, he moved his hand to turn it off; but as he did so, the shop bell rang, and the fat man entered the shop.

'*Kali mera*, barber,' he said. 'I'm afraid I'm late. I intended to be with you earlier, but a matter of business took my attention. I see you're ready to attend to more important matters yourself; but will you indulge me by delaying your departure and cutting my hair, since I'm here? In short, will you make an exception, and take a thirteenth customer to-day?'

The barber smiled.

'What are rules for, if not for breaking?' he said.

The fat man seemed cool in the heat. His suit – loose-fitting, yet beautifully cut of a close-woven, nutmeg-brown cloth, finished with deep-umber buttons – held no creases, and there was no redness in his cheeks. Removing his jacket, he folded it shoulder to shoulder, revealing a lining of fine Chinese silk, striped in pale lemon and mint-green. His shirt, a polo shirt with a small crocodile on the breast, was perfectly matched to the green of the lining. The barber found the fat man almost elegant, but his elegance was compromised by his footwear: old-fashioned, white-canvas tennis shoes.

The fat man laid first his holdall, then his jacket, on the chairs where, earlier in the day, Costas and Vassilis had waited.

'I wonder if, before we start, we might order coffee,' he said. 'I notice there's a *kafenion* next door. If you'll order, I'll gladly pay.'

'What'll you have?' asked the barber.

'Iced coffee with milk, no sugar.'

'I'll join you,' said the barber, and left the shop.

The fat man crossed to the shelf beside the barber's chair where, alongside the colognes, Sostis kept his products for male grooming – moustache wax, balms for inflamed skin and shaving rashes, brilliantine, hair wax and styling gels, and an unlabelled bottle with glue-like, tarry contents the fat man could not identify. He picked up the bottles and jars that most interested him, unscrewed their lids, read their labels and sniffed at them. Then, becoming bored, he moved to a poster pinned to the wall – a photograph of Norwegian fjords – and lowered his glasses from his eyes to study it, seeming intrigued by every detail.

When the barber returned, the fat man pointed to the poster.

'This is a remarkable picture,' he said. 'Quite beautiful. Quite foreign.'

'A customer sent it to me,' said Sostis. He placed two glasses of iced coffee on the counter before the mirror. 'At least, I assume it was a customer. I cut the hair of foreigners from time to time. We don't communicate much; I speak little English, or German, or whatever. But this poster arrived one autumn, with a note which said *Thank you*, and a photograph of a man and woman, both very blond, and an address in Trondheim. I didn't recall them, but I drew my conclusions. When the weather grows hot, the picture goes up. Just to look at it cools you down, don't you think? Even though the sky is blue, you can tell that the water's cold as ice, that the air is fresh and crisp. And look at those colours! When I'm bored, between customers, I picture myself in a little boat out on that water, fishing with a rod and line, and all the great cold-water fish I'd catch. The water there must be deep enough to hold gigantic fish. That's true even here, in our much warmer waters. For winter, I have a poster of Tobago I begged from the travel agents. White sand and coconuts. So you see, for me, the grass is always greener.'

'You have plans to travel to these places?'

'No, not me. I'm not a travelling man, these days. The truth is, for me, there's no place like home.'

The fat man sat down in the barber's chair. The ring Sostis had found was, the barber noticed, still on the fat man's little finger. The fat man sipped at his coffee through a straw; the thick foam at its top was pale and creamy, the coffee beneath was cold and rich, with floating ice cubes tinkling on the glass's rim.

Sostis threw a cape around the fat man's shoulders and tied the black ribbons behind his neck.

'So,' he said, 'what'll it be?'

'A trim, no more,' said the fat man. 'You've an appointment I'm keeping you from. The fish don't like to be kept waiting.'

The barber placed his hands in the fat man's hair and pulled it gently, extending the curls to show their true length. Their texture was soft, like the silky hair of children, and where it was still black the colour was glossy as crows' wings. As he let the hair fall, it gave off a faint, nostalgic scent, of hay meadows, grass and flowers warmed by the sun; and the scent disturbed some memory in the barber, a happy memory just out of reach, which suddenly he regretted having lost. He spent a minute in trying to recall that time and place; but the more he reached out for it, the more distant the memory became.

When he came back to himself, the fat man was watching him in the mirror. Behind his glasses, his eyes were large, the colour of them uncertain.

'What do you think?' he asked.

'You have very fine hair,' said the barber, 'which it would be a crime to lose. You're not a short-back-and-sides man. I'll take an inch off all over.'

'Excellent,' said the fat man. He sipped again at his coffee, enjoying its coolness. 'Business has been brisk today, I hope? You were ready to leave in good time for the fishing, if I had not detained you.'

'I had a prompt start,' said the barber. 'In fact with the gentleman – if gentleman is the right word – you and I discussed. Aris Paliakis. He was my first customer this morning.'

'Our property-developing friend,' said the fat man.

'That's him. He talked about his plans. There's to be – if he gets his way – a whole village, it seems. A ghetto of villas for foreigners.'

'I'm surprised,' said the fat man, 'that he's considering more development, now that his current project has gone so badly wrong. I saw the local paper.'

'The wall collapse? Work's halted there, of course. An investigation's in progress, they say; it seems to me none's necessary. Ask any man in the street, they'd tell you the reasons for that disaster – corner-cutting, unlicensed gangs, cheap foreign labour. But old Paliakis, he doesn't seem worried.'

'Why wouldn't he be worried?'

The barber laughed.

'You and I know, friend, how these things go. A lunch here, a gift there, a credit to a bank account or cash stuffed in an envelope, and papers get lost. The case will be forgotten. The same will happen with his new development. He's got friends in the Chamber of Commerce, one in the Planning Office – they call him Alfieris, his first name I don't know. The man is bought and paid for; he'll speak up for Paliakis at the highest level. He's another customer of mine, as charmless as Paliakis himself. Birds of a feather, the two of them. Cutting Alfieris's hair is like cutting the hair of a snake, and as pointless; he has none to speak of, so what he has, he has me shave very short, so his baldness seems deliberate. It's his moustache that is his vanity; the man is as in love with that moustache as he is with himself. Only a government officer would have so much time to spend preening. He's a man you'd never trust, the kind of man who'd stamp on butterflies.'

On the floor around the chair, cut curls lay in one-inch lengths, but the fat man's hair looked no different.

'What do you think?' asked the barber. 'Shall I take more off? You'd never know I'd touched it.'

'Just as it should be,' said the fat man.

The barber removed the cape, and brushed a few stray hairs from around the fat man's neck. The fat man drained his glass of coffee and, pulling on his jacket, took twenty euros from his wallet and handed it to the barber.

'Keep the change,' he said.

'Many thanks,' said the barber, smiling.

'I'll come fishing with you one day, if I may.'

'My pleasure. You know where to find me, any day of the week.'

The fat man picked up his holdall. As he opened the door, the shop bell rang.

'Do you perhaps know,' he asked, with one foot in the street, 'where I might find Mrs Paliakis?'

'A grand house, not too far from here.' The barber gave the address. 'Are you going there?'

'That's my intention.'

'Then perhaps you could return Mr Paliakis's property.' Sostis picked up the key and broken chain from the counter, and held it out to the fat man. 'This is his; he always wears it. I found it on the floor here this morning, after he left.'

'My pleasure.'

The fat man took the key and chain, and slipped them in his pocket.

'When you go there,' said Sostis, 'beware of the dog.'

The fat man raised his eyebrows.

'The Paliakis family,' he said, 'does not strike me as being one for animals.'

'Even so,' laughed the barber, 'be warned. The woman's well guarded. You'll find Mrs Paliakis keeps a most unusual pet.'

Twelve

As the fat man drove along the track to his villa, the early afternoon blazed hotter than midday. In the olive orchard adjoining his garden, the cicadas were in full voice; the orchard's grass was dry and dead as straw, and of the same soft gold. A donkey tethered to an iron stake flicked ears and tail to rid itself of flies; the olive trees themselves were broad-trunked and twisted, riddled with hollows, and ancient enough, said the people of Palea Chora, to remember the days when Midas wore an ass's ears himself. At the roots of the trees, an old woman cleared weeds from earth so dry it rose in puffs of dust at her hoe blade; she wore a wide straw hat against the sun, and against the adders, black wellingtons on naked legs and feet. As the fat man passed, she paused in her work and held both hands up to her eyes, like a mariner on the lookout for first landfall; recognising the fat man, she raised a hand to him in flat-palmed greeting.

On the verandah, the table was spread with a blue cloth, and laid for lunch in the shade. As the fat man took his seat, Kokkona brought out Greek salad and a plate of squid fried golden-brown, a jug of water from the well and a bottle of Mythos beer, chilled so the condensation sat in drops on its shoulders.

The fat man removed his nutmeg-brown jacket and draped it round the back of his chair.

'Sit with me,' he said. 'Talk to me whilst I eat.'

In the wicker chair she favoured, a piece of fine crochet work lay on the well-worn cushion. With fingers slowed by the first aches of arthritis, she worked on a string of daisies and a scalloped edge. In the distance, the sea was pale in the heat-haze, a line of subdued blue where the buff-coloured land came to an end. Beneath the olive trees, the donkey raised its head and brayed, lips pulled back over its monstrous teeth as though in devilish laughter.

The fat man seasoned his food from a pot half salt, half rice grains to absorb the damp. Squeezing a segment of cut lemon, he dribbled juice over the squid. He poured wine vinegar on the salad, and olive oil the light, clear green of moss. From a still-warm loaf of bread, he tore off the crusty end, and began to eat.

The tomatoes, picked from the garden, held both the sun's warmth and the plant's essence in their flavour; the feta was white and sharp, musky with sheep's milk. The red onion was hot and pungent; the squid was crisp to bite, the flesh tender and succulent with the freshness of the sea. The bread's crust was a pleasing contrast to its yeasty softness; the beer was cold and cooling, and excellent refreshment against the saltiness of the food.

'A first-class lunch, as always,' said the fat man, choosing a piece of green pepper from the salad.

'Spiros caught the squid this morning,' said Kokkona. 'He brought it here himself. He was sorry to miss you.'

'I had business in town,' he said. 'One or two matters have come to light. It seems there's someone with an interest in Gabrilis's land.'

She tugged at the crochet work with the hook, forming another petal on a daisy.

'You surprise me,' she said. 'There's little enough value to it. Gabrilis – God rest him – worked hard on it for decades, and it never gave him much of a return. It's stones and dust, and all on a slope. If you know someone looking for farmland, my brother-in-law's a piece he'd like to sell.'

'Ah, but Gabrilis's land has a feature that makes it unique, Kokkona *mou* – it boasts a wonderful view. And a view, these days, is worth much more than melons and honey. The gentleman with the interest thinks he can sell that view. He believes this coast would benefit from some new residents. He wants to build homes for foreigners – I presume, to keep them here permanently, and secure their income.'

'A new crop, then,' she said, shrewdly.

'Indeed.' He glanced at the old woman hoeing at the roots of the olive trees. 'A crop you don't have to weed or water; a crop that comes to you, and looks after itself. Quite a neat concept, don't you think?'

'No,' she said. 'That view's been there, unspoiled, since time began. It isn't for anyone to sell it off and profit from it. Besides, who'd think of ruining such a place?'

'Aris Paliakis.'

She laughed.

'I should have known. Of course it would be Aris Paliakis who would come up with such a scheme. He's a man who'd sell his own grandmother, if she were still amongst the living.'

A wasp hovered at the neck of the beer bottle. The fat man wafted it away and refilled his glass, placing the empty bottle across the table. When the wasp returned to the bottle, he let it crawl there undisturbed.

'Your opinion of him coincides with that of others. The

family name I know, but this particular Paliakis has built himself up in my absence.'

The daisy she was working on completed, she unwound more cotton thread from the ball, and began to form the centre of the next.

'Of course you remember the name. Around here, the Paliakises are famous; the family fortune's given much to talk about, over the years.'

The fat man frowned.

'There was an interesting story, wasn't there?' he asked.

'Indeed there was. Of a fortune that went missing, and was never found.'

The fat man smiled.

'Remind me,' he said. 'But if this is going to be one of your longer tales, Kokkona *mou*, let me light a cigarette before you start.'

He reached into his pocket and took out a pack of cigarettes – an old-fashioned box whose lift-up lid bore the head and naked shoulders of a forties starlet, her softly permed platinum hair curling around a coy smile. Beneath the maker's name ran a slogan in an antique hand: *The cigarette for the man who knows a real smoke*. Producing a slim gold lighter, he knocked the tip of a cigarette on the table, lit it, and laid the cigarettes and the lighter beside his empty plates.

'I'm ready,' he said. 'Let the story begin.'

'Time was,' she said, laying her crochet work in her lap, 'that Paliakises were pitied. Then there was a time Aris was admired for his success. Now, most won't give him the time of day. It doesn't bother him. The balance of his bank account is all he cares about.'

'Why did people pity him?'

'It wasn't only him they pitied, it was all of them. The

family was for years a laughing stock. Though it should have been otherwise. His grandfather on his father's side made money. He was an Aris too, with this Aris being named for him, of course. And true to his grandfather's memory, he keeps both name and spirit alive. Their love of money is in the blood, and Aris is his grandfather's disciple.

'Now some say different, but I say this: the way his grandfather made his money was very simple. He had a store on the edge of town – long gone now, of course, knocked down for new development. He sold feed and farm implements. Anything you needed, old Paliakis would supply, from a bag of corn for your chickens to a wheelbarrow or a saddle for your donkey. My grandmother would take me there as a girl, and I remember all sorts of odds and ends – cheese strainers and rope and buckets, fence posts and ointments for your goat's mastitis.

'The villagers were all shepherds and small farmers, but Paliakis had a businessman's mind. And happily for him, he had a monopoly, too – for miles around, no competition for his store. So everything he sold, he sold at a premium price, and made a little extra profit on each item. And bit by bit, he salted his profits away. You'll hear, maybe, he bought this bit of land, or that, but I don't think so. There was nothing so grand. There didn't need to be.

'For some years, Paliakis kept his money in the bank, in the way most people do. In those days, my grandmother's neighbour was cashier at the National Bank, so it was common knowledge what he was worth. And by middle age, it was plenty; by today's measures, not much, perhaps, but believe me, Paliakis was very comfortable. Or should have been. You may have guessed by now, the money wasn't for spending. A dry stick he was, and tight as tight could be. Money in the bank there was, but his kids went about dressed almost in rags, and the family lived on lentils and oranges, same as the rest of us.

'And then, one day, Paliakis and the manager of the bank had a disagreement, and the disagreement grew into an argument. Maybe Paliakis believed the manager was cheating him; the reason they fell out was never clear. The manager refused to talk about the matter; not even my grandmother's neighbour knew what had been said. But whatever the reason, old Aris Paliakis marched home, marched back to the bank with a stout wooden box, demanded all his savings, piled the cash into the box and took it away.'

The fat man drew on his cigarette, and flicked the ash from its end. He seemed thoughtful, but kept silent.

'Now, what happened to that box was the subject of speculation for years,' went on Kokkona. 'Paliakis's children claimed they didn't know; so did his wife. In the *kafenions* and the tavernas and the churches, they discussed its where-abouts endlessly. Some said it was under the bed, some said under the floorboards, some said buried in the garden. But no one doubted he would keep the box close by. That was the nature of the man.

'Years went by, the children grew up, and Paliakis became an old man. But he still opened up the shop every day, and he still made a few drachmas extra on everything he sold. And still the mystery of where those profits went remained. What people said was in that mysterious missing box! Gold, jewels, the deeds to all kinds of property – in the folklore of the village, it grew and grew, until it was a box no longer, but a treasure chest!

'And then, very suddenly, Paliakis died. Young Aris was still at school, and suffering badly. The whole family was teased about Grandpa's fortune, taunted because they saw none of it. But Aris always hit back at his tormentors by saying he knew exactly where the box was; Grandpa, he said, had told him. Well, if he had, young Aris kept it to himself; and if he hadn't, no doubt the old man meant to tell them all one day. But he left it too late. Without warning, he was gone; caught out in a storm, he took the only shelter he could find, beneath a pine tree and – pouf! – a flash of lightning took the tree, and him with it. Folks made plenty of that, of course, him being taken by fire. The devil, they said, had come to take his own.

'So then the treasure hunt began in earnest. Of course Paliakis's children – Aris's father particularly, being the eldest – turned the house upside down. They ripped up floorboards, they smashed cupboards; they went down the well and drained the *cisterna*; they took the plaster off the ceilings to check the roof timbers and dug up the garden foot by foot. Nothing. The box wasn't there.

'Still, to this day, it's never been found; and the not finding of it was a tragedy in itself. Paliakis's father believed all his life he'd find it; he believed it so strongly he never bothered to make anything of himself. Everywhere he went, they called after him, *Hey, lucky, found that box?* He didn't care, until he ran out of places to look for it. He took to drink, and went to an early grave, destitute; from a young age it was the grand-children who paid the bills, and took care of their mother. I remember the mother. She was a miserable woman. *You can't spend wishes*, she used to say.'

Kokkona picked up her crochet work.

Finishing his cigarette, the fat man ground it out in the ashtray.

'So where did our Aris Paliakis get his start in life?' he asked. 'To build his empire, there must have been seed money. A little capital, at least.'

'Now that,' she said, 'is a mystery, too. He made it somewhere, though not round here. He disappeared for a while, and came back with his pockets lined: not stuffed, you understand, but with enough to make a start in a small way.'

'And did no one ask him where he'd made this money?'

'Oh, you can ask a Paliakis all you like, but if they're not telling, you waste your breath. Old Grandpa Paliakis taught them that.'

'He has a family, I believe.'

'He has a wife who suffers with her nerves, a highly-strung, difficult woman. And two sons. One he put through university, made him a lawyer to cover his backside. The other's another matter. He had it in mind to be a racing driver – not those proper racing cars, but rally cars – and as a hobby, it proved expensive. He took himself all over the place – Italy, France – to take part in the races; but there were no wins, only repair bills. This past year, I hear, Paliakis refuses to pay, and Kylis has joined the family business. Though what his contribution is is hard to say.'

The fat man picked up his box of cigarettes and opened the lid, as if considering lighting another, but he closed the box without doing so. As he slipped the box and his lighter back into his pocket, his fingertips touched the key the barber had given him.

'I read a story in a newspaper recently,' he said. 'It came from Thessaloniki, and as a cautionary tale, you'd be hard-pressed to invent a better one. A second-hand dealer hunting for antiques found his way into a house scheduled for demolition, and found a mummified body in the bedroom. The dead man was elderly, and quite forgotten by relatives and neighbours; the pathologist believed he'd been dead for eighteen months. When police searched the house, they found, in drawers and cupboards, the evidence of wealth – bank books and bond certificates, with holdings worth, when they were added up, two million euros. Clever enough to make himself a fortune, he wasn't smart enough to make sure someone in the world cared if he lived or died. I can foresee a similar end for Aris Paliakis, if he doesn't take care.'

For a few minutes they sat in silence, and the fat man watched the honey bees, busy even in the heat around the delicate spikes of lavender and the blush-pink roses of which he was so fond.

'I think,' he said at last, 'it's time for my siesta.'

He made his way around the house, to where a hammock was stretched between two evergreen oaks, whose deep-green foliage gave shade cool as a cavern. With some agility, he bounded into the hammock; and soothed by the cicadas, made drowsy by the beer, with his hands folded on his ample stomach, in no time at all he was peacefully dozing.

Thirteen

One hour after dawn broke over the placid sea, the sky's pale pink was yielding to strengthening blue. At the harbour, the fishing boats had tied up; the fishermen in their sterns were red-eyed and unshaven, dirty with oil and blood. Repairing yellow nets, tinkering with engines and greasing seals, replenishing fuel tanks with diesel, they called to one another as they worked, exchanging banter, bumming cigarettes, swapping tales of the ones that got away on last night's sea.

The fat man strolled along the moorings, half-listening to the fishermen's stories: a dolphin floating dead at Ayios Yiorgos (*The only good dolphin's a dead dolphin, fish-thieving bastards every one*), a shoal of fat sardines caught by someone's cousin, rumours of an unlicensed boat confiscated by the *limanarcheio*, the coastguard – *Koproskila!* – up the coast. They watched him, but with only half an eye, not curious enough to comment on him when he'd passed.

The fat man walked close to the boats, scanning their modest catches: a few long-nosed garfish, slender as rope, some silver-scaled bream and a good haul of shrimp, one or two octopuses, slimy and slithering, half a bucket of whitebait, a leopard-skinned conger eel. And, in the last boat on the line, the fat man saw what he needed: three scorpionfish, vermilion and dangerous, clear, round eyes bright, and still staring as in life.

The fisherman at the prow was naked to the waist and tanned to leather; he was hauling up buckets of seawater, swilling it over the deck planks to keep the wood from shrinking. His manner was surly, his breath smelled of alcohol and aniseed. A cigarette dangled from the corner of his mouth, and his eyes were narrowed to slits, from smoke, or from the sun, or from mistrust; but when the fat man drew out a banknote, he flicked the cigarette overboard, and offered a sly smile.

But, knowing the price of fish, the fat man bargained hard. With his purchases tied up in a carrier bag, he wished the fisherman *kali mera*, and made his way along the harbour-front to where stone steps led down to a narrow, pebbled beach.

Sitting on the steps, the fat man took out his penknife and, one by one, dealt with the fish. The guts he threw out to sea, then he rinsed his hands in the shallow water, rubbing in citrus-scented ointment from the bee-embossed tin to take away their stink.

At the *kafenion* Aktaion, the waiters, puffy-eyed from hot, sleepless nights and too much ouzo, swept the street-dust from beneath the tables and laid out the napkin-holders, the laminated menus, the glass ashtrays still wet from rinsing. Dressed in fresh, white linen with his hair still damp from combing, the cook leaned on the counter turning the pages of *Taste* magazine; at his feet, the stock delivery – fruit juice and bottled water, salted peanuts and a tray of sticky baklava – waited untouched for his attention.

On FM107, the 8 o'clock pips signalled the news, and the cook turned up the volume on the radio. The headlines were of the heatwave stifling Greece.

Passing the counter with a broom, one of the waiters called out to him.

'What are they saying, Chef? Rain before lunch, snow by evening?'

The cook grunted, and slapped away a fly crawling on his hand.

'More of the same,' he said. 'Thirty-nine degrees, and the power stations all out. Too much demand for air conditioning. Used to be when it got hot we all left town.'

On his way outside, a second waiter paused to listen.

'Another easy day for you, though, eh?' he said. 'What are they saying, only fruit and water?'

'Fruit and water, my backside,' said the cook, turning the pages of his magazine. 'It'll be coffee all day, as usual, and they'll still want to eat. It's not in their nature to take good advice.'

'Ten dead nationally, I heard,' said the waiter, 'and a little child in Navplio. That's tough.'

'Yes,' sighed the cook, 'that's tough on someone. Why didn't they just take the kid to the beach? When you've finished sweeping that terrace, you can give me a hand carrying this delivery out the back.'

The radio slipped into a melancholy ballad, and the cook looked with sad eyes towards the sea, as if the song brought to mind someone too far away but not quite forgotten.

On the *kafenion*'s terrace, the fat man surveyed the four customers already seated. All were at separate tables, all had briefcases and wore the summer uniform of businessmen: plain, short-sleeved shirts, pale cotton trousers and loafers on bare feet. But though the uniforms were identical, one man was unique in his current occupation. Three of the men had spread papers on the table and, with the anxious energy of the self-employed, talked fast and loud into mobile phones, already brokering deals. The fourth man sat quite relaxed in his chair, his legs stretched before him and crossed at the ankles, reading this morning's *Ethnos* and smoking a pungent cheroot. His head was shaved bald, his moustache was flamboyant and waxed, precisely trimmed over the lips, twisted into sharp, sabre-curved points at the sides of his mouth.

The fat man took a seat at the table beside him. Hanging the knotted bag containing his fish on the back of his chair, tucking his holdall beneath his feet, he laid his cigarettes and a matchbox on the table, and picked up the menu.

Outside a small electrical shop across the street, an aged lorry rattled up to the kerb. Leaving the engine running, the driver jumped down from the cab and sauntered into the shop, a clipboard tucked under his arm. The noise from the truck was loud; every panel on its body rattled, and its exhaust pumped oily, noxious clouds towards the *kafenion*, soon overcoming even the smoke of the moustached man's cheroot. Theatrically, the fat man waved a hand before his face to disperse the fumes, glancing sideways to catch his neighbour's eye; but the moustached man seemed oblivious, absorbed in an article in his newspaper.

The street was narrow, with no room for traffic to pass. Soon, a taxi carrying a smartly dressed matron rounded the corner, and pulled up behind the lorry. Only a few seconds passed before the taxi driver blew his horn. There was no response. The taxi driver turned to his passenger and spoke, then blew his horn again. Again, there was no response, and so he blew his horn a third time.

Then, the taxi door burst open, and the driver – a florid, obese man in a heavy sweat – stood in the street, hands on hips and cursing viciously. He looked up at the lorry's empty cab and along the street; seeing no lorry driver, his eyes settled on the owner of a *periptero*, who sat, arms folded and interested, on a stool behind his counter, waiting for a drama to develop.

'Where is this *malaka*?' demanded the taxi driver, jerking his thumb at the lorry.

With a Judas smile, the *periptero*'s owner pointed to the sign over the electrical shop, just visible above the lorry's roof. The taxi driver moved quickly, gut wobbling, between his taxi and the lorry's rear end, and disappeared; his matronly passenger, well-coiffured and made-up, but in very dated style, called after him.

'Where are you going, *kalé*? Twenty minutes, didn't you say? You'll make me late!'

Raised voices from the electrical shop – the angry voices of two men – stopped her complaints. The fat man's eyebrows lifted slightly at the language; the moustached man laid down his newspaper and looked, frowning, across the street.

'What in God's name is going on?' he asked the fat man.

'A dispute over parking,' said the fat man. 'Nothing more.'

The shouting within the shop was reduced to one voice, and the taxi driver, face purple and murderously set, reappeared behind the taxi. At his counter, the cook had forgotten his magazine, the waiters had stopped sweeping and, standing together, leaned smiling on their brooms. As the taxi driver passed his passenger's window, she reached through the open window to grasp his arm.

'*Ela, kalé!*' she whined. 'My sister's waiting to be taken to the boat! If it sails without us, what will we do?'

But the taxi driver heard nothing above the lorry's rumbling and rattling. Marching past his car, he hauled himself into the lorry's cab, and slammed the door shut. Finding the right gear with difficulty, he released the brakes and moved the lorry slowly up the hill, leaving its space at the kerbside vacant.

As its wheels began to turn, the shouting from the electrical shop abruptly ceased, and in a moment a bewildered shop-keeper and the lorry driver, red-faced with rage, appeared. The lorry driver threw his clipboard to the pavement and ran shouting after his lorry, which was indicating and making a right turn into an alleyway, where, once off the street and with only its back-end visible from the *kafenion*, it braked with a hiss of air, and stopped. Immediately, the taxi driver jumped down from the cab, and disappeared at a run along the alleyway.

The driver reached his lorry, and slapped its side as if the lorry itself were culpable, before he, too, disappeared, still shouting, in pursuit of the taxi driver.

The watchers waited, until, to their surprise, the taxi driver appeared at the far side of the *kafenion*'s terrace, emerging from between two buildings at a very brisk walk. Of the lorry driver there was no visible sign, though his abuse still echoed loud between the alley walls. As the taxi driver hurried panting across the terrace, the laughing waiters offered their applause.

But, with a single shout from where the taxi driver had appeared, the lorry driver emerged from the alley. Not looking back, the taxi driver broke into a shambling run, and soon reached his taxi, whose engine, like the lorry's, was still running. Sliding into his seat, he let in the clutch and was quickly away, grinning at the impotent lorry driver, gesturing with the side of his hand at his genitals in a valediction which said, triumphantly, *Eat my balls*.

The waiters returned smiling to their sweeping. The cook lit the burners on the gas stove, calling out to the waiters he was ready to start; and one of the waiters put away his broom, picked up a wooden tray, and approached the first of the businessmen for his order. The moustached man turned back to his newspaper; but before he could begin to read, the fat man interrupted him.

'A bold plan, but effective,' he said genially. 'It's gratifying to see Greek ingenuity at work, don't you think?'

Over the top of his paper, the man regarded him, his annoyance at the fat man's interruption clear in his face.

'I beg your pardon?' he said.

'The taxi driver. It's good to see such a fine example of Greek ingenuity.'

'Ingenuity?' The man lowered his paper and gave a cold smile. 'What you call ingenuity, I'd call theft.'

The waiter stood between them.

The moustached man addressed him without offering any greeting.

'Greek coffee, medium-sweet, a double,' he said.

The fat man smiled at the waiter.

'*Kali mera*,' he said. 'I'll have the same, no sugar, if you would be so kind.'

As the waiter crossed whistling to the kitchen, the moustached man again made as if to resume his reading; but again, the fat man interrupted him.

'I have to correct you on that point,' he said. 'The taxi driver had no intention of permanently depriving the lorry driver of his vehicle. Intent is crucial in these matters. No theft was committed.'

Across the street, the lorry driver was haranguing the blameless shop proprietor, who stared miserably down at the pavement. As the moustached man regarded the fat man, his lip lifted in an unmistakable sneer.

'You're a lawyer, then,' he said.

The fat man laughed.

'A lawyer? No,' he said. 'I have some knowledge of the law, picked up over the years. But a lawyer, no. Though I have often thought I would thrive on the drama of the courtroom. A little drama is something I enjoy; and happily I find that, wherever I travel, there's something of a drama going on. Sometimes it plays like theatre, as here, this morning; sometimes you have to watch more closely. But I'm never disappointed. There are as many dramas as the human race has members. Sometimes, a little digging's necessary. But what I find when I dig would take a lifetime to tell.'

The moustached man grimaced, as if concerned the fat man might begin that lifetime's stories now, and that he, an unwilling listener, would be condemned to listen. Once more, he bent to his newspaper, but once more, the fat man interrupted him.

Flipping open the lid of his cigarettes, he held out the box. 'Cigarette?'

The moustached man shook his head, and held up the remainder of his cheroot.

'Forgive me,' said the fat man. 'I hadn't noticed you were smoking.'

He chose a cigarette, picked up the matchbox and then seemed to change his mind. Laying the box back down on the table, he drew his gold lighter from his pocket and put the delicate flame to the cigarette tip.

The waiter brought them coffee and iced water; beneath their ashtrays, he slipped a till receipt. The fat man smiled and thanked him, whilst the moustached man sipped immediately at his cup, showing slight annoyance, as if the coffee wasn't perfect but only adequate.

The fat man tasted his coffee, and replaced the cup in its saucer.

'Excellent,' he said. 'There's nothing quite like the first coffee of the day. Don't you agree?'

The moustached man fixed his eyes on his newspaper, and made no reply.

'I'm so sorry,' said the fat man, 'you must think me very rude. I haven't introduced myself. Hermes Diaktoros, from Athens. The name is my father's idea of humour. He was a classical scholar.'

He held out his hand, and reluctantly the moustached man took it, though the contact he made was brief.

'Manolis Alfieris.'

The fat man assumed an expression of thoughtfulness.

'Alfieris,' he said. 'Alfieris. The name's familiar to me. Have we met before?'

'I don't believe so, no,' said Alfieris.

'No, I don't think so either,' said the fat man. 'And yet . . . Perhaps I've heard your name in connection with business. Tell me, what line are you in?'

Alfieris straightened himself in his chair as if about to make an announcement, leaned forward and stubbed out his cheroot.

'I'm with the Planning Office,' he said. 'Area Director, as a matter of fact.'

The fat man slapped his leg.

'I knew it!' he said. 'A government man! I had you down for it as soon as I saw you. You know, in my experience, smart men always get themselves into government jobs, and the smartest of all go for local government.'

Alfieris's face filled with mistrust as if anticipating being the butt of some joke. But the fat man leaned towards him, his index finger to his nose, encouraging discretion.

'I work for the authorities myself, as a matter of fact. Look around you, and anyone can see your choice was the smart one.' He indicated the businessmen alongside them. One had covered his table with invoices, turning it into a makeshift office; another frowned as he studied a dispatch slip, drawing heavy lines through items not received; the third spoke urgently into his phone, demanding to be put through immediately, his foot tapping with the stress of being made to wait. 'That life's not for you. You've made a much better choice, wouldn't you say? No unpaid overtime, no worries about bankruptcy, or profits, or competitors. As long as you turn up and do the job, you can go home at the end of the day and forget all about it. A well-paid, secure job for life, and a big, fat pension at the end of it. Quite a gift, wouldn't you say?'

Alfieris said nothing, but watched as the man on the phone swore and cancelled the call, slamming the phone down so hard his coffee slopped into its saucer.

'An absolute gift,' repeated the fat man. 'And yet, would you believe there are those who aren't happy with such a gift? It's interesting that we were just now talking of theft, because there are people – and I'm sure you're aware of this, if you have a few years' service under your belt – who abuse their positions of trust, who take advantage of their positions to line their own pockets further. Yet amongst office workers, we're reluctant to call it theft. We call it corruption. And corruption is my line, Manolis. In certain government departments, it's rife.'

Perhaps startled to be addressed by his first name, Alfieris blinked, and leaned forward to drink from his coffee cup. Then he looked at the fat man as if what he had heard had warmed his interest.

'Are you here on official business?' he asked.

The fat man turned his head to left and right, glancing over his shoulders as if ensuring no one stood within earshot.

'Strictly between us,' he said, 'we've had a tip-off. Regarding your offices, as a matter of fact. It's a happy coincidence, meeting you; I have your department in my diary for later this week. We have no names yet, obviously, or we'd have cleared out the offenders already, but we have no doubt we'll root them out. My powers are considerable: I can go anywhere, view any file, ask any question of any employee. I can access your staff's personal bank details; that's where we usually find our evidence. And I'm supported by an impressive network: I have spies everywhere. The powers that be are determined to crack down; but that's between you and me. If word gets out I'm in town, the pigeons'll fly the coop. As Director, obviously you have a right to know, but I'm sure you understand it's crucial you say nothing to your subordinates at this stage. Can I rely on you, Manolis?'

Alfieris gave no immediate answer. Taking the till receipt from beneath the ashtray, he glanced at the amount he owed, as if about to leave; but after a moment, he slipped the receipt back into its place, and faced the fat man.

'If I am available,' he said, 'you will, of course, have my full cooperation.'

'You have my word I will not add to your workload,' said the fat man. 'All the resources I need, I bring with me. I have my spies, and they are always invaluable in identifying offenders. And I have these!' He pointed to his right eye. 'My own eyes are my most precious tools, and it is on them that I rely. Of course, I cannot promise there will be no unpleasantness. The police are always involved, and there will be prosecutions. But the disruption brings huge benefits – a department entirely free of those who bring government offices into disrepute.'

Behind the *kafenion*, the town hall clock struck the quarter-hour. The fat man looked at his watch.

'You must forgive me,' he said. 'I am due to meet the District Auditor in a few minutes, and she's not a woman who likes to be kept waiting.' He held out his hand; with reluctance, Alfieris took it. 'We'll be meeting again very soon, Manolis. Please be reassured, you may rely on me absolutely to remove whatever rot your offices conceal.'

Leaving coins to pay for his coffee beneath his saucer, the fat man pocketed his cigarettes and lighter. Taking his bag of fish from the back of his chair, he picked up his holdall and made his way between the tables, thanking the waiters as he left.

Alfieris watched until the fat man was out of sight. His newspaper lay folded on the table, his coffee was half-drunk and cold in its cup. The fat man, he noticed, had left his matches behind.

For a while, Alfieris sat. The tables around him filled with customers and the waiters moved amongst them with loaded trays, until the air lost the smell of the sea and took on instead the smell of breakfast.

Absently, Alfieris took a cheroot from his shirt pocket, then reached across for the fat man's matchbox. Exotic in design, it was painted with a scene from some mythology: a woman in a sari and a turbaned man embraced beneath a palm tree, where an unlikely, slavering tiger hid amongst the leaves. The manufacturer's name was in a script he couldn't read. It was a pretty object, an ideal gift, he thought, for his new mistress, who had a taste for foreign tat, matryoshka dolls and Chinese porcelain.

The matchbox gave no rattle, but inside it something moved.

Alfieris slid open the lid.

Six bright fish eyes stared up at him, their irises fiery orange, the pupils black, and blind.

In Alfieris's mind, the eyes saw everything.

As he left the *kafenion*, he seemed preoccupied. He left no money to pay for his coffee, and when the waiter wished him *kali mera*, Alfieris made no reply.

Fourteen

Gazis sat at the canteen window looking down towards the town hall, where the mayoral car stood in the *No Parking* zone, the driver at its wheel reading a morning paper, biting from time to time into a warm apple pie.

The coast road was busy, and traffic moved slowly. A youth on an overpowered motorbike zoomed recklessly around a tour bus, dodging an oncoming delivery van. The youth, casual in sunglasses and sandals, wore no helmet. Gazis considered noting down his number, but no pen was to hand, and he admired, just a little, the youth's boldness in passing the police station at speed and helmetless. Perhaps, though, it was not boldness that made him brave, but knowledge; perhaps he knew the habits of local policemen. Most of the morning's shift were here in the canteen, enlivening themselves with strong coffee and sugared doughnuts, indulging in a little gossip before the day's work began.

Gazis drank the last of his bitter coffee. Overhead, an electric drill screamed as electricians worked on the air conditioning. Petridis was silent, chewing on a ham-and-cheese roll.

On the far side of the street, a pedestrian waiting to cross from the promenade to the town caught Gazis's eye: Hermes Diaktoros. Gazis watched him, judging him to be unwilling to take risks; rather than choosing his moment to run between oncoming cars, the fat man had troubled to walk to the zebra crossing, where he stood on the first faded white stripe, looking from left to right for a gap in the traffic. There was, Gazis believed, no question of the traffic stopping; but as he watched, the fat man placed a white-shoed foot on the second black stripe, and held up his hand in a command. Immediately, the traffic slowed for him to cross. The fat man was surprisingly nimble on his feet, and in a moment he reached the town-side pavement. There, he hesitated, seeming to think, until quite suddenly he looked directly up at the window where Gazis sat and, meeting his eyes, raised a hand in greeting.

Startled, Gazis raised a hand in return, and the fat man gestured to him, pointing first at Gazis, then at his own lips, with a curling of the fingers as if to pull Gazis towards him: *Ela na sou po* – Let's talk. The most commonplace of signs in the Greeks' silent language, from one as refined as the fat man it was unexpected; and the gesture so surprised Gazis that, without hesitation, he rose from his seat to comply.

As Gazis pulled on his beret, Petridis's breakfast was still unfinished.

'Meet me downstairs in five minutes,' said Gazis, leaving the table. 'And pick up the car keys on your way.'

'Sergeant Gazis,' said the fat man. 'I was passing, and I thought I'd enquire if there's any progress on my friend Gabrilis.'

'You were passing very early,' said Gazis. 'Did the heat keep you awake?'

'On the contrary, I slept extremely well. My house is always cool, regardless of the temperature outside. I had some early business to attend to, so I was up and out with the sunrise. In fact I was out so early I caught the fishermen before they left for market and I bought some fish. Perhaps you would accept it, as a gift.'

He held out his knotted bag of fish, but Gazis held up his hand in refusal.

'I can't,' he said. 'It's not appropriate.'

'Oh, surely you can. It's nothing special, I'm afraid: only scorpion fish, but enough to make a soup. In my opinion, soup is the only way to eat *skorpios*. I paid for it before I remembered my housekeeper won't touch it; she fears the spines, not because of the pain of their sting, but because of the bad omen of being spiked. She is too superstitious, in my opinion, but you don't strike me as a superstitious man. Come, take them. It's not as if I'm still a suspect – or am I?'

'It may be only *skorpios*,' said Gazis, 'but anyone watching me take the bag won't know that. They'll be thinking lobsters, oysters – in short, a bribe. And anyway, whatever my own opinion, I can't confirm you're not a suspect until we've someone else to charge. Which, at the moment, unfortunately, is not the case.'

'Has there been any progress?'

'Progress, in truth, is slow.'

'No news at all?'

'Not good news, no.'

'Are you prepared at least to tell me what the bad news is?'

The policeman considered for a moment.

'You'll be discreet, I'm sure,' he said, 'because any indiscretion will get me a reprimand. The fact is, you'll be unsurprised to hear we've no support from CID. Their view is that the case is hopeless. I see their point of view: only an idiot would take the offending car in for repair at this stage. They'll find another form of transport for a few weeks – a moped, or take the bus even – and claim engine trouble, or waiting for parts, if anyone asks. Waiting for parts is a national pastime, as you're aware. It could easily account for a vehicle being six months off the road. And when enough time has gone by for people to forget that we were interested, they'll get the body-work fixed. Or scrap the vehicle. Or simply do nothing, and drive it with the damage still on it. If it were me, that's what I would do.'

Petridis appeared in the doorway. Seeing Gazis with the fat man, he approached, adjusting his holster on his hip as if its weight were uncomfortable.

'Happily,' went on Gazis, 'my partner and I are more optimistic. Aren't we, Petridis?'

'Sir?' He nodded towards the fat man. '*Kali mera sas.*'

'I'm telling Mr Diaktoros that you and I are making the Kaloyeros case our personal crusade. I was about to tell him of your excellent idea, which CID didn't have the brains – or inclination – to come up with. Now you're here, why don't you explain it yourself?'

'Petrol stations,' said Petridis. 'If the vehicle involved is still on the road – if – it will need petrol. So I suggested we visit every petrol station in the area, asking them to look out for a white vehicle with recent damage on it.'

The fat man regarded Petridis with admiration.

'An excellent plan!' he said. 'And let me make it even more effective. Tell the proprietors there is a reward at stake. I will personally – anonymously, mind – pay 1,000 euros to anyone who comes forward with information. A little incentive to do the right thing never hurt. Well done, Constable.'

Gazis placed a hand on the young man's shoulder.

'He has a policeman's mind, this one,' said Gazis. 'With the right guidance, there's a great future ahead of him.'

'With the right guidance,' echoed the fat man. 'But yours is a profession with many traps.' He held out the bag of fish to Petridis. 'I've been shopping already this morning, Constable, and I've foolishly purchased fish I'm unable to use. Will you take it off my hands? It's only *skorpios*, but there's a good soup there. A light fish soup is perfect for this overheated weather.'

Without hesitation, Petridis took the bag.

'Many thanks,' he said. 'My aunt makes excellent soup.'

'Tell her to beware of the spines. *Skorpios* is a crafty fish, even when dead.'

'You're right there,' said Petridis. 'My cousin caught one once, and it got him right in –'

'Never mind that now,' said Gazis, shortly. 'Go and find somewhere cold for your fish. Ask them in the canteen if there's space in the fridges. Give me the keys. And be quick. We're already late.'

As he left them, the fat man caught Gazis's eye.

'He's a good lad, truly,' said Gazis.

'Perhaps a word,' suggested the fat man.

'Perhaps. Now, if you'll excuse me.'

'Of course,' said the fat man. 'You've work to do. You'll get in touch, if there's any news, if there's anything I can do?'

'I'll be glad to,' said Gazis.

Gazis turned away towards the police station, but the fat man stopped him.

'I want to thank you,' he said, 'for the interest you are taking in this matter. I'm not a fool, and I know to all you busy men Gabrilis Kaloyeros is just another file to be processed, another case to be either solved, or shelved.

But to me, he was much more than that. Over the years, I have lost many good friends, and that has made me value those remaining all the more. Gabrilis had virtues which are, these days, quite rare. He was generous, and humorous, and gentle. I miss him deeply, and so I place great value on your assistance. I'm pleased to have you as my ally.'

For a long moment, Gazis looked into the fat man's eyes, and felt he saw there the pricking of many griefs.

'You may trust me,' he said, 'to do my very best.'

'And I am grateful,' said the fat man.

Now Gazis left him. The fat man made his way back across the busy road, and for some time wandered alone along the promenade, watching the mighty ships far out at sea.

Petridis was gone some time. Gazis waited in the car, engine running, windows tightly shut to hold in the coolness from the air conditioning. The short-wave radio was almost silent, crackling intermittently with units reporting their positions and intentions.

Gazis was eager to make use of this quiet hour. They were booked to check security at a factory where two break-ins had been reported; more important to Gazis were the petrol-station visits he and Petridis planned.

For the fourth time, he checked his watch. The patrol car parked beside him pulled away, its driver and his partner too deep in argument to acknowledge him, and Gazis smiled: he knew the men, and knew the argument would concern basketball.

When the town hall clock struck the half-hour, he was ready to go and find Petridis; but Petridis appeared in the staff doorway, and headed towards Gazis across the car park, moving slowly in heat that was already debilitating.

Petridis took his seat beside Gazis. His face was pale beneath its tan.

'Where the hell have you been?' asked Gazis.

Petridis held up his right thumb; its upper joint was wrapped in a neatly tied bandage.

'Don't tell me,' said Gazis. '*Skorpios*.'

'One of the motherfuckers got me. The girls in the canteen wanted to see what I had in the bag.'

'I'll just bet they did,' said Gazis.

'I'm in terrible pain, sir. The girls say you've to take me to the clinic for a painkilling shot.'

'Those *skorpios* are tricky little bastards, aren't they?' said Gazis, starting the engine. 'What was it doing, playing dead? That's one of their best tricks. Didn't they teach you anything on that island of yours?'

'It was dead enough,' said Petridis. 'Gutted. Eyeless, too. But the spines were sticking out through the bag.'

'Have you got them out?'

'One of the girls used her eyebrow tweezers. She made me suck the poison, and she put some iodine on it. She said it might get infected.'

Gazis slipped the car into gear and moved it towards the road.

'I'm told,' he said, 'that the pain is worse if the fish has been eating crabs. What do you say, Petridis – had your *skorpios* been eating crabs?'

'A steady diet since birth.' Petridis lifted the edge of the bandage to inspect his wound. 'It's swelling up; the girls say I'll need antihistamine. There's a clinic on Mavrokopoulos Street. That's the closest.'

On the radio, a call for service came through: a collision between a motorbike and a pick-up carrying eggs. The dispatcher sounded amused.

'Responding units, take a frying pan,' she said.

'Tell her we'll take that,' said Gazis. 'ETA three minutes. Put the lights on.'

'What about the clinic?'

'If you asked your grandmother, she'd tell you to piss on your thumb,' said Gazis. 'Sometimes, the old cures are the best. Anyway, a bit of suffering builds character. Learn from it. You're lucky it's only *skorpios* that's bitten you. There are sharks that bite far worse than that in this job, believe me. Look out for the sharks, son. You'll find them in the least expected places.'

As Gazis pulled out into the traffic, Petridis turned on the blue lights.

'You can put the siren on, if it'll cheer you up,' said Gazis.

Petridis flipped the switch.

'What about the bad luck it'll bring me?' asked Petridis. 'What's the cure for that?'

'Don't worry about it,' said Gazis, raising his voice above the siren. 'In my experience, if there's any bad luck coming to you, it's only what you've brought on yourself.'

All morning, Paliakis waited for Alfieris's call, until, impatient and tired of waiting, he called Alfieris's office. He'd called there a dozen times before; but this time, something was different. The direct line to Alfieris's desk did not ring out; instead, Paliakis heard the clicking of redirection, and a computerised female voice asked him to hold the line. Tapping his foot in irritation, he waited.

As he was about to hang up, a young woman answered.

'*Parakalo?*'

'Who is this?'

'This is the Planning Office, Chartomeni speaking. How may I help?'

'I want to speak to Mr Alfieris. Isn't this his number?'

'Mr Alfieris is out of the office today.'

'When will he be back?'

'I don't have that information.'

'Where is he, then? Where can I contact him?'

'I can't say.'

'This call is urgent. I need to get in touch with Mr Alfieris today. Now.'

'I'll put you through to his department. Maybe someone else can help you.'

'It's a personal call.' He hesitated before the lie. 'I'm his cousin.'

'Oh.'

'So where is he?'

'You say you're his cousin.'

'Second cousin.'

'Then I'm surprised you didn't know. Mr Alfieris called this morning to say his mother's been taken ill. He's gone to be with her. He may be gone some time; a stroke, apparently. If you're family, I expect you'll have the contact details.'

Paliakis didn't thank her, or say goodbye. Hanging up the phone, he placed his elbows on his desk, and gripped his temples with his forefingers, as if his head was aching badly.

The barber's directions were clear and, parking near by, the fat man found the address he sought quite easily, on a quiet street in the inner suburbs, where old cobbles showed through worn tarmac and the grounds of the great houses stretched an entire block. The street itself lay in the shade of mature trees whose roots lifted the pavements; the gardens were hidden behind high stone walls crowned with spiked iron railings. In the past, the street had been, no doubt, the home of wealth and privilege, and a sense of genteel colonialism still endured. But the grandeur was faded. Where the pavements met the walls, the dead leaves of last winter still lay in drifts, the flaking paint on the railings was yielding to rust, a garden glimpsed through a gate had run amok, its wildly blossoming beauty overwhelming its planned geometry.

The gate to Paliakis's house stood half-open, but not, the fat man judged, because some recent visitor had left it so. The same dried leaves that littered the street lay behind it and in front; clearly the gate was stuck, yet no one had troubled to oil its hinges or clear away the winter's debris so it could be opened wide and unobstructed.

The fat man pushed through the half-open gate, where a narrow flight of stone steps led upwards. Crushing dead leaves beneath his feet, he climbed between fortress-solid walls supporting steep banking, where the overhanging limbs of shrubbery left the stairway in dimness that chilled.

At the stairs' head, the ground levelled into an expansive lawn of frail and fading grass, crossed by two stone paths set in a crucifix. Where the paths intersected stood a marble fountain – a figure of a once-splendid Poseidon, who clasped the upright body of a huge fish, its mouth gaping to emit a surge of water. But no water splashed over the fish's carved scales into the fountain's basin; the basin was cracked, and the fish's scales were crusted with dry, yellowing lichens and mosses. Poseidon's hand had lost one elegant finger, and the only sign of water was the fresh green of the grass around the fountain's base, where somewhere underground the plumbing leaked.

The fat man followed the path, first to the fountain, then towards the front of an imposing house, whose door was framed by pillars inspired by Rome. Its windows, too, were classical in proportion, designed for maximum light; but all – except for two on the ground floor – were covered with louvred shutters sealed with cast-iron bars. Flanking the doorway were two tall planters in the shape of urns, but the earth in them was hard-baked and barren, with no sign at all of flowers or greenery.

Beneath the portico, the fat man applied the lion's-head knocker, its banging echoing through the house as in the high halls of museums. There was, for a short while, silence; in his pocket, the fat man touched the small key on its slender chain. Then the door opened.

The fat man's most genial smile was, fortunately, ready; it hid his surprise at facing a priest. He was tall and gaunt, with long hair fastened in a knot at the nape of his neck and shiny with grease where it was pulled tight on his scalp. From his face, the fat man thought him somewhere in his thirties; but some medical condition affected his skin, drying and dusting it with powdery whiteness, and giving him the fine lines of an older man; in places – on his forehead, in the hollows of his cheeks, on the tops and lobes of his ears – the skin was red and flaking, and slick with ointment. His grey summer cassock was clean and pressed; around his neck a wooden cross hung on a leather thong.

The priest held the door with his hand, where his condition was, apparently, worse, and the irritated skin was scratched in scab-lines spotted with fresh blood. The disfigurement was unfortunate; without it, his hands were elegant as the stone Poseidon's.

'*Oriste?*' he said.

'*Kali mera sas,*' said the fat man. 'I'd like to speak with Mr Paliakis, if I may.'

'Mr Paliakis is not at home.'

'Mrs Paliakis, then.'

The priest hesitated.

'May I ask your business?'

'Would you please tell Mrs Paliakis I have some property of her husband's that I would like to return?'

The priest moved silently down a hallway furnished with an ornate chest and carved chairs, dated as the furniture found in cheap, rented rooms, but polished and cared for. The fat man studied a monochrome photograph framed on the opposite wall: a handsome man with an expression of great self-importance stood behind a plain, unsmiling woman, a proprietorial hand on her shoulder; the background was the façade of this house. There were fly-spots on the glass covering the photograph, and the hallway was dark with gloom; dust-motes descended through the sunlight let in by the open door.

Soon, the priest returned, beckoning the fat man across the threshold and waiting outside the room he was to enter. The fat man closed the front door behind him and crossed the black-and-white-tiled floor; the priest stood back to let the fat man pass, his arm extended in the manner of a gracious host.

The fat man stepped into a *salone* in the old-fashioned style. The ceiling was high, with a chandelier at its centre, and the coving was ornate with moulded patterns; but the ceiling plaster was ruined at one corner by water, the damage a penetrating stain in varied shades of brown. The polished floorboards were covered by a hand-knotted Turkish carpet, intricately patterned and clearly of some age; but in places, where well walked on, the wool was worn away, exposing the sack-like fibres of its backing.

On a long sofa (a match, the fat man noticed, to the out-of-date hall chairs) sat a woman; she faced an unshuttered window with a view towards the faded lawn and the neglected fountain. She did not stand to greet the fat man, but held out the back of her pale hand to be taken (or, in an earlier age, politely kissed). Her chin was raised in what seemed an accustomed pose of haughtiness, or vanity. If vanity, thought the fat man, the vice was justified; though fading now, her face retained a quite remarkable beauty, a feminine loveliness not commonly seen, a little blighted by the appearance of fragile health the fat man suspected was of nervous, rather than physical, origin. Over her shoulder, she wore her glorious hair, black and silver, brushed and gleaming, looped through itself in a loose knot on her breast and ending in soft tapering on her lap.

As seemed to be required, he took her fingers carefully in his own, released them and, placing his feet together, gave a small bow.

'Madam,' he said solemnly, 'thank you for receiving me. I am Hermes Diaktoros, of Athens. I came hoping to return some property to your husband; but the *pappas* tells me Mr Paliakis is not at home.'

Beside her, a chessboard spread on a low table held the pieces of a game at an early stage. The priest picked up a paperback book – *Moves of the Masters* – from the arm of a chair and, sitting, held the book as if reading; but his eyes, the fat man noticed, did not travel along the lines of print, and the priest himself was very still, and listening.

Mrs Paliakis touched the sofa seat beside her.

'Please, sit, Mr Diaktoros,' she said.

'I don't wish to intrude. If I had known you had a guest, I would have called another time.'

She gave a smile that swept the coldness from her face.

'Father Babis's visit here is extended,' she said. 'It would be difficult to find a time when he's not with me. Please, sit. Can we get you something cold to drink?'

'Thank you,' said the fat man. He sat. The sofa was hard, packed with horsehair; the bones of its frame dug into his back.

'Babis,' she said to the priest, 'would you fetch us some iced tea? And some of those almond biscuits from the bakery.'

The priest looked warily at the fat man, and hesitated for a moment before rising from his chair. As he left the room, he made no noise at all.

'Father Babis and I are united in our faith,' she said, 'in our belief that God will reward us in the next world for our sufferings in this one. He is my very good friend. Of course you are thinking it is a strange household where the mistress keeps a tame priest, and you would be quite right. But my husband makes no objection, because my husband is very rarely here. I'm afraid your journey was wasted. You'd do much better, always, looking for Aris at his office. Babis will write down the address for you.'

'A journey to find myself in such lovely company could never be wasted, Mrs Paliakis.'

She laughed, her delight in his compliment as great as her amusement.

'You're a flirt, Mr Diaktoros,' she said. 'Happily, Babis isn't here to see it. He takes the matter of my honour very seriously. And please, call me Ourania. I like to be reminded of the Paliakis name as little as possible.' The fat man's eyebrows lifted a degree. 'Don't be shocked. The disaster of my marriage is common bar-talk in this town. They embroider and embellish it, of course, and can't resist including impropriety between myself and Babis; but the basic facts can be obtained quite easily, in any *ouzeri*.'

The fat man smiled.

'There would be no point at all, madam, in running after bar-room gossip when one is taking tea with the horse's mouth. Though a mouth less like a horse's would be hard to picture. If you'll forgive another compliment.'

She returned his smile; her beauty seemed quite perfect.

'Was that a compliment?'

'It was. I, too, am mindful of your honour. If I were not, I would leave you in no doubt that a compliment was very much intended. With regard to the gossip, you put me in a difficult position. I confess to a growing interest in your husband, and as such would be intrigued to know about your marriage. But to ask a lady about such private matters is, of course, a gross impertinence, and if I did so, you would be quite entitled, in my view, to throw me out.'

'I wouldn't throw you out,' she said. 'Visitors – interesting visitors – are rare here, so we must be careful to hold on to those we have. And, as I've said, the state of my marriage is common talk. If you are going to take an interest, I'd rather you had the facts from me.'

'You haven't asked me why I have an interest.'

'Having no interest in Aris myself, I'm sorry, but your reasons don't interest me.'

'But you have no idea who I am. I might wish him harm.'

'In what way, harm? Plainly you're not a thug who'd put him in physical danger; you're not a man, I'm sure, who'd use your fists. If you are the police, or the tax man, or a creditor, then I assume you have good reasons for digging into his background. There's no doubt in my mind that, if Aris is in trouble, he's brought it on himself.'

The priest re-entered the *salone* carrying a tray, which he laid on the table beside the chessboard. In silence, he handed a glass of tea to Ourania, and offered her biscuits, which she declined. To the fat man, he indicated he should help himself.

The fat man bit into a biscuit – crisp on the outside, soft at its centre and tasting of marzipan – and sipped at the chilled, mint-flavoured tea. The priest resumed his seat, and took up his book; again, the fat man noticed, his eyes did not travel the lines of print, but fixed on one spot on the page as he listened.

Finishing his biscuit, the fat man watched through the window, where a sparrow pecked at the moss between Poseidon's toes.

'This is a beautiful house,' he said.

Ourania laid down her glass.

'I love this house dearly,' she said, 'and yet it is the root of all our troubles. And of course it is not what it was; but then, neither is its mistress. It was built in the late nineteenth century, and for many years it played its part in the best Arcadian society – parties and dinners, actors, writers, singers. There are photographs, upstairs . . . My father acquired it when his business began to do well, and I was born here. It was my dowry.

'Aris knew this house as a boy, and dreamed of living here. When *his* businesses began to do well, he made enquiries as to who owned it, and so discovered me. He wooed my father before he wooed me. Many young girls, I believe, have the reverse experience, being themselves regarded as the prize. It was not so with Aris, though I didn't know it at the time. He was charming; I thought he loved me. My father respected Aris; he admired his ambition, his lust for making money, because it matched my father's own. Aris had a little money at that time, but nothing compared to my father. When he married me, Aris thought, I'm sure, that he was set for life. He had big plans he thought he'd execute with Father's cash.

And I had a role to play, of course; I was to bear the children who'd found his dynasty. It was an old story, but I was young, and didn't know it.'

Her voice betrayed her self-reproach.

'Ignorance in youth is not a sin,' put in the priest suddenly. 'You're too hard on yourself, Ourania.'

She smiled at him, and touched him gently on the back of his hand, in no way repulsed, it seemed, by the ugliness of his skin.

'You're right,' she said. She smiled at the fat man. 'Father Babis and I differ somewhat on God's role in our lives, Mr Diaktoros. It's my belief He should be always benevolent. I see it as His job to do His best for us, in every possible way. It doesn't seem unreasonable to me that those of us who keep faith with Him should reap some kind of benefit: a pleasant life, with minimal disappointments and distresses. Babis says my view of Him is childish, and with that view I'm destined always to be cross with Him because He won't do what I want. He says God's role is to test us to our limits, that our time here is not to be a bed of roses, that the bed of roses comes in the next life. I know the next life will be better, of course; but still a part of me hopes for happy days now. I can't believe it was intended to be all a vale of tears. What do you think?'

The fat man scratched beneath his ear, and pursed his lips in thoughtfulness.

'You ask an age-old question,' he said, 'debated by philosophers for centuries. But I agree with both of you in part, and neither of you in some things. It's my belief this world was made to test us, but that we can create, to some extent, our own outcomes, by taking care of how we act and think. And if there is injustice, I believe that sometimes help will come. But there are other factors, too. Sometimes we are affected by the actions of others close to us, and the consequences of those actions can impact on us very deeply. In other words, some suffer undeservedly. In such circumstances, Father Babis is right; we are tested to our limits. The answer, then, is to rely not only on help from the Divine, but from your fellow humans: family, community and friends. Do you understand this, Ourania?'

'I don't agree with you!' she said. 'God should be kind! And I know Aris would disagree with you, too. He helped himself, and found himself thwarted by fate. He put his heart and soul into his scheme to marry me, and my inheritance. But two weeks after our wedding, my father died. His death was very sudden, an accident. He left a shoelace untied, and tripped over it coming down the stairs. He broke his neck. It's a sorry little story in itself, but the sorrier for Aris; so early in our marriage, he wasn't in Father's will. I already had the house. The money went to my brothers, and Aris was the enemy to them. They saw him for the fortune hunter he was. So there we were: a wife he didn't love, and a house he couldn't afford to maintain. I was a poor bargain, in the end; not a blank cheque, but a drain on his resources.'

'But you have children, I know. Did they not bring you closer?'

'He didn't like the noise they made, or their demands on his attention. They were a joy to me, of course, though in the end they make their own way. Kylis we see very little of here; he rents an apartment in the town, where he can take his girlfriends. And Pandelis, when he is home, always has work. He takes life too seriously. He should make time for lighter things. For love, and life.'

She looked out across the garden; there was sadness in her face.

'Forgive me, Ourania,' said the fat man quietly, 'but a stranger like me might suggest – with respect, with the very greatest respect – that you might do well to take your own advice.'

The garden seemed to hold her attention, but in her eyes, he caught the glistening of tears.

'Babis.' She turned to the priest. 'Would you be an angel, and fetch my tablets? I feel a headache coming on. It's this heat; it affects me very badly.'

The priest laid down his book, and left them. The fat man stood, and wandered to the window. A brightly coloured butterfly flew close to the fountain but, finding no greenery there, fluttered away.

'You know he's in love with you,' he said. He turned to face her. 'Why not leave here, and start somewhere new?'

'Who?' Her expression was puzzled.

'Your priest, Ourania. The deity he worships is you.'

She shook her head, and smiled.

'No. You're wrong. Babis is a true holy man, a celibate. His ambition is to follow the monastic life, to devote himself entirely to worship.'

'So why, then, is he here?'

'He feels bound by duty to me. I am a millstone round his neck. He sees me as his earthly responsibility, and I feel guilty that he won't leave me.'

'And what would release him from that responsibility?'

She hesitated.

'I really don't know.'

'And if he left you, how would you feel?'

'Lonely. I would be all alone.'

'I think you are right about his calling, that he is a holy man, a true believer. But, happily, the priesthood does not demand celibacy from its recruits. Most are not suited to it, and most do better work as family men, as village priests working in communities, dealing with life there – births, marriages, and deaths. It would be no disgrace for him to take such a position.'

'He held such a position, in our local priesthood. He found the people difficult to deal with: all hypocrites, he says, all shallowness and show.'

'Quite right. But surely that's the priest's role, to bring the godless closer to God? And with a companion to support him – with a wife – perhaps he'd be more tolerant of their short-comings.'

'You're suggesting me.'

'I'm suggesting you.'

'I'm already married, Mr Diaktoros.'

'Your husband does not deserve you. The church permits divorce. Take advantage of it.'

'My mother would turn in her grave.'

'The dead do not turn, Ourania. Rather, they would strongly recommend you make the very most of all the time you have here. I must go, but please consider what I've said. This house is beautiful, but it will be your mausoleum if you let it. Sell it. Move away. You may find before long, anyway, you have reasons not to want to stay here.'

He crossed the room, and stood before her. She held out her hand, as before; this time, he took it, and, lifting it to his lips, lightly kissed it.

'It's been a pleasure,' he said. 'Truly, a pleasure. And try to remember this one thing, Ourania: if the gods sometimes seem unjustly cruel, in time they will make reparation.'

Outside, the heat was intense. Across the street, behind a wall, children shrieked and splashed in a swimming pool, their laughter happy and uplifting. But the fat man's mood was sombre. He was considering the tangled threads of life; why was it sometimes so, he thought, that the righting of a wrong did not settle the scales, but created only crueller injustices?

Fifteen

For Gazis and Petridis half an hour of their shift remained, so instead of taking the fast road, Gazis chose the long way back to town. Petridis watched the passing scene – tourist apartments, olive groves, an open-air Chinese restaurant beneath a red pagoda – and hummed a song Gazis knew from the radio. Reaching Platea, Gazis braked for the speed limit, and ahead, Petridis pointed out another petrol station.

Gazis pulled on to the forecourt alongside the pumps and turned off the engine.

'Fourth time lucky?' he suggested.

Petridis looked around.

'Doesn't look like much of a place to me,' he said. 'We could be their only customers this week. This month, even.'

The petrol station sat, stubborn, scowling and grimy, on a site which had no doubt been at the heart of the coastal village until the village had metamorphosed into a spreading resort. Surrounded now by neon-lit bars, fast-food joints and shops stocked with suncream, foreign newspapers and leather sandals, the one-man business was not thriving amongst its new neighbours. The sea view from the pumps was gone; the new hotels had bought the views along with the land, and now their high walls hid the beaches from the streets.

The strip was quiet in siesta. From the poolsides at the hotel rears, the shrieks and screams of children were loud. From one of the empty bars came the persistent throb of club music; no one was there to hear it but the barman.

A large notice – black on red – announced ATTENDED SERVICE. A dirty sponge for washing windscreens floated in a bucket with no handle. Gazis looked at the glass in front of him, spattered with the sun-baked corpses of dozens of insects. The policemen waited. Of the service advertised there was no sign.

'They'll be sleeping,' said Petridis, after a while. 'Who wouldn't be, in this heat?'

'Go inside and talk to them,' said Gazis. 'I'll see if I can get some of this mess off the windscreen.'

On the forecourt, the stink of petrol was sharp. Gazis pulled the sponge dripping from the bucket and slapped it on to the windscreen. The water was warm, above blood-heat, but the drops that fell on to his forearms felt cool. The afternoon meltemi was beginning to blow; it stirred the heads of the geraniums dying in the concrete containers which divided the carriageway from the forecourt.

Hands in pockets, Petridis sauntered over to the station's small shop. A beverage fridge blocked the window; its stock was running low. On the ice-cream freezer lay a piece of cardboard torn from a packing case, where a child's hand had written in black marker, *Ochi pagota: No ice-cream.*

Petridis took a lemonade and a Mars Bar from the fridge, calling out to Gazis and holding them up. Gazis shook his head.

Inside, the shop was dark but not cool. A rotating fan merely caused the hot air to move in waves that carried a whiff of overripe fruit, its source a box of bananas with skins more black than yellow. Beyond the half-empty shelves – canned tomatoes, tinned mackerel, Spam – a door into the living area stood ajar; the conversation Petridis heard was from the TV, characters in crisis on the familiar afternoon soaps.

'Is anyone there?'

The volume of the TV was lowered, but no response came; all was still behind the door, as though someone waited in silence, listening. He called again, and a woman's voice, weary and annoyed, answered.

From behind the shelves came a woman, flabby and untidy from long-term motherhood, hard-eyed from penury. Seeing Petridis's uniform, she looked out at the police car, where Gazis was rubbing hard at the baked-on flies. The navy-blue beach shoes on her bare feet were too big, a man's size; in these she shuffled to the cash register.

'*Oriste*?' She folded her arms across her drooping breasts, her sullenness suggesting a visit from the police was unwelcome. 'You wanting petrol?'

'Just these.' Petridis held up his lemonade and chocolate.

'One eighty.'

Petridis found the right change. Opening the till drawer, she slid in the coins without thanking him. In the back room, a child wailed – *Mama, Mama, he hit me!* – but she made no reaction, seeming immune to the whining. Refolding her arms, she looked defiantly at Petridis.

Petridis popped the top of his lemonade and drank from the can.

'It gets hot,' he said, 'in that car all day long.'

She glanced out to where Gazis had moved on to the headlights.

'It's hot everywhere,' she said, without sympathy.

The wailing came again – *Mama, Mama, he's hitting me!*

Turning towards the door, she yelled, 'Shut up, the pair of you! You're giving me a headache!' She turned back to Petridis. 'Anything else?'

'As a matter of fact,' said Petridis, 'there is. We're making enquiries for a car involved in a traffic accident. We're looking for a white car with damage, probably on the wing. Have you seen a car like that in the past few days?'

Without hesitation, she shook her head.

'Are you certain?'

'Look, *kalé*,' she said, 'many cars pass through here, all the colours of the rainbow. How do you expect me to remember one particular car?'

Petridis drew a card from his shirt pocket.

'If you do see a car like that, I'd appreciate a call,' he said. He laid the card on the counter. She looked at it, and at him, as if both were things distasteful.

'Thanks for your cooperation,' he said. He opened the forecourt door. 'There's a reward, by the way, for any information leading to an arrest in the case.'

The door banged shut behind him; he was at the car before she called after him.

'Wait a minute, *kalé*. What reward would there be?'

Gazis straightened up from washing the headlights and dropped the sponge into the bucket.

'Let me,' he said to Petridis.

Approaching the woman, he smiled.

'There's a good reward, madam,' he said. '1,000 euros.'

'Cash?'

'If you wanted cash, I'm sure that could be arranged.'

'And my name wouldn't be mentioned? I don't want anyone coming after me.'

'We always protect our sources. Your anonymity would be guaranteed.'

'There was a car like that this morning. Bad damage on the passenger wing, the headlight all smashed. A white car. Mainly white, at least.'

'What make?'

'How do I know what make? One of those little Italian things. Or Japanese.'

'Did you notice the registration? Was it a local car?'

''Course I didn't notice the registration. When I'm at the pumps, I'm watching the gauges. But it shouldn't be hard to find; you could go there right now. It had *FM107* in great pink letters all over it.'

'Thanks very much indeed,' said Gazis. Climbing into the car, he was frowning.

She called after him.

'Hey, *kalé*! What about my reward?'

'If it comes to anything, we'll be in touch. We know where to find you.'

Gazis switched on the indicator, and pulled on to the carriageway. In the rear-view mirror, the woman – hands on hips and complaining – grew small.

The fat man used the telephone at a kiosk, inserting a phonecard bought from the proprietor and dialling the number from memory.

Ilias Mentis's secretary answered promptly. As she spoke, fingers rattled a keyboard in the background.

'I'm afraid he's stepped out of the office,' she said. 'Can I take a message?'

'Please tell him,' said the fat man, 'that Hermes Diaktoros called.'

'Ah, Mr Diaktoros.' The fingers on the keyboard stopped their work; instead, he heard the rustling of papers. 'He left a message for you, in fact. It's here, somewhere . . . He asked me to say, if you called, that the paperwork is giving him no problems, except for a little stickiness. Does that make sense to you?'

The fat man smiled.

'Perfect sense,' he said. 'Please tell Ilias I'll call for more news when I'm able.'

Paliakis's restaurant was closed for a private party. Alongside the balcony wall, where the view across the rooftops to the harbour was unimpeded, three tables were pushed together and covered with white linen cloths; the places were laid with the gold-trimmed banqueting china, the silver-plated cutlery and the crystal glasses only normally brought out for weddings. The canvas-and-teak chairs were made comfortable with cushions; the calico awning was extended, cutting out the glare and making the balcony seem shady and welcoming. The cold, effervescent water was imported from Italy, the bread sliced in the baskets was still warm from the oven. Two bottles of dark, Cretan wine were already uncorked; two more of good Rhodian white were chilling in ice-filled buckets. There were packs of American cigarettes in the ashtrays, opened and with one cigarette peeping out in invitation, and book matches advertising the restaurant were ready to strike.

The waiters had laid seven places, but only six men sat down to eat.

Aris Paliakis took his seat at the head of the table. Pandelis and Kylis, as instructed, took the chairs opposite, leaving the seats closest to their father free for his guests. Paliakis gestured to his right, where Councillor Routsis from the Mayor's office and Mr Horiatis from the Department of Agriculture were to sit; Mr Fitrakis, from the Department of Archaeology, took a chair to his left.

At once, Sotiris the waiter brought the first dishes – small shrimp fried whole with garlic, creamy, rose-pink taramasa-lata, red peppers stuffed with feta and baked to scorched softness – and laid them down the centre of the table, where the civil servants' forks could easily reach them.

As Sotiris poured wine and water, Paliakis raised his glass, and spoke.

'Eat, gentlemen,' he said. 'As my honoured guests, I am pleased to offer you a little something from my restaurant. Please, eat. And *kali orexi*.'

Horiatis carefully stubbed out the last inches of a noxious cigar and, tucking its remains behind his ear, speared a shrimp and chewed, the shrimp's crisp tail crackling between his teeth. Councillor Routsis dipped bread in the taramasalata; as he popped it in his mouth, blobs of pink cream caught on the ends of his untidy moustache. Fitrakis drank down half a glass of red wine, and slid an oil-slaked pepper on to his plate.

Kylis leaned across to his brother, and spoke behind his hand.

'Which one is which?' he asked. 'They all look the same to me.'

His wineglass untouched, Paliakis sipped at the Italian water. He retracted his lips in a smile, revealing his gold tooth.

'I'm sorry Mr Alfieris is unable to join us,' he said. 'He has, unfortunately, been called away on urgent family business. But he and I have spoken at great length, and he asks me to give you his firmest assurances that he supports my plans wholeheartedly. From a planning point of view, he sees no objections whatever to what I propose. Or should I say, gentlemen . . .' His smile grew broader, showing more teeth. '. . . With your assistance, he sees no insurmountable objections.'

A shadow of disappointment crossed Councillor Routsis's

face. He had done business with Alfieris before, and had looked forward to a discreet passing of cash-filled envelopes on his departure. With the tip of his middle finger, he pushed his glasses back to the bridge of his nose to focus on the plate Sotiris was bringing from the kitchen: delicate lamb chops, grilled over wood and sprinkled with oregano and fresh lemon juice.

'It is unfortunate he can't be here to tell us so himself,' he said. He reached across to help himself to chops; noticing there were few, he added a fourth to his plate. 'You'll forgive me for saying so, but I'll need to hear it from Alfieris's own mouth that he has no objections.'

'The lamb is from my own small flock,' lied Paliakis. 'I know you'll find it excellent.'

By Fitrakis's hand, Sotiris laid down a plate of octopus, the seared, burgundy limbs sliced to show the clean white flesh within, its aroma savoury and tempting.

Fitrakis dug in his fork, and chewed.

'I must agree,' he said. 'The final word is always with the planners. Without Alfieris's agreement, it would be impossible for me to give any kind of approval.'

At the end of the table, Pandelis was attentive to every word; the food on his plate was barely touched. Kylis's plate remained empty; he poured himself more wine, emptying the last of the red into his glass. As Sotiris passed close, Kylis tapped him on the forearm.

'Open two more,' he said. 'Keep it coming.'

'You've seen the site, of course?' asked Pandelis.

'I've studied the maps,' said Fitrakis, taking more bread. 'The site is regarded as quite minor, and isn't well documented. But it's scheduled for excavation, when funds allow. That in itself presents problems, as Alfieris is no doubt well aware.'

For a long moment, Paliakis regarded him.

'Problems have solutions, though, do they not?' he said. 'I have often found, in business, that the solution is financial. I am sure that, given the correct level of funding – the right remuneration to the consultants involved in the project, is what I mean – any problems, of scheduling or anything else, can be overcome relatively easily.'

Fitrakis smiled. A piece of charred octopus skin was stuck to his incisor.

Horiatis emptied his wine glass; at Paliakis's signal, Sotiris hurried to refill it.

'Of course,' said Horiatis, 'we none of us want to stand in the way of progress, or commerce. We are all experts in our own fields, and men of business, too. I believe we all have sympathy with what you want to achieve. But there are olives on the land; it's designated for agricultural use, and that's another problem. Without Alfieris's help, getting a permit to remove the trees will be an insurmountable obstacle, in my opinion. I recommend you wait until Alfieris can be consulted. Perhaps we could all meet here again, when he is back in the office.'

The three guests' cheeks were flushed from wine, and their eyes travelled lustily over the remains of the food.

'I agree,' said Councillor Routsis.

'I think that would be best,' said Fitrakis.

'I'm afraid from what he said that he may be gone some time,' said Paliakis, 'and I am naturally anxious to press ahead. The scheme is important to the local economy; it will provide employment for our leaner winter months. With the red tape taken care of quickly, the first phase could easily be complete by spring. But, of course, you are all professionals in your fields. Consultants, if you will. Outline for me again, in simple terms, your main objections to the scheme.'

'The scheduled excavation,' said Fitrakis.

'The olive trees,' said Horiatis.

'The lack of Alfieris's written consent,' said Councillor Routsis.

'And if there were no trees? If there were no archaeology?'

Councillor Routsis laughed, and shrugged.

'Well, obviously, in such a case the matter would be greatly simplified, of course,' he said. 'Much more straightforward. If only such a thing were possible.'

'The paperwork would be a mere formality,' said Horiatis.

'We might consider it, even in Alfieris's absence,' said Fitrakis.

Paliakis bowed his head.

'Gentlemen,' he said, 'I must thank you all for your invaluable advice. Allow me to offer you coffee, and French cognac. And you are right – we must certainly set a date to meet again. I have the promise from a contact of mine of a carcass of wild boar from Turkey, prime quality, well-flavoured meat, and I would be honoured if you would join us here to share it.' He raised his wine glass, from which he had not taken a single drop. 'A toast,' he said. 'To good friends, and good business. *Yammas*.'

The civil servants were slow to depart, remaining at the table until the afternoon was at its close and the shadows were growing long. Councillor Routsis stumbled on the steps; Fitrakis clasped Paliakis's hand and pulled him to his chest, like a much-loved brother.

Paliakis shut the street door behind them and rejoined his sons at the table. Kylis was keying a text message into his phone; Pandelis wrote in a small leather-bound diary with the tiny pencil from its spine.

Paliakis sat back in his chair, spread his hands on the white linen cloth and looked from one of them to the other.

'Well?' he asked. 'What d'you think?'

Kylis pressed a button on his phone and flipped it closed. Pandelis did not look up from his writing.

'It's a no-hoper,' said Kylis. 'For God's sake, give it up, Papa. There're other sites that'll do just as well, without all the complications.'

'You miss the point, my boy,' said his father. 'Or rather, two points. One is, if we play a careful game, this land is ours for free. No upfront capital cost, and a very significant saving. And secondly, we are aiming at a discerning market, a wealthy clientele. And wherever they come from, those kinds of people are not going to pay premium prices for property on zoned building land with a view of more houses just like theirs. They want a *real* view; they want the sea. And that's what we're going to give them. What do you think, Pandelis?'

Pandelis closed his diary.

'Kylis is right,' he said. 'Give it up, find another site. Without Alfieris, it's hopeless. There's too much risk. For some reason, he's run out on you, and these buffoons won't act without his say-so. Give it up, Papa. Look elsewhere. I've heard of a site further south where the developer's gone bankrupt. It'll be cheap; the permissions are all in place. We could drive over and have a look.'

'No!' Paliakis slammed a fist down on the table, rattling the silverware on the china plates; a red flush of anger spread up over his cheeks. 'Am I the only one who sees the obvious? They gave us the solution! They practically advised us what to do! Forget Alfieris: we don't need him. In fact, not using him is another big cost-saving. Maybe he was never to be trusted; I always had my doubts. You two, I hope, I need not doubt.'

He glanced towards the kitchen, where Grigor was slicing tomatoes for the evening's salads and Sonya was drying glasses on a cloth. Of Sotiris there was no sign; but Paliakis, anxious he should not be overheard, kept his voice low.

'The solution is both simple and very cheap,' he said, 'and what is more, there need be no delay. A little boldness and a little vision are all we need. So pull your chairs up close, and I'll tell you exactly what we're going to do.'

Sixteen

'I've been meaning to call you,' said Dinos.

He led Petridis into the *salone* of the small apartment, spreading his arms to invite Petridis's approval.

'So,' he said, 'what do you think?'

'It's great,' Petridis said. It wasn't his true opinion: he found the modern, Scandinavian-style furniture unattractive; the red-upholstered sofa trimmed with pale beech was too plain, the light from the angular, chrome lamps was too dim, the stainless-steel kitchen was too clinical, and the pictures on the walls – all geometric lines on primary colours – he could make no sense of.

Through sliding glass doors, the view from the balcony was of rooftops and more apartment blocks, of the lighted windows of quiet streets, and, at a distance, where the starry sky grew black, the undulating line of the mountains. On the balcony, two wrought-iron chairs were pulled up to a table, where Dinos had left his glass – a long, clear drink poured over ice – and an expensive mobile phone.

'You want a gin and tonic?' asked Dinos. 'Or Scotch? There's cold beer in the fridge.'

'Nothing for me,' said Petridis. 'I just called in to give you this.'

He held up the roll of banknotes he'd found in his trousers. Dinos looked at the money, then at Petridis, and laughed.

'What's that for?' he asked. 'Go and sit on the balcony, man, and I'll get you a drink.'

'It's yours,' said Petridis. 'You gave it to me to look after, the other night.'

Throwing back his head, Dinos laughed again, and clapped Petridis on the back.

'Island boy,' he said, 'you're something else! Go on, sit down, have a drink. We'll have a couple here, then go and find some girls. I've got a yearning for something blonde. You had yourself a Swede yet? I know a bar where they hang out and man, they're easy pickings! Sit down, I'll get you a beer. And this' – he snatched the money and stuffed it into Petridis's shirt pocket – 'is yours.' He turned towards the kitchen. 'Pass me my drink, will you?'

Petridis stepped on to the balcony and picked up Dinos's drink, dropping the cash on to the table in its place.

In the kitchen, Dinos crouched by the fridge, choosing the coldest beer.

'Heineken OK?' he asked. 'I seem to remember you got through a few of those, the other night.'

Petridis stood Dinos's glass on the counter.

'Your money's on the balcony,' he said. 'I have to go.'

Dinos popped the top of the can, and held out the beer to Petridis. When Petridis didn't take it, he stood it on the counter, and picked up his own drink.

'Where're you running off to in such a hurry?' He drank from his glass, grimacing as he swallowed. 'I overdid the gin,' he said. 'I should use more tonic. So – are you on duty, or what?'

'No,' said Petridis, 'but I have plans. I just came to bring your money. That's all.'

Dinos leaned back on the counter and, regarding Petridis quizzically, folded his arms.

'Is it really possible, island boy, that you don't get it? Or has someone told you to give it back? I wouldn't want to think you've been discussing our private business.'

'No one's told me anything,' said Petridis. 'It's your money, I'm returning it.' He checked his watch. 'I have to go.'

He took a step towards the door, but Dinos, with a hand placed on his forearm, held him back.

'Before you go,' he said, 'let's you and me sort this out, George. The money's a gift to you. A gesture of respect, if you like. A token of our working relationship. So pick it up on your way out, use it and enjoy it.'

Petridis's expression was startled.

'Working relationship?' he asked. 'What working relationship?'

Now Dinos's laugh was derisive.

'Don't play that game with me, George,' he said. 'We're friends now, right? Don't play hard to get with me. I'm not a rich man, you know that. I've paid what I can afford. There's no reason to be greedy.'

'Greedy?'

'Look, I knew your predecessor a long time. We worked well together, and I'm sure you and I can too. I don't ask for much, just tip-offs so I can be first to the nationals. That's where the money is, in my game: exclusives. It's not money for nothing, agreed, but it's easy enough. Exclusives only come from the inside. And I'll look after you, whenever I can – concert tickets I'm always good for. Perk of the job.'

'Perk of whose job?'

'Mine, and yours. That's the point, surely? For God's sake, George, I thought you understood all this when you gave me the name on the hit-and-run!'

'I shouldn't have done that.'

'No harm done. Has Gazis been getting at you?'

'Gazis has nothing to do with it.'

'You shouldn't worry about him. He's nobody.'

'He's my superior officer,' said Petridis, stiffly, 'and I am bound by duty to report this conversation to him.'

Dinos laughed.

'Oh, he's a superior officer all right! Whiter than white! What do you think, George, all your superiors are like Gazis? All your colleagues aren't on the take? Why d'you think they put on the uniform in the first place? Come on – this is a joke, isn't it? Drink your beer, and let's take ourselves out somewhere. Forget Gazis. What he doesn't know won't hurt him. You have to take care of yourself.'

On Petridis's thumb, beneath the ragged edge of a sticking plaster, the site of the scorpion-fish's sting throbbed.

'No,' said Petridis. 'It's not about me. My job is to care for the community.'

'Community! Were you drinking before you got here?'

Petridis drew out his wallet, placing a banknote on the counter as he spoke.

'I'm giving you this back, too: the twenty you gave me out at Loutro. That makes us square. See you around.'

Dinos took the note; Petridis turned again towards the door.

'Don't go rocking any boats,' said Dinos to Petridis's back, 'because that would be stupid.'

Petridis turned again and faced Dinos; he took several steps towards him, so the two men stood very close.

'I'll tell you what,' he said, 'we'll make our last deal. You don't say anything to Gazis tomorrow about my being here – not a word about the time we spent together – and I won't rock any of your boats.'

Dinos's eyes brightened.

'Tomorrow? What's happening tomorrow?'

Petridis set his face to cover his indiscretion, but the blood flushing his neck and cheeks betrayed him.

'Nothing,' he said. 'Tomorrow, or whenever you see him, is what I meant.'

'Liar!' said Dinos. His smile was broad. 'Come on, tell me. What's going on tomorrow?'

'I have to go.'

'Tell me,' said Dinos, 'or you might find I let something slip to Gazis. Accidentally, of course. Which makes me wonder if now might be a good time . . . I have something interesting to show you.'

Smiling, he crossed to the balcony, glancing back over his shoulder at Petridis, like a coquette. From the table, he picked up the mobile phone; as he returned to the kitchen, his eyes were on the phone's diminutive screen, his thumb working the keypad, scrolling through images.

'Here you are,' he said. 'This'll bring back memories.'

He held the phone up to Petridis's face. On the screen, a video clip was playing. The focus was poor, the background dim, but the man in the foreground was definitely Petridis, the woman clearly Haroula. Petridis recalled the scene only vaguely, like the remnants of a dream: Haroula on her knees, her face in Petridis's exposed crotch, his hand on her head, pressing down, and in the background, people laughing, applauding.

The clip ended. Petridis's face was hot with shame, and anger.

'There're more,' said Dinos. 'The stills are brilliant. You want to see them? I could download them to my laptop; we'd get the finer details. We could post them on the web! Email them to your friends! Would your mother like to see them?

Your grandmother? That girlfriend of yours? The Chief Constable? That would bring a smile to his fat face, wouldn't it – a new recruit getting the treatment from a known prostitute. Come on, George – let's have a look at the rest!'

'Fuck you.'

Again, Dinos laughed.

'Not me,' he said. 'I'd say the one who's fucked – in every sense, my friend – is definitely, unquestionably, you. You want a drink now? Because you look to me like you could use one.'

Petridis's eyes glistened with the start of tears, and to hide them he turned towards the door, but Dinos, with a predator's instinct, sensed weakness.

'Hold on, there, George, not so fast. We haven't concluded our business.'

Petridis faced him; stripped of any maturity by his misery, he seemed no older than a schoolboy.

'I said we were friends, didn't I?' asked Dinos. 'You can trust me, one hundred per cent. If you've got to go, too bad. Just tell me what's happening tomorrow, and you have my word Gazis won't hear about any of this. Promise.'

Petridis didn't speak.

Dinos held up the phone and, smiling, waggled it in the air.

'It's about the Kaloyeros death, the hit-and-run,' said Petridis. 'We're coming to talk to you about it. That's all.'

'Me? Why on earth do you want to talk to me about that?'

'Because you were there. You were in the neighbourhood.'

'That's it?'

'That's it.'

Dinos pressed keys on the phone.

'Have a look at this one, George,' he said. 'This is one your granny'd really enjoy!'

In despair, Petridis shook his head.

'OK,' he said, 'OK. We got some information, an FM107 car, with damage on it. We've got a witness.' He paused, and seemed to think, and slowly his expression changed. 'You know, I bet your car's downstairs, isn't it? No need to wait until tomorrow – we could go and check it now, couldn't we? Because I'll tell you what I think, *friend*. I think it was *your* car our witness saw. I think you were involved. I think you know a lot more about the old man than you've said.'

But Dinos smiled, holding up both hands to stop Petridis.

'Sorry, George, but I think you just put two and two together and came up with five. Or even six. I've nothing to hide. Just ask me, and I'll tell you. Yes, there's damage to my car, and yes, it was my fault. Like a fool, I pulled out in front of some guy. So if you're going to arrest me, arrest me for bad driving. I was at the Kaloyeros scene because I'm an ambulance-chaser. Gazis knows that; I do it all the time. Wherever there's a blue light flashing, old Dinos isn't far behind. It's my job.' A shadow of doubt passed over Petridis's face. 'For the record, you'll be pleased to hear the station manager wants my balls for it. And the guy I hit isn't very happy either. And yes, I do have his contact details, so you can go and talk to him, if you've nothing better to do, and ask to have a look at his car – a very nice car, unfortunately – and you'll find I'm telling the truth. Which means I've just saved you and Gazis from making fools of yourselves, doesn't it?'

For a long moment, Petridis regarded him.

'I'll take those details from you,' he said.

Dinos smiled.

'I can tell you're going to be a first-class policeman,' he said. 'You trust no one.'

'I'm learning to trust only the trustworthy,' said Petridis. 'As Mr Gazis says, the trick to this job is not getting eaten by sharks.'

*   *   *

The night was warm and still, and the scent of the white-flowered jasmine had yielded to the woodsmoke rising up into the branches of the almond tree. Watching his father-in-law from a comfortable chair, Gazis sipped at his beer. Seated on the low, three-legged stool from which he used to milk his goats, the old man laid the sardines on the grill, brushed them liberally with oil and dropped a few small twigs of mountain oregano on to the glowing charcoal, so the woodsmoke conceded in its turn to smells of seared fish and burned oil, and to the sweeter smoke of herbs. The juices from the fish hissed on the coals; by the old man's feet, a cautious cat crouched, waiting.

Through the open window, Gazis heard the rattle of cutlery as his wife found knives, forks and plates none of them would use. She liked things to look right, but all of them would eat the fish with their fingers, and spit out the bones. A late supper on a summer's evening was meant to be that way, and his father-in-law would grumble at her for trying to flaunt the old tradition: that fish (and chicken, and women) should be taken with the hands. And his wife would say, *We may be peasants still in our hearts, but there's no need to let the neighbours know it, if they should call.*

She came out into the garden now, kissing her father lightly on the top of his head as she passed, and he smiled up at her, grateful for her affection. At the table where Gazis sat, she began to set three places, smiling at Gazis to stop him saying, *Don't bother*; and so he gently shook his head, and sipped again at his beer.

And then, the doorbell rang.

In quiet triumph, she patted Gazis's shoulder.

'See?' she said. 'We have company. Make sure the table's properly set.'

Together, Gazis and the old man watched her go back inside the house.

'Who the devil's that, at this hour?' asked his father-in-law. 'I don't think it can be anyone for me.'

Gazis had already recognised the figure following his wife into the garden.

'Don't worry, Father,' he said. 'It's no one for you.'

Gazis was frowning. Unless he took care, this visit might end a pleasant evening, spoil it with some emergency, with something left undone, with information sought by colleagues or superiors.

And by the look of Petridis, the matter was serious. His usual smile was absent, his shoulders were stooped and, as he stood before Gazis, though the light of the lamps was distorting, it seemed possible that the boy had been crying.

'I'm sorry to interrupt your evening, sir,' said Petridis.

'You won't interrupt my evening,' said Gazis, lightly. 'Whatever your errand, I shall make it a matter of personal pride to refer you, in under a minute, to someone far better qualified to handle the matter than I am. All my years of service have not been for nothing. I can pass a buck faster than a government minister. State your business, and I'll name you a suitable person to handle it.'

Petridis sighed, and his sigh had depths worthy of long despair, or hopeless failure; it seemed the more melancholy to Gazis, who usually enjoyed Petridis's smiling optimism.

'I'm afraid it's personal, sir,' said Petridis.

'Personal?'

'About me. There's something I have to do, and I want you to be the first to know.'

'You're not getting married, are you? There isn't some outraged father somewhere with a gun to your head?'

'No, sir. Nothing like that.'

'Well, come on, then. Sit down and let's have it. What'll you drink? The beer's cold. Or my father-in-law makes excellent lemonade.'

'Nothing,' he said, taking a seat across from Gazis. 'Truly, nothing.'

Turning the fish on the coals, the old man watched Petridis with the same interest the cat showed in the fish. Gazis gave him a slight shake of the head, and the old man feigned indifference, poking the ashy charcoal with a stick.

'Let's hear it, then. What's on your mind?'

Now, there could be no doubt: Petridis's eyes were filled with tears.

'I've given it a lot of thought,' he said. 'I've been riding round for hours, thinking about what's best. And I've decided there's only one possible course of action. I'm going to resign.'

'Resign!' Gazis repeated the word so loudly that the old man, startled, dropped his stick to the ground. In the kitchen, Gazis's wife paused in cutting up a lemon. 'Why on earth would you want to resign? You have the makings of an excellent officer! The force needs you! I thought you loved the job!'

'I do, sir. But I've screwed it all up. I've screwed it all up so badly, there's no other way out.'

Gazis frowned.

'Tell me,' he said.

A tear fell on Petridis's cheek, and he shook his head.

'I can't.'

'Tell me, George,' said Gazis. 'Tell me, and we can fix it.'

'It's too bad to be fixed. And shame prevents me from telling. You must take my word that my only honourable option is to resign.'

'Shame is a good thing,' said Gazis. 'It persuades me more strongly still that you will make an excellent policeman one

186

day. Shame tells me you understand the difference between right and wrong. Now listen to me. There's nothing you can tell me that will shock me. Nothing. Whatever you've done, I've seen it before. Every kind of vice known to man – and a few you'd never think of – has passed before my eyes over the years. If you've committed a sin I've not run across before, I'll slap you on the back and call you a genius of invention. So tell me, and let's see what's to be done.'

By the fire, the old man was lifting fish on to a plate.

'You want some sardines, friend?' he called out to Petridis. 'They're fresh this morning.'

'Not now, Father,' snapped Gazis.

But Petridis answered the old man politely.

'In a while,' he said. 'Thank you.'

'I caught them myself,' said the old man, proudly.

'Just give us five minutes,' said Gazis. 'There's some police business we have to take care of.' He turned back to Petridis. 'For God's sake, George, tell me and let's get this sorted out. The department can't afford to lose you.'

With great reluctance, Petridis told his tale: the concert and the whores, the money and the photographs, the night in the cheap hotel. When he finished, Gazis stared for a moment into Petridis's face, then leaned across and cuffed him on the ear.

Petridis flinched, and rubbed at the side of his head.

'I do that in your father's absence,' said Gazis. 'It's what he'd do if he were here. But he isn't here, so for now I'll be a father to you. You're right, it isn't good; in fact it's a sorry, bloody mess. May I assume, too, that it was you who leaked the details of the Kaloyeros death to the press – to that radio station, at least – before official notification was given?'

Sadly, Petridis nodded.

'He told me he would hold it until it was official.'

'And you believed him.'

'At the time, I had no reason not to.'

'But you have good reason now. You gave him a way in, and because of the kind of man Dinos is, he has followed up his advantage. Now he thinks he holds all aces. He's wrong. But before I go any further in extricating you, I need to know you're committed to my rules of policing. My rules are not the same as the scum that join the force to line their pockets. Dinos is right – there are a few of them. My rules are these: no gifts – not even fish, not even a cup of coffee – no favours, no activities you wouldn't tell your grandma about. No blind eyes, no unproven prejudices. And no indifference. We treat every case, every victim of every crime as if they were our first, or our last, which is the one we'll be remembered for. Do you understand me?'

'Perfectly.'

'Then have a drink whilst I do some thinking. Father, bring some of that fish, *kalé*! You'd better stick to lemonade, George; you'll be riding home later. The first step, at least, is clear: we'll haul friend Dinos in and find out if he was driving that damaged car that has the radio station's logo on it.'

'I was coming to that,' said Petridis, dejectedly. 'He's off the hook. He admitted the damage was down to him; he had an accident downtown. I've got the details of the guy he hit.'

Gazis smiled.

'So what did I tell you? A policeman through and through. Even in adversity, you come up with the goods.'

'But that leaves us with no leads, and me still in a mess, with no leverage. If he publishes my pictures . . . Oh, Christ – what will my mother say?'

'With luck, your mother need never know. Things may look black now, George, but remember, the darkest hour is always before dawn.'

'I'm sorry to bring you this trouble, sir – more sorry than I can say.'

'As my mother used to say, youth and a cough cannot be hidden. You're proof of that, at least. Now make the old man happy, and eat his fish. I have some thinking to do. We need to plan our way, before Dinos decides to make use of his advantage.'

The fat man left glass and bottle on the verandah table and, slipping his Turkish espadrilles back on to his bare feet, made his way along the marble-tiled passageway to his bedroom. The book he had forgotten lay on the bed, but before he picked it up he seemed to have another thought, and left it there.

Kokkona had lit the lamps and, taking one from the dressing table, he knelt down on the rug, and shone the lamp beneath the bed, where its weak light threw deep shadows amongst the items stored there. He reached out for the little ring box and, rubbing away any dust with his thumb, opened its lid. Its white satin lining bore the name of a jeweller in Naxos, but the ring it held was of little obvious value: a narrow gold band set with a single diamond chip. For a moment, the fat man studied it, then closed the ring box and returned it to its place.

Stretching out his arm, he moved the boxes and packets, until he uncovered a parcel hidden by the rest, and pulled it forward into better light. The parcel had the look of being too long in transit: the brown paper that wrapped it had lost its crispness and showed damage at the corners; the twine that bound it was fraying and discoloured. There were several addresses, in various inks and handwriting, all but one struck through; the last address was the fat man's own, at this villa. For a moment, he studied the fastenings on the parcel, the knots in the twine and the adhesive tape. All was intact.

The fat man smiled. Leaving the parcel to the front of the others, he stood and replaced the lamp; then, picking up his book, he made his way back down the passageway, closing the bedroom door behind him.

Seventeen

When Petridis left Gazis the hour was late; evening had already become night. Gazis had said little, and in Petridis's ears his reassurances lacked confidence. Gazis spoke of 'having words', of 'applying gentle pressure', but these solutions seemed weak weapons against such serious threats: blackmail and exposure for Petridis, and disgrace, potentially, for the entire police force. Already, worry gnawed at him. It was an unwelcome experience to carry secrets known by another – an antagonistic other, with every motive to use the knowledge against him. For the first time in his life, Petridis had an enemy.

The seal on the half-bottle of Scotch in his saddlebag was unbroken; swiftly developing maturity told him there was no room tonight for dull thinking, or for more of the irresponsibility and immorality alcohol had induced. He rode slowly through Gazis's quiet suburb, where families sat late in gardens and on balconies, talking away the night's heat, or slept in closed-up rooms cooled by air conditioning.

Reaching the mountain road, he opened up the throttle and let the motorbike move fast, speeding along dark roads he had rarely travelled. At first, the climb was steady, a slow incline rising above the coast's resorts; there, the hotels blazed with light, their English names in neon and quite legible in the distance. Behind them, the sea was empty blackness. Petridis took a right turn, and faced instead the darkness of the mountains. The unknown road was unpredictable in his headlight, and he took the twists and bends with care. As he passed an isolated taverna, a waiter stacking the plates of the last diners squinted out at him; seeing nothing but the headlight, the waiter raised a hand anyway, in case Petridis was a local boy. Petridis didn't notice; his eyes were on the road as he rode on, heading for the particular nowhere he was travelling to.

And then, at the brow of a hill, he found it: a small, domed church set in a high-walled courtyard lit by ornate wrought-iron lamps. Outside the walls, the dark branches of a great oak spread black shadows over dusty ground. Petridis parked the bike beneath the tree and, turning off the engine, listened for a moment to the quiet of the night. Set into the courtyard wall, a spring trickled water into a moss-covered trough, where three tin cups were chained to a carved-stone shelf. Petridis filled a cup and drank the clear water, which held the cold of rock and the green taste of the moss.

The courtyard gates were heavy with bars fit for a prison, so the small, white-painted cross at the heart of each seemed insignificant. Unlatching the right-hand gate, Petridis passed through it to a flight of wide stone steps, whose freshly whitewashed edges fluoresced in the light of the lamps. Climbing the steps to the church's high arched doors, he turned the cast-iron ring that should have opened them, but the doors were locked. He sat down on the topmost step, on stone still warm from that day's sun, and, placing his face in his hands, he wept.

The night moved on. In the highest branches of the cypress trees, a light breeze stirred; a scrawny, feral cat crouched at a rat-hole. The moon reached its zenith and began its decline, and the patterns of the infinite galaxies shifted, though imperceptibly to the human eye. Petridis's mind drifted away and returned, via long meanderings into his past and his intended future, to his present dire difficulties; and as he wandered, his thoughts grew darker, and that darkness deepened, until it seemed a single choice was open to him. To end it all was the only honourable exit – yet even that solution had its difficulties. It must seem like an accident, or it would bring its own, worse, shame, and for those he left behind the certainty of his damnation. A mountain climb and his footing missed, or an overbold risk on a busy road: either of these methods would do. As he considered methods and practicalities, his fear grew, but his determination to find the courage to save his family's honour matched that growth. There was nobility in early death. Dishonour and disgrace could only be a lifelong stigma.

The night remained quiet, but against the barely heard whispering of trees and the trickle of the spring water, somewhere, at a distance, more water ran, a stream or summer-depleted river. Aching from long sitting on hard stone, he got stiffly to his feet, and followed the sound of water. At the back of the church, a larger courtyard lit by similar lamps spread to a surrounding wall, where a stone bench ran all around its base. Kneeling on the bench, he peered down over the wall into what seemed, in the darkness, a bottomless ravine. The water, he judged, was down there, at some unthinkable distance: a river which had, through eons, cut the gorge sides, but now ran slow, and impotent.

The place seemed perfect, the opportunity a gift; and yet he lacked the courage to make the jump. His fear, though, was not of death: he worried for his physical body. What if his remains were never found, or couldn't be retrieved? He couldn't bear the thought of lying down there, unsanctified and unburied, chewed at by animals, rotten with maggots and worms. He wanted a Christian burial; he wanted his place with his relatives, in the cemetery he knew, where his mother would visit and talk to him and candles would be lit for his soul. He slumped on the stone bench, his back against the wall; he lacked more tears to weep, and so, exhausted by misery, soon lay down to sleep.

Slowly, sleep came, and as it did so a thought came to his mind that he considered lucidly before he let it go. It was his culture that insisted on proper burial, that made the rites and rituals so essential to him; it was the same, he knew, for everyone who was brought up in the faith.

Which made it very unlikely that, if Gabrilis Kaloyeros's death was an accident, his killer would have left him there to rot. And that, in turn, suggested that, to make sure Mass had been said for Gabrilis, the killer would, quite likely, at some point have revisited the scene.

On an alleyway in the old heart of the town, a light shone in only one window. Climbing from the Pony, the fat man heard the rhythm of dance music from neighbouring streets, the loud shouts of foreign voices, and the inharmonious singing of several drunks. In their direction, the sky glowed with polluting light which hid the stars; but to the west, where there was only the sea, the constellations were clear on the darkness of their natural background, and he fixed his eyes there for a moment, admiring their familiar, brilliant beauty.

Then, walking around the car and opening the passenger door, he lifted a parcel from the seat. It was the parcel from the floor under his bed, but the addressee was not now the fat man. Written in heavy black capitals, a white adhesive label covered the villa's address, redirecting the package to Aris Paliakis, at No. 40 on this street.

The fat man took the parcel in his arms, and carried it towards the building where the light burned. At street-level, the building housed a shop selling women's shoes; at the window on the first floor, a naked light bulb dangled. Alongside the shop, the fat man found a door bearing a brass plate engraved with just three words – *Paliakis and Sons* – and, passing through it, was faced with a short staircase. Nimbly, he climbed the stairs and, on the first-floor landing, stood and listened. Behind the left-hand door, there was slight movement, and here the fat man knocked; but without waiting for an answer he turned the handle, and walked straight into Paliakis's private office.

Paliakis looked up from the untidy stacks of paperwork that filled his desk. The room was very hot, the window closed against the music and the singers, and, under the thick smoke of cigarettes, the air held the odour of Paliakis's sweat. The collar of his shirt was loose at the neck, the cuffs were pushed up over his wrists; his eyes were pink with strain, purplish and swollen with fatigue beneath. In an ashtray, a neglected cigarette burned. On the desk amongst the disordered papers a vending-machine coffee was half-drunk and cold; a packet of Petit Beurre biscuits, its Cellophane ripped open, spread crumbs over the documents.

Paliakis stared at the fat man, who, freshly showered and cheerful, seemed cool in beige Chinos belted with Italian leather (*The buckle*, thought Paliakis, *must surely be gold-plated*); his polo shirt, in pale lemon-yellow, had a tiny galloping horse embroidered on the breast. On his feet, the old-fashioned canvas tennis shoes he wore were spotlessly, pristinely white; his smooth-shaved face was fragrant, and the scent stirred a memory in Paliakis – the blossom of orange trees, perhaps, or cherry. But, though he tried to grasp it, the memory slipped away, and, recovering from his surprise at the intrusion, he glared at the fat man.

'Who the hell are you?' he asked.

Somewhere outside, a clock began to strike.

The fat man gave a friendly smile, and laid the parcel on the desk, covering the papers Paliakis had been annotating with a pencil.

'*Kali spera sas*,' he said. 'My name is Hermes Diaktoros, of Athens. And you are Aris Paliakis. I am pleased finally to meet you, Mr Paliakis.' He held out his hand, but Paliakis made no move to take it. The fat man, still smiling, gave a small shrug of indifference. 'My apologies for calling on you so late. I have tried to call on you before, at a more reasonable hour; perhaps your wife has told you?'

'State your business,' said Paliakis shortly. 'I'm a busy man; I'm not here for your entertainment.'

'Do you mind if I sit?' Without waiting for Paliakis's assent, the fat man did so, and, because the parcel on the desk was now obscuring his view of Paliakis, he shifted it to the left, disturbing the stack of papers it was sitting on. Paliakis frowned. 'I'm making a delivery,' went on the fat man. 'This parcel is for you.' He patted the parcel almost with affection, as a child might pat the head of a friendly dog.

'Excellent,' said Paliakis. 'You've made your delivery. *Kali nichta sas*.'

The fat man smiled more broadly.

'I'm afraid it's not that simple,' he said. 'You and I have much to discuss before we open it.'

Paliakis frowned again, deepening the lines of bad temper in his face.

'We? I'm sorry, Mr . . .?'

'Diaktoros. Hermes Diaktoros.'

'Mr Diaktoros. What exactly is the nature of your business? It's late, I have a great deal still to do, and I would appreciate it if you would leave.'

'All in good time. Take care with your cigarette there. It's so easy to start fires accidentally.'

The fat man pointed to the ashtray, where the burning cigarette had dropped its length of ash on to the desk and its smouldering stub had fallen into the mess of butts which filled the ashtray. For a long moment, Paliakis regarded the fat man, then, grim-faced, ground out the smoking stub.

'I'm trying to cut down myself, although I feel no better for it,' said the fat man. 'Perhaps because my health, overall, is excellent. For a man of my age, I'm pretty sprightly.'

Critically, Paliakis studied him – the bulk suggesting overweight, the owlish glasses, the greying hair – and found himself speculating on the fat man's age. But it was impossible to determine. Paliakis would have guessed at fifty; and yet the fat man's unlined skin, his muscle-tone, his optimism, suggested he might be considerably younger.

'What do you want?' he asked. 'Is this about money?'

The fat man slapped his broad thighs, and laughed.

'Straight to the nub of it, Aris, straight to the nub! Indeed it is, yes; it is about money. But then, with you, everything's about money, isn't it?'

'If you've some claim to make, speak to my lawyer.'

'Pandelis? How interesting you describe him as your lawyer rather than as your son. Is that how you see him? As a tool to be used to get rid of annoyances like me?'

'My son is an excellent lawyer.'

'And, you're thinking, he'll make short work of me, whatever my business. But he can't help you this time, Aris. My business is with you alone. It's personal.'

'State it, then, and be done. I'm a busy man.'

'I'm here to return some lost property.'

From his pocket, he took the little key and broken chain brought from the barber's. In the palm of his hand, he held it out across the desk. The band of the gold ring rescued by Sostis from the sea glinted on his little finger. 'Your talisman, I think.'

He turned his palm, and the key slipped off on to the desk. Paliakis picked it up, dangling the key at the end of its chain.

'Where did you find this?'

'You left it at the barber's.'

'The fool broke the chain.'

'The chain had a weak link. You lost it, the barber found it, and I'm returning it to you. It is customary, I think, to thank those who have done you such a favour.'

'Then I thank you.' Paliakis gave an insincere smile, and moved to slip the key into a drawer. But the fat man held up his hand to stop him.

'Just a moment,' he said. 'Am I right in taking you for a superstitious man, Aris? Are you hoping the return of your lucky key will bring a swift end to the problems of an unlucky week? Is this the key to your Midas touch – the object that turns everything you touch to gold? Your bad luck has nothing to do with the key, of course – your difficult week is a product of your own making.'

'I'm afraid I have no idea what you're talking about. It's just an old key of no value. Are you wanting some reward? Ten euros, no more.'

He reached down to the same drawer in the desk, where a little money was sometimes kept.

'Petty cash?' asked the fat man. 'For the key, maybe. But how much for the box the key fits?'

Paliakis took his hand empty from the drawer, and slid it shut.

'Box?' he asked. 'What box?'

The fat man smiled.

'This one,' he said, slapping the parcel. 'My delivery. It's addressed to you. Go on, open it.'

'Is this some kind of joke?' Paliakis asked. 'Who sent you?'

'I am here to deliver this box, and a message. The box came to me in a convoluted way, but it was intended, always, for you. A gift, I understand, from your grandfather.'

The fat man's words lit Paliakis's eyes with interest but, pretending nonchalance, he kept them from the parcel. His hand went again into the drawer, and drew out a fifty-euro note, which he laid on the desk before the fat man.

'I thank you for your trouble,' he said. 'But if this is, as you say, a gift from my grandfather, then I'm sure you'll understand the opening of it is a moment when I'd enjoy some privacy. So, if you wouldn't mind . . .'

'Of course, you want me gone so I don't see what's in there. You don't want me to tell what I've seen. But believe me, my discretion has always been absolute. And I already know what's in the box.'

'You opened it?'

'Without the key? No. My knowledge is from word of mouth.'

'Whose mouth?'

'Is that important? Come, hurry up. Your impatience will make you burst a blood vessel.'

Paliakis's face was growing redder; his heart raced, and there was a lightness in his head. The fat man folded his arms and, with this gesture of his visitor's stubbornness, Paliakis decided to delay no longer. Taking scissors from a pencil stand, he cut the fraying string and into the brown paper, which, dried out and somewhat fragile from many years, tore easily, like tissue. He ripped the paper off, and dropped it to the floor.

It stood before him: a plain box of polished olive wood, its brass hinges dull, and in the lid, a small keyhole, just right for Paliakis's key.

On his upper lip, the sweat stood in beads, and he was smiling, strangely and so broadly his gold tooth gleamed. He fitted the key to the lock; it turned quite smoothly, as if the lock had only recently been oiled.

Paliakis hesitated, then, with both hands, he slowly raised the lid and looked inside.

The smile left his lips, the deep lines of a frown came to his forehead. Reaching into the box, he took out what was there: some photographs, and a sealed envelope, addressed with a single word in ink, whose black pigment had faded to burgundy. The word was *Aris*.

The fat man, forgotten, was relaxed in his chair, his expression showing amusement, and interest.

One by one, Paliakis studied the photographs. Of different sizes and finishes, three were in black-and-white, three in the unsubtle colours of photography's earlier days. All, it seemed, had been taken at a similar time, but on different occasions. As he finished with each one, he laid them out in two rows of three, and when he was done, he studied all six together.

The first photograph showed a house amongst other houses, a village house; a wooden handcart stood by the door, a chicken pecking round its wheels. Then, a picture of two people, a man and a woman, in clothes and hairstyles of the sixties. Beneath the shady branches of a tree, the woman was seated on a kitchen chair, shielding her eyes as she looked into the sun; beside her, the man lay in a truckle bed, a pillow at his head, his body covered in a blanket made up of knitted woollen squares sewn into patchwork. The woman smiled, trying for levity for the camera, her hand resting affectionately on the man's shoulder; but the man's face was serious, his dark eyes shadowed by a fall of glossy black hair.

Another picture: the same scene, at the same time, but the woman's place was taken by another man, and the chair had gone. This man crouched by the truckle bed, clasping the lying man's hand in a self-conscious handshake. Next, a small boy of four or five years old stood alone and proud before the camera, his belly out, his grin wide; but, even in black-and-white, stains showed on his little shirt, his shorts, too big, were drooping, and his naked calves and feet were pale with dust. There, again, the black-haired man, a picture taken in a bedroom, where the man lay flat, still unsmiling, in an old-fashioned, carved wooden bed, a white sheet up to his neck, his arms stiff at his sides. And lastly, the woman and the child, though somewhat younger: he a toddler, both standing, and the child reaching up, grasping the woman's fingers to be sure he didn't fall. The woman, Paliakis noticed, wasn't pretty, and her smile was not wholly natural, as if she had posed reluctantly, and a moment ago had shyly refused her cooperation.

Paliakis's eyes lingered on the picture of the two men. He picked it up, and brought it closer to his face to examine their faces.

'Do you know those people?' asked the fat man.

Paliakis shot him a look which damned his impertinence; but then he answered.

'This man.' He indicated the standing man. 'I believe it's my grandfather.'

The fat man lowered his head in acknowledgement.

'It is indeed,' he said. 'Aris Paliakis. The man for whom you are named.'

Again, Paliakis looked at him.

'How do you know him? What has this to do with you?'

'Let me explain it like this. Your grandfather gave this box into my family's care. We have been a kind of *poste restante* facility – with delivery to be made if the message were ever required. Which, in my judgement, it now is.'

Paliakis held up the envelope.

'So you know what's in here?'

'I do indeed.'

'So tell me, Mr Diaktoros.'

'Read, and discover for yourself.'

Paliakis ran his finger under the envelope's edge; the old glue had no adhesion, and the envelope opened without tearing. Inside was a letter: three pages on paper ripped from a spiral-bound book, the fragments of the torn holes untidy at the edges. The handwriting was cramped and careful, as if penned by a hand unused to writing, and marred by clumsy crossings out, not for misspellings but for rewording, as if to improve the phrasing of a thought.

My dear grandson,

I write this on the advice not of a friend, but of a man whose judgement I have come, in a short time, to respect.

If you receive this letter, the news is bad; you have followed in my footsteps, and gone too far in a dream of wealth and money.

As a man of middle age – you know already – I did something which made me, in the eyes of that small-minded community I called home, a legend. In our village, a man could be a legend for very little – for growing a giant cucumber, even, or surviving a fall from a rooftop. Is it the same still? Perhaps it is.

In fact, what I did was very ordinary. I closed my bank account, and moved the cash elsewhere. There. In bald terms, my boy, it's not the stuff of legend. It was not an action, though, that they could understand, and so they gave all kinds of meanings to that simple act, multiplying my holding to a fortune in the process. I knew what they said afterwards, because they told me. The argument with the banker became his theft, embezzlement, the fortune in the box became gold pieces, land deeds, a treasure map. Fools!

I believed that, given time and silence from me, the legend of my hidden fortune would die. But your father, of course, was its truest believer, though I told him a thousand times there was nothing to it. You seemed a bright lad as a youngster, and I believed you would make something of yourself without the need for me to interfere. It seems now I may have been wrong.

So here's the truth, my boy, and you won't like it. I kept silence on the whereabouts of my fortune because there was none. The argument with that idiot at the bank was simple: I told him I was giving my money away. The man was apoplectic; he seemed to take my madness, as he called it, personally. But I had learned all I needed to know about money, though the lessons were hard-learned. You know, in your heart, what I learned, though you may have difficulty believing me. Firstly, money buys you nothing of true value. Secondly, there is only one exception to this rule. Sometimes, you can use money to buy peace of mind, and the easing of suffering, and by that means you can free yourself from its influence.

The man in the photographs is my cousin, Nikolas. As boys, he and I were inseparable, the best of friends. Friends are something I never had, in later years. I hope you do not suffer the same lack. Friends keep your feet on the ground, and make you stay true to yourself.

Nikolas married, and had a son. And then, by the worst luck possible, he fell down a well and broke his back. A letter reached me from his wife and I – sick with my money fever – was disposed to ignore it. But I had a visitor who persuaded me of the right thing to do. They had my money, most of it. It went, I think, on doctor's bills and pain relief, and schooling for the boy.

My message to you, dear boy, is this. Look around you, see what you have of value, and cherish it. Trade money for time, and use your time wisely. That's the way to happiness. Do what you love, and be content. Listen to an old man's words. Respect the messenger who carries this letter. Sometimes a stranger has insights those who know us well can't see.

Good luck to you, Aris my boy,
Your most affectionate
Grandfather

Aris laid the letter on the table. Picking up the photographs one by one, he dropped them in the litter bin by his feet, amongst the screwed-up paper and the empty coffee cups.

'Bad news?' asked the fat man.

'If you'll excuse me now,' said Paliakis, 'I have work to do.'

'Your grandfather says nothing of interest in his letter?'

'My grandfather, it seems, was a bigger fool than any I've yet met.'

'Why so?'

'Not a sound businessman at all, but a sentimentalist. Now, if you'll excuse me.'

'I believe your grandfather, in his later years, was a very generous man. I heard of several who benefited from his generosity in time of need, though he was careful, I understand, to keep his generosity to himself. I expect he feared the unworthy beating a path to his door – the idle and the lazy. Was your father lazy, Aris?'

'My father was a drunk.'

'But what made him a drunk? A lust for easy money your grandfather saw fit to frustrate?'

'You seem to know a lot of my family's history, for a stranger.' As he said the last word, he remembered the same word at the end of the letter. He looked at the fat man with curiosity. 'What is your business here, specifically?'

'Specifically, since you ask,' said the fat man, 'your well-being.'

Paliakis laughed, the dry laugh of a man who has been unamused for years.

'My well-being is my concern, and mine alone,' he said. 'Don't patronise me, sir. I need no concern from you, nor from my sainted ancestor. *Kali nichta sas.*'

'Your disappointment is keen,' said the fat man. 'To have the grail you have been seeking all your life laid before you and find it is not gold, but dust, is hard. But my advice to you is this: seek diamonds in the dust. Because they are there, in your grandfather's words. Listen to him, and change your path.'

'Change my path? What can you mean? I'm a highly successful man. Why ever should I change my path?'

Now the fat man laughed.

'Is this success, then: to be alone in this office, whilst the rest of the world is out there, with friends and family, relaxing on this wonderful summer night? Is this success, the threats of legal action from the immigrants your penny-pinching has left injured? The scheming and the bribery, the looking over your shoulder to see who might be catching up with you? The enslavement of your children in this shabby enterprise? For what? There is no time to enjoy your money; your sickness compels you to make more, and more, and more. I remind you, Aris, of ancient Midas, the king of all fools – a man who wished for all he touched to turn to gold, as you do. His wish was granted: and before the week was out, he was a desperate man, dying of hunger and of thirst, weeping for the children whose living bodies he had turned to golden statues. You have the Midas touch, perhaps – you think you do, for certain – but be careful your fate isn't his, because there will be no Apollo to reinstate your children if you damage them with your greed.'

'My children, sir, are none of your business.'

'No. You have made them tools in *your* business, though, have you not? Like you, they have no time for love, or family; they are too busy on their missions serving your golden empire. Listen to me, Aris. You are about, I think, to step across a line you should not cross, from corruption to more serious crime.' Paliakis opened his mouth to object, but the fat man raised both his hand and his voice. 'Do not interrupt me. I know more than you would like me to know of your activities, and I am here to warn you that if you proceed, the consequences will be dire. My strong advice to you is this. Go home now, and sleep; tomorrow, take a boat and go fishing. Spend a few hours alone, away from all this, and consider what you have become, what road you're walking. Take your grandfather's letter, those photographs, and consider very carefully which way to go. Whether you know it or not, you're at a crossroads. I caution you to make the right decision.'

Without offering them to the fat man, Paliakis took a cigarette from a near-empty packet of Marlboros. Striking a lighter, he put the flame to the tip, inhaled, and, with a noise like a sigh, blew the smoke from his nostrils.

'With your interest in my well-being, you'll tell me, no doubt, I smoke too much,' he said. 'But I don't care. You seem to know plenty about my business, but you know little enough about me. So let me tell you. I used to have a sister, Chrissoula. Pretty as a picture, with a smile that could light up a room. And she adored me. I was her big brother, her protector. One year after my grandfather was taken, when I was nine and she was four, she died. There was no money for the medical care that would have saved her. My father was a lush, a drunk, who spent his life waiting for the contents of this box' – he swiped at it with the back of his hand – 'this stinking box to save him. It didn't save my father, and it didn't save my sister. And I never believed – not for one minute – that it would save me. I expected nothing from it, if it was ever found. Now here it is, and I wasn't disappointed. What my father, God rot him, didn't understand, was this.' He leaned across the desk to stress his point. 'It's every man for himself. My father hadn't the wit to realise you grab what you can before someone else grabs it. I had to make my own start in life, because no start was given to me. My legacy was being a laughing stock, a treasure hunter's son; my legacy was castles in the air, and empty dreams, and a dead sister. My first challenge was to work out how a young man with ambition can make a start, when – as I learn tonight – my grandfather gave my legacy to strangers. How was I to get a foot in the door, to get on to that ladder? Where could I find the seed money I needed to get me started? I know what they say here, that the money I used to get a foothold, I stole. But that's not true. I got my capital honestly, if such a bargain can ever be an honest one. I sold the only commodity I had: I sold myself. I took myself to a city far from here, and I found the places to go, and before the week was out, I had a patron. Patron! That was his word. He was a queer, a *poustis*, a married man, respected in public office by day, a rampant sodomite by night. I close my eyes, sir, and I feel his hands all over me still. You may imagine how it was, if you've the stomach for it. We made a devil's bargain, he and I; he bought a year from me, a year of my life, a year of my body. The bargain was a poor one: still, after all this time, he haunts me. The day I left, I left him bleeding on the floor; how he explained the bruises to his wife, I'll never know.

'But I had my seed money. It bought me a start and a marriage contract. Another poor bargain, that; she's like a tap with money, a tap that won't turn off. In spite of her, I succeeded, the boys were educated, my empire – as you put it – grew. But complacency – there is no room for that. You counsel rest, and fishing, and so I know immediately you are no businessman. A tight hand on the reins at all times – a tight hand, and a programme of diversity. A business interest is always vulnerable; disaster looms round every corner. A wall collapses, and the vultures clamour for compensation; a new restaurant opens on the same street as mine, and my own may close tomorrow. The game, sir, is constantly in play. Fishing is for fools, and bankrupts.' He slammed shut the lid of the box. 'Take the goddamned box, and bury it with my grandfather's bones. He did me no kindnesses! He left his own son an empty dream and his granddaughter a pauper's death. With wise investment, we might have had a life of comfort, all of us. His fickle charity condemned us to misery and degradation.'

'His gesture was to an old friend – a relative – in great need, and with no means to help himself. His message was to embrace the simple life.'

'My father's life was simple: the next bottle, the next drink. Mine is more complex, as you seem to know.'

'If you had no interest in the box, why did you wear its key around your neck?'

'I took it from my father's neck, before we buried him. I wore it to remind me of his stupidity, and of my grandfather's malice in leaving him to dream. I wore it as I'll wear it still – to remind me dreams are futile. Hard cash buys you all you need.'

'You are bitter from your degradation, of course. But do not blame the world for choices you made. There was no compulsion to sell yourself. Your own lust drove you – lust, and greed for money. You could have taken a steady job, grown savings over the years, but you were impatient. And there was no compulsion to marry a woman you neither loved nor respected to get at her father's money. You lied to her, and him, about your affection for her; you made her deeply unhappy. Your greed has brought unhappiness at every turn. Now you are writing the same prescription for your sons. You will not set them free to learn what in life has true value, and they dare not cross you. You're teaching them to fear the same things you do – the loss of wealth. But it's a poor father who loves his sons so little his greed comes before their happiness.'

'How dare you say I do not love my boys!'

'I don't say that. What I do say is, you love your money more. You have enough now, Aris. To keep amassing more is to take a path as erroneous as your father's. Your mistakes are from the same root, just different flowers.'

'When they call me Onassis, then I'll have enough. Maybe then.'

'Consider again,' said the fat man. 'Reread your grandfather's words. Listen to what he says. His nature and yours are remarkably similar, and he was persuaded of a better course. As the proverb goes, painless poverty is better than embittered wealth.'

'Believe me, there is nothing painless about poverty! You do not strike me as a man who has ever suffered hardship, and I have made sure my boys have escaped it, too. Poverty is the bitterest fruit you'll ever eat, and I'll not put it in my sons' mouths! What could ever be better for them than a solid foundation for their future? Answer me that!'

'A happy present. A present where you value them, truly value them over your own morbid fears. That's what's at the base of your obsession, Aris; not their well-being, or their future, but your own terror of a return to poverty. Of being a laughing stock.'

Paliakis shook his head.

'Please, go.'

As Paliakis drew again on his cigarette, the fat man stood. A moth flickered around the light bulb, casting small, moving shadows on the lid of the olive-wood box.

'Consider what I've said, Aris,' said the fat man. 'Maybe we'll meet again.'

He turned to leave, but in the doorway he stopped.

'There is another matter I wanted to mention,' he said, 'regarding the legal heir of the land near Loutro, at the Temple of Apollo. Have you traced him yet?'

Palikais blew smoke towards the fat man.

'Land?' he asked. 'What land?'

'Have it your way,' said the fat man. 'But I give you notice, there is a legal heir. I strongly advise you to beware of him. Do not attempt to steal from him, or he will steal from you in return. And when he steals, he always takes the same thing; he will deprive you of whatever in life it is that you most value.'

Not yet dawn, but the sky was growing light, fading the stars like a mirage and vanishing the moon. Somewhere near by, a car engine was running. Disturbed from his uneasy doze, Petridis opened his eyes. The engine stopped. With silence restored, Petridis closed his eyes, rubbing his temples to sooth the violent pain in his head. His mouth, dry as pillow feathers, had the foul taste of rubbish. And he was still here. The memory of his difficulties was immediately restored to his consciousness; but the solution which had seemed so obvious only hours before seemed madness now.

Another sound: a car door slammed. Someone was here: some warden, he thought, come to light the oil lamps in the church. Too weary to rise, he stretched out on the stone bench to ease the stiffness in his muscles, listening to slow footsteps on the church steps; but, as he waited to hear a key turn in the lock, the footsteps continued, alongside the church, towards the rear courtyard. As a figure rounded the corner, the silhouette was both distinctive and familiar, and Petridis, embarrassed, rose quickly to his feet. Now close to him, the figure spoke, seeming to recognise Petridis with some surprise.

'Constable Petridis!' said the fat man. 'This is most unexpected! What brings you here?'

Confounded, Petridis gave no answer, and so the fat man went on.

'I expect your reasons are the same as mine. I come here often to watch the sunrise. My house is just a kilometre away, through the village. If I wasn't lazy, I would walk here, but as I see it the wheel was invented for good reason. Before they built this fine church of St Philipas, this place was sacred to Helios, god of the sun – did you know that? A worthy spot indeed to watch him ride his chariot into the sky.' He glanced at his watch. 'We've a few minutes to wait – but look, the show's already begun.'

Beyond the courtyard wall, across the ravine, the sky had faded from black to deepest mauve, and below that, a military grey. And there, splitting those sombre colours, a line of fire appeared, flaming so fiercely it burned the eyes.

'See, he's waking up. Always on time. We could take him as an excellent role model, couldn't we?' The fat man laid his holdall on the stone bench and, unzipping it, withdrew a large

Thermos flask and a short stack of paper cups. 'I've brought coffee. You'll join me, I hope.'

'I must go,' said Petridis.

'Go? But the show has barely started!'

The fat man filled a paper cup and offered it to Petridis, who, thirsty and tempted by the coffee's aroma, accepted it. Strong but smooth, the warm drink took the ache from his muscles and seemed to clear the fatigue from his brain.

The fat man poured coffee for himself and, sitting down on the stone bench, stretched his arm along the wall, looking east to where the sun would rise. In the growing light, he had the bright-eyed look of a man with a clear conscience and a good night's sleep behind him. It was a look Petridis recognised; before last night, he had seen it many times in his own mirror. He rubbed at the light stubble on his chin; his bloodshot eyes were stinging.

'Cigarette?' The fat man held out a box to him; on the lid, a platinum-blonde starlet pouted.

'I don't smoke.'

'Good for you.' The fat man lit himself a cigarette. 'I'm cutting down myself.' He popped his lips, and exhaled a perfect smoke-ring, which hung for a moment in the air, then, shifting and expanding, drifted slowly skywards. 'My party trick. You know, there's a funny story about this place I think you'd enjoy. There was a man a few years ago – not from the village, an out-of-towner – who got himself into some difficulties, I believe of a financial nature. Or with some woman. The nature of the problem is not important. Whatever was troubling him, he decided there was only one honourable solution – suicide.'

Petridis's cup was at his lips. At the fat man's words, his hand gave a small jerk, tipping hot coffee into his mouth and down his windpipe. He stifled a choking cough, but the fat man appeared not to notice; his attention seemed on the horizon, where the fiery line was growing in breadth and spectrum – tangerine-orange, grenadine-red.

'He came here by night, thinking to pray,' went on the fat man, 'but as is usual in so many Christian places, he found the door locked against him, the church being keener to protect its physical assets – its silver and its brass – than to provide a place of comfort for pilgrims with aching hearts. So, drawn by the sound of running water, he found his way to this spot, and thought it the perfect place to do the deed – a chasm with a river at its bottom to wash away his broken body, so he would never be found. So over he went.' The fat man laughed. 'What a fool!'

He drew on his cigarette, and gazed again at the breaking dawn.

Petridis waited for him to continue, but the fat man said no more.

'So what made him a fool?' asked Petridis.

The fat man laughed again.

'Look and see!'

In the weak light, Petridis peered over the wall. Just three metres down ran a terracotta drainage pipe, the water trickling through it echoing like a distant river.

'There's your great river and its chasm,' laughed the fat man. 'Fortunately, he chose a Saturday night. When the congregation assembled for Mass on Sunday morning, they heard him calling from where he'd fallen. A broken ankle, a bruised ego and a sore head from the whisky he'd drunk to give him courage. No lasting damage; and he survived to work out his problems like a man. More coffee?'

Petridis held out his cup.

'But some problems can't be fixed,' he said, miserably. 'Some mires are too deep, and can't be crawled out of.'

'Spoken like a young man unused to facing difficulties.' The fat man poured him coffee. 'When you reach my advanced age, son, you'll realise there are very few problems a thinking man can't get the better of. Forgive me for asking, but are you perhaps having trouble with a young lady?'

'In a manner of speaking. But she wasn't so young, and she wasn't worth the trouble.'

'A broken heart?'

'A broken life. I can't say more.'

At the horizon, the sunrise was entering its full glory.

'A splendid show,' said the fat man, then, more quietly, 'I assure you of my absolute discretion. You may trust me implicitly. What enters these ears as a confidence will never leave through this mouth.' Petridis fixed his bloodshot eyes on the fat man's which, behind his glasses, seemed large and owlish. There was compassion there, understanding, and the possibility of sympathy. 'I may be able to help you, George, but only if you first – how can I put this? – admit your sins. In the – predictable – absence of a Christian priest, consider me a substitute. We are, after all, on Orthodox soil.'

'I told Sergeant Gazis. He couldn't help.'

'On the contrary, I suspect Sergeant Gazis is, at this very moment, working on plans to bail you out of trouble. But with respect to him, he doesn't have my arsenal of weapons at his disposal. In very many areas, my influence is considerable.'

Petridis sighed, and told his story again. The fat man listened without interruption, watching the blooming dawn.

'The worry of exposure gnaws my gut,' finished Petridis. 'Already I'm changed. My life changed for ever in one hour.'

'You feel you are in this man's power.'

'There were things I did as a kid – taking a hundred drachmas from my mother's purse, playing practical jokes

214

on the next-door neighbour. I broke a favourite piece of Mother's china, once. My brother knew it all, and sometimes, in spite, or if I refused some favour, he'd snitch. The punishments I got were terrible to me – a slap from my mother's hand, banishment from meals until Grandma complained about stunting my growth. But it was my mother's disappointment in me I couldn't stand. I hated her not to think well of me. And that, you know, is how it is now. Exposure amongst strangers I can stand. Hell, down at the station they'll pat me on the back and tell me, *Well done, son, you're a randy lad and one of us – too bad you got caught*. There'll be handshakes and drinks all round on my way out the door. A hero, I'll be to them. No, it's not them I care about. Except for Sergeant Gazis.

'It's those at home I can't face, and it's not my own shame, but theirs. How would Mama face the sniping when the news comes from the mainland that her son's disgraced, and fired from the police force? How could she go to church, knowing what they were whispering behind her back? How could my father play poker at the *kafenion* where I was the butt of every joke? How would I face my grandmother, when she couldn't keep her disappointment from her smile? And Yorgia, my lovely Yorgia! She'll cut me in the street, as if she and I never met, as if I never kissed her in the dark . . . I can't face them. I can't face my own heartbreak when I think of all I've wasted – the interviews, the examinations, the weeks at the academy. One night in the wrong company, and I pissed it all away! How will I bear it, when I hand back the uniform I was so proud to wear: the shirts my aunt presses just so, my cap and the badge I've polished . . .'

He stopped. Overhead, a waking jay cackled in the branches of a pine tree.

'Your gun,' said the fat man. 'You're thinking of your gun.'

Petridis looked down at his hand; he seemed to see the weapon there, black and menacing, to feel its weight, its coldness, its potency.

'It was given to me for protection,' he said.

'To protect the public,' corrected the fat man.

'My loved ones are the public.' Hatred for Dinos filled Petridis, sweeping away good sense and reason, and seeming to empower him.

Shaking his head in admonition, the fat man laid a hand on Petridis's forearm, and at his touch the hatred was diminished; but a residue remained, as if a stain on the policeman's character were spreading, and in his heart he understood that, where his new enemy was concerned, Constable George Petridis could not be trusted to do his duty to protect him.

'Violence is a certain road to ruin your life,' said the fat man. 'Don't think of it again.'

'Are you suggesting my life is not already ruined? I am no longer fit to be a serving police officer. I am compromised. I have compromised myself. There's no way out of the mire that I can see.'

'But my eyes see better than yours,' said the fat man. 'Long experience of life gives clearer vision. If you wish to sink into your mire, you are at liberty to do so. But if you wish to be hauled out, I offer you my hand. And our immediate concern is anyway not you, but Sergeant Gazis. In my assessment of the man, it's likely he'll move heaven and earth on your behalf. In other words, he's likely to do something both precipitate and unwise. Though he means well, of course.'

'What do you think he'll do?'

'That remains to be seen. But he is not a man to watch you fall out of the sky and do nothing, wouldn't you agree? Still, the day's only beginning, so we have time. Are you on duty today?'

'This afternoon, at 5. But how can I face it?'

'You'll face it. And no more coffee. What you need is sleep. Is there any news at all, by the way, on my good friend's death?'

Petridis explained about the damage on the radio station's car.

'But it was Dinos. He gave me the address of the guy he hit. So that's a dead end.'

'You have the address he gave you?'

Petridis found the paper in his pocket.

'No one has been there yet?'

'There's been no time.'

'Excellent. Leave it to me. Look!'

A slender sector of the sun had risen above the horizon, its brilliance filling the sky.

'Great Helios is always punctual,' said the fat man, referring again to his watch. 'Your problems may seem overwhelming to you, George, but Helios has seen it all before. Nothing new under the sun, as they say! Trust me, and trust Sergeant Gazis, because we are both friends to you. You have been honest in your confession and your admission of your fault, and your sins are weakness and bad company, not worse. Trust me for a day or two, and, one way or another, we'll haul you out of the mire. Now, ride carefully on your journey home, and then sleep. Don't be late for your shift. And whilst you're sleeping, you can be assured I have everything in hand.'

Eighteen

In the radio station's lobby, FM107 was piped through speakers. As Gazis entered, he caught the last words of a commercial for a bank. Last year, this building hadn't been here; contractors' tools still littered the unplanted flower-beds, and the car park was marked with the clay-drawn tracks of heavy plant. The offices' design was contemporary, modelled on the modern architecture of Northern Europe and fronted with smoked glass, which, from outside, mirrored their surroundings: similar office blocks half-completed, a new service road, a Toyota dealership. Inside, the glass's tint reduced the sun's glare so efficiently it leached the blue from the sky, the heat from the day, the season from the year, so if he hadn't walked in from enervating heat Gazis could not have said, looking out, whether it was mid-winter or high summer.

At a curved reception desk, a girl with blonde curls to her shoulders (who, Gazis suspected, might be quite plain without eye make-up and lipstick) wished him a sullen *kali mera*.

Gazis smiled, but the girl did not smile back.

'I'd like to speak to Dinos Karayannis,' he said.

'Who shall I say wants him?'

'Thanos Gazis. Sergeant Thanos Gazis.'

'Take a seat.'

She pointed to a sofa upholstered in chocolate-brown leather. On the wall above its back was a gallery of steel-framed portrait photographs of the station's DJs, all labelled with their names and work-shifts: *Vassilis Kakamoutsos, Early Morning Call, Panayiotis Rondis, Midnight Express.* Through unseen speakers, the broadcast ran on; the commercials over, this shift's DJ talked fast about nothing at all. His voice was smooth, dark and deep. Gazis looked up at the wall of portraits, and found the voice's owner: a middle-aged man, whose obesity and drooping jowls could not be hidden by soft focus.

'Mr Gazis.'

Dinos stood behind him. His ponytail hung halfway down his back, the hair on his scalp pulled tight; his T-shirt showed the emblem of a French designer. He was smiling but, as he held out his hand, his eyes were wary. Gazis looked at the hand. When he took it in his own, Dinos's smile grew broader.

'I wouldn't have known you, out of uniform,' said Dinos. 'You look different. Shorter. So what's going on – have you transferred to plain clothes?'

'I'm off duty.'

'This isn't an official visit, then? But it can't be a social call, I'm sure.'

'You and I have business. Is there somewhere we can talk?'

Dinos shrugged.

'Follow me.'

He led Gazis through an office, where the air was blue with the smoke of cigarettes. Five women sat at desks heavy with paperwork; all wore headsets, and talked loudly into their microphones. Gazis heard dates, times, prices, days of the week. At the centre of the office, a man with his shirtsleeves rolled up over the elbows spoke angrily into a phone.

'Advertising sales,' said Dinos. 'The lifeblood of this station. Without these ladies, FM107 would cease to exist. The media is so glamorous, isn't it?'

Exiting the office, they followed a short corridor, passing a door on their left labelled *Newsroom*.

'That's my office,' he said, jerking his thumb towards the door. 'And there . . .' He pointed two fingers in a pistol towards a door ahead of them. 'That's the engine room – the broadcasting suite. We can talk in here.'

Gazis followed Dinos into a small lunch room, where the sink was full of unwashed china and the light on the drinks vending machine flickered on and off, the ashtray on the table overflowed with butts and the upholstery on the cheap chairs was stained. Beside the water-cooler, a mop stood in an empty bucket; Gazis smelled chlorine bleach, and the mustiness of growing bacteria. The smoked-glass window showed a view of the car park; looking out, Gazis saw his own car baking in the sun.

'You want something to drink?'

'Nothing,' said Gazis.

'Sit down.'

'I'll stand.'

Dinos leaned on the sink, and folded his arms.

'So,' he said, 'are you going to tell me what this is about?'

'Petridis,' said Gazis. He watched Dinos's face for his reaction; there was nothing there, except, perhaps, a slight narrowing of the eyes. 'George Petridis, my constable. You know Petridis, don't you?'

'Vaguely.'

'Don't give me any crap,' said Gazis quietly. 'I've had his side of the story. Now I want yours.'

'Story? I don't know any story.' He dug for change in the pocket of his shorts, turning his back on Gazis to feed it into the drinks machine. 'Sure you won't have anything?'

'Very sure.'

Money rattled in the machine; Dinos pressed a button, and a can of orange soda thumped into the dispenser. Popping the top and drinking, Dinos turned back to Gazis.

'I'm sorry, Mr Gazis, but I have no idea what you're talking about.'

'Then I'll explain. The way he tells it, he's been getting into bad company. Yours, amongst others.'

Dinos shrugged, and drank again from his can. Now, Gazis read something in his face: bravado, or insolence.

'We hung out one night. Is that a crime?'

'More an error of judgement on his part,' said Gazis. 'But the actual crime came later. Last night, in fact.'

Dinos raised his eyebrows.

'If there's been a crime, lucky you're on the case, Mr Gazis.'

'Don't mess with me, Dinos.' Gazis's voice was cold with anger. 'Blackmail is an ugly business. It's the kind of crime only scum would sink to, wouldn't you say?'

'I'd say that was open for debate. And I'd say, if someone has some leverage, they should be entitled to use it. Especially if someone else has made an error of judgement, as you put it. Business is business.'

'Compromising a young man's career is a very dirty business indeed.'

'If there's been any compromising, it needed no help from me. Your man compromised himself. What did you take him for, some kind of choirboy?'

'In a manner of speaking. The innocent are the most easily corrupted.'

'He's a man like any other. Is he some relative of yours? Is that what this is about?'

'He's no relative to me. He's a young man with a very bright future, which I'm not going to let you screw up.'

'Well, now. It's interesting you mention futures, because that's exactly where my eyes are – on my future. You know how it is. To get where I'm going, I need contacts. Sources. That's the business I'm in – good, reliable sources. There's no need to get excited, Mr Gazis. Press and police have worked that way for ever.'

'There's a difference between a mutual exchange of information and extortion.'

'Extortion! That's a very strong word. Who's extorting anything?'

'You are.'

'How so?'

'Photographs.'

Smiling, Dinos nodded.

'Now we get to it. He's told you I have some interesting pictures. And he's right. They'd make a great story. *The policeman and the whore*. It's no big deal. He knows I won't write it. We have an understanding.'

Gazis shook his head.

'No. There'll be no understanding between you and him. That's why I'm here.'

'To threaten me? To bully? That would be the icing on my cake, wouldn't it? You threaten me, and I'd really have a story worth writing. Go ahead, beat me up. It's the big break I've been waiting for.'

'I know that. That's one reason it's not going to happen. The other reason is, it's not my style. I'm not here to threaten, Dinos. I'm here to trade.'

'Trade? What on earth could you offer me in place of pictures of a policeman screwing a whore?'

'What happened about the money?'

'Well, in fairness to George, he brought the money back. I don't think he knew he was meant to keep it. Perhaps you're right about his innocence. But I just happen to have a picture of George stuffing banknotes in his pocket. People would draw the wrong conclusions, obviously. But you're getting things out of proportion; I've no intention of publishing. And I've no idea, either, why he came crying to you. It's between me and him. It's just a little insurance policy I've taken out to encourage him to use me as his exclusive media contact. Nothing more.'

'It's plenty more. It's the end of his integrity as a serving officer.'

Dinos laughed loudly.

'Integrity! Mr Gazis, you never cease to surprise me! There's so little integrity in your line of work, why expect it in George? Present company excepted, of course. It's well known you're a candidate for canonisation. But your colleagues . . .'

'There are some good men in there. And Petridis is going to be one of them.'

'Maybe, maybe not.'

'No maybe. We're going to trade.'

'Are we? Well, you'd better have something good to offer.'

The door opened, and the receptionist entered, hooking blonde curls behind her ear. As though Dinos were not in the room, she acknowledged Gazis with an inclination of her head. Opening a wall cupboard, she reached up for a packet of coffee from a high shelf, drawing Dinos's eyes to the stretched curves of her body: thighs, buttocks, breasts. Closing the cupboard, she clutched the coffee to her chest, and turned to leave.

But Dinos stopped her.

'You're still mad at me,' he said.

She lifted her chin in a show of disdain.

'I'm not mad at you,' she said. 'Why should I be?'

He placed his orange soda on the table, and crossed the room to stand close to her, keeping his voice low as he spoke. But the room was small, and Gazis caught every word.

'I told you how it was. She came on to me. I'd had a drink. I'm sorry.'

'You're always sorry.'

'I'll make it up to you. I'll take you to the beach this afternoon.'

'I'm busy.'

'Don't be busy. I miss you, Mina.'

'You should have thought of that before you tangled yourself up with her.'

He leaned in closer and, placing his lips to her exposed ear, whispered something Gazis didn't catch.

As Dinos stepped back, Mina was smiling.

'Come on,' said Dinos. 'I'll take you to the beach. You choose where we'll go. Kastro. Let's go there. I'll pick you up at 3, 3:30. OK, *agapi mou*?'

For only a moment, Mina hesitated.

'If you're late,' she said, 'it's over.'

'I won't be late.'

She left them, pausing in the doorway to adjust the neck of her blouse, where the lace of her bra was showing.

'Stupid,' said Dinos, as the door closed. 'Stupid, but compliant.' He moved back across the room, picking up his soda. 'You were saying something about a trade. What you hadn't said was what you're actually trading.'

Gazis held Dinos's eyes.

'Me,' he said. 'You can have me.'

Dinos laughed.

'And what on earth would I do with you, Mr Gazis?'

'I'll be your story.'

'You? I'm sorry to have to tell you, but there's no story in you.'

'There is if you substitute me for Petridis. It'll work, if the photographs aren't very clear. Change them digitally, if you like. Swap my face for his. Then tell me I'm not a better story than Petridis. He's a rookie with a few weeks' service. Him going to the bad is only a little story. But me, I've got thirty years, and two years to my pension. True or not, the general public'll believe I've been on the take all that time. Whoring, too. You'll bring down a senior man. There'll be repercussions. Investigations. You'll make the nationals.'

Dinos's expression showed shrewd, calculating interest.

'Now, why on earth would you do that?' he asked. 'Is it possible I've misread you all this time? You're looking for a percentage on the story, aren't you?'

'You'd never understand my reasons, Dinos. I don't want a cut. Take it or leave it. You'll take it, of course. And to make it even sweeter for you, I'll tell you something else. If I retire now – of course they'll let me retire quietly, if they can get away with it – I'll lose a quarter of my pension.'

'Quarter of your pension? You've gone mad.'

'Maybe.'

'Why on earth would you sacrifice that – sacrifice yourself – for a boy you hardly know?'

'Because I do know him. He'll be a great policeman one day. And he'll come back and get you. That's the part you need to understand. If I know Petridis, you won't be comfortable in this town ever again.'

'So what? Who'd need this town? You'd be my ticket out of here.'

'So do we have a deal?'

'I think we might.'

'OK. Buy me a soda, and I'll tell you how we're going to play it.'

As Dinos searched for change, Gazis crossed to the window. In his face was sadness he wanted to hide, and he looked out across the new road to where a building crew sat resting in the shade.

Alongside Gazis's car, a red Namco Pony pulled into an empty space.

'What'll you have?' asked Dinos. 'Coke, orange, lemon?'

'Lemon.'

Gazis watched as the fat man climbed from the Pony and looked around. Close by was a white car with a pink *FM107* logo splashed down its sides; the damage to one wing was significant. As the fat man bent to examine the car, Gazis smiled.

He turned to Dinos.

'Someone's taking an interest in your car,' he said. The fat man was scraping the damaged paintwork with a penknife, catching the flakes of paint in an empty matchbox. 'Looks to me like he's taking paint samples.'

But Dinos didn't hear; he was already on his way outside.

Gazis followed slowly. By the time he reached the car park, Dinos had finished shouting at the fat man and was on his way back into the building.

As he and Gazis passed, Dinos glared.

'Was this a set-up?' he asked. 'You bastards!'

'Set-up?' asked Gazis, but Dinos was gone.

Gazis stood by the fat man. The sun was hot on his back.

'You seem to have upset Dinos,' he said.

'It would seem so,' said the fat man. 'But, as I tried to explain to him, I am merely working on a process of elimination.'

'He'll calm down.'

'I was coming to see you later,' said the fat man, 'so I consider it lucky – though unexpected – to find you here.'

'I had some business to discuss with Dinos, as a matter of fact.'

The fat man looked at him long and hard.

'I hope you have done nothing hasty, or rash,' he said.

Gazis did not reply.

'Not to worry,' said the fat man. 'What's done can often be undone.' He held out the matchbox. 'May I give this into your care? These paint samples are important for our process of elimination. As I said to Dinos, elimination of the innocent is as important a part of this process as conviction of the guilty. I'm afraid I have ruffled his feathers. I shall call on him again later, and hope to convince him my intention was not to offend. In the meantime, even I am feeling the heat, so I shall take myself for a swim.'

'Perhaps you can kill two birds with one stone,' said Gazis. 'I believe Dinos has a date at Kastro beach later on. You could buy him an ice-cream by way of apology.'

The fat man smiled.

'In the meantime,' he said, 'please take no further action in the Petridis business. I think you'll find matters will work themselves out, without your further intervention.'

Gazis frowned.

'Young Petridis and I have become quite good friends,' went on the fat man, 'so I'm aware of his current difficulty. And when I speak to Dinos, I'm convinced I can persuade him to see reason.'

'You're welcome to try,' said Gazis. 'But if you fail, he and I have come up with a solution of our own.'

'There'll be no need for that,' said the fat man, shortly. 'Goodbye, for now. I'll be in touch, when I've spoken to Gabrilis's killer.'

Gazis was startled.

'Do you know, then, who is guilty?'

'Oh, yes,' said the fat man, 'I know who's guilty. Believe me, I have him very clearly in my sights.'

On the way to the beach, the fat man had planned a short detour, but the address on Petridis's piece of paper was hard to find. Twice, the fat man drove through the village, and found no road by the name he'd been given. Turning round, once again, at the village outskirts, he saw a young man tinkering with a motorcycle's brakes and, winding down his window, asked for directions.

The young man knew the house well.

'A good kilometre from here,' he said. 'Just keep driving. You can't miss it.'

Where the mountain foothills began, the villa stood in isolation, the high, iron railings that surrounded it spiked with fleurs-de-lys, like the fences around embassies or palaces. Its wide gates were open to the road, and the fat man drove through them, along a driveway where dried, dead weeds filled the cracks in the concrete.

The house, when he reached it, was grand but unattractive. A failing lawn spread to the railings, the lines of the original lengths of turf lifting at their parched edges, the surviving grass sparse and pale, kept barely alive by water from a hosepipe that lay, coiled and dribbling, in the house's shadow. The fat man saw no native trees, no bushes or shrubs, no flowerbeds within the garden; but on the land all around, crickets sang in the thriving wild grasses, as if Nature's nose were pressed up against the fence.

Beside the front door was an electric doorbell, but above it, hung on a crooked nail hammered into the frame, was a sheep's bell with a length of cord attached to its clapper. The fat man rang the sheep's bell, whose tinny rattle seemed in keeping with the foothills' grasslands. For a minute, he waited, but the sheep's bell brought no answer; behind the door, a vacuum cleaner droned. Stepping up again to the door, the fat man pressed the electric bell. Immediately, the droning of the vacuum cleaner stopped.

A woman opened the door, her lips set in down-turned lines.

'Yes?'

'*Kali mera*,' said the fat man. 'I'm looking for Mr Manos Vrettos.'

'He's not here.'

'When will he be back?'

'I don't know.'

'Mrs Vrettos, then?'

'I am Mrs Vrettos.'

'A moment of your time, then, *kyria*. I'm here in relation to a car accident I believe your husband had recently. He's mentioned it to you, I'm sure.'

'Oh yes, he mentioned it,' she said sourly. 'And I know you're not from the insurance, because he let the insurance lapse.'

'As a matter of fact,' said the fat man, 'I'm working with the police.'

She pulled a frown, which drew deep wrinkles on her brow.

'It's not a police matter, surely?' she asked. 'It was straight-forward, Manos said, the other guy's stupidity. And of course we have insurance. My husband wouldn't drive without insurance. But still, I think it would be better if you came back when Manos was here.'

'But I'm here now, *kyria*, and truly I need only a few moments to clarify a point or two. I would consider it a great favour if you would save me the return trip.'

'What can I tell you?' she asked. 'I wasn't there.'

'But you know how the accident happened?'

'I know what he told me. He said he wasn't to blame. Manos was on Chimaras Street; he'd been to the bank. He was driving slowly – so he says – with other cars ahead of him. And this other guy was waiting at the junction, in a side-street. Manos says he must have had an aberration of the brain. The cars ahead of Manos he let go by, and as Manos approached – bam! – he pulled out straight in front of him.'

'Was there much damage?'

She laughed.

'Manos's beautiful car, his BMW! He cares more about that car than he does about me. Now it's got the front all caved in. Of course he can't find the time to get it repaired, not in tourist season. It'll stay like that until October, or beyond.'

'Was there much damage to the other car?'

'I haven't seen it, so I couldn't really say. Manos daren't drive fast, not in that beloved car. But he hit the guy side-on, on the wing, so I'm sure the other car had something to show for it.'

'And can you tell me, Mrs Vrettos, what colour is your husband's car?'

'Black,' she said. 'My husband's car is black.'

Nineteen

Four o'clock, and, as the heat-wearied families of foreigners prepared to leave Kastro beach, with the cooling of the day the Greeks were arriving. In the water, a group of army conscripts threw a frisbee; a grandmother and grandfather released, reluctantly, the hands of a small and precious grandchild, and watched, nervous and interfering, as he splashed joyfully in the shallows. In the car park, Greek cars took the places of those rented by Europeans, and the barmen changed the music, from the tedious pounding of club anthems to the ethnic rhythms of Greek pop. At the beach bar, the slender-limbed, bronzed Italian girls tossed their salty hair like mermaids, and demanded juices and French water from the barmen, whilst overeager English girls with sunburn red as scalds competed for the men's attention by ordering too many cocktails. The air smelled not of the sea but of frying food; the hot sand was churned with footprints and trampled castles.

Far along the beach, the sand turned into gravel, then pebbles, then into the steep rocks that marked the beach's end. In the shade of those rocks, the fat man waited. A plush, navy-blue towel was spread beneath him; his swimming shorts were damp, his hair was drying into curls. His tortoiseshell-framed sunglasses had a discreet American logo on the arm; their lenses were tinted teak-brown but, although the tint was subtle, somehow behind the lenses his eyes could not be seen. On his little finger, the ring Sostis had returned to him glinted ostentatiously.

His spot was carefully chosen. The rocks had a clear view of the car park on the flat cliff tops across the bay, where his red Namco Pony, unique amongst the other cars, was parked close to the entrance from the coast road.

At 4:15, a white car with a blaze of fuchsia on its side drove slowly past the Pony, and reversed into a nearby space. As the fat man watched, a man and a girl climbed from the car: Dinos and Mina. Dinos lifted a sportsbag from the rear seat, Mina swung a backpack to her shoulders, and together they walked down to the beach.

The fat man waited. Near the beach bar, where a wooden changing cubicle stood beside a fresh-water shower, Mina kissed Dinos on the cheek, and left him. Dinos came on along the beach; free from Mina, he surveyed the women as he walked, smiling at the Italian girls at the bar, calling out to a German girl stroking suncream on her thighs. Passing the sunbeds and umbrellas, shifting the equipment he carried from hand to hand, he walked to where the sand turned to shingle; there, he paused and looked about him, but, seeing no place to his liking, came on further still. By lying face down on his towel, the fat man made himself anonymous. Attracted by the rocks' shade, Dinos moved closer and closer until, just a few feet from where the fat man lay, he dropped his sportsbag on the pebbles, together with his flippers, a harpoon gun and a belt of lead weights.

He pulled off his T-shirt and, letting it fall, removed the shorts that covered his swimming trunks, then slipped off his sandals to stand barefoot on the beach. From the sportsbag he took out a snorkel and mask, and a net bag to hold the catch he hoped to make. He touched a fingertip to the harpoon trident's prongs to check their sharpness and, with the gun still unloaded, pulled the trigger twice to check the mechanism; satisfied, grimacing with the effort, he forced the trident down into the barrel. He bent then to pick up the belt of weights; but, as he was about to clip it on, the fat man got to his feet, and spoke.

'*Yassou*, Dinos,' he said.

In surprise, Dinos turned.

'We've met before,' said the fat man. 'This morning, at your office.'

He took a step closer to Dinos, who squinted into the sun, trying to identify the man behind the glasses.

'It's you,' he said. 'What the hell were you doing with my car this morning?'

'Just routine,' said the fat man.

'What do you mean, routine? Are you another policeman?'

'I have been working with Sergeant Gazis, but no, I'm not a policeman. I've been making independent enquiries – into the death of my friend, Gabrilis Kaloyeros.'

Dinos snapped his fingers, recalling the memory.

'That's where I've seen you. You were there, when the ambulance turned up. You were there when Gazis found the body.'

'I was indeed there, but it wasn't Gazis who found the body. It was I, and it was a moment I shall never forget. Gabrilis was a good man, and a true friend to me for many years. He did not deserve that lonely, painful death.'

'My sympathies. But what does that have to do with my car?'

'It was a white car that killed Gabrilis, as you know, since – I believe – Constable Petridis contacted you, asking you to include in your news bulletins a request for help in tracking down that vehicle.'

Dinos shrugged, and bent to fiddle with the cable connecting the trident to the harpoon gun, rubbing at a blemish with his thumbnail.

'He may have asked me. I really don't remember. We get requests like that all the time. Everything from lost dogs to runaway wives. A stolen tractor, once. We don't put them all on the air.'

'They don't all relate to murder, though, do they? This one did. And yet your station didn't run the appeal.'

'Didn't we? And not murder, surely? Manslaughter, at worst. I'm sorry, but as far as we're concerned, it was just a traffic accident. A tragedy to those that knew him, of course; but to the world at large, my friend, just one of those things.'

He looked across the beach. The fat man followed his eyes, to the bar where Mina stood chatting with two swimsuited girls.

'Your friend has found companions.'

'She talks too much, and I'm ready to go. She won't know where to find me.'

The fat man gazed out over the sea.

'What are you after, out there?'

'Anything I can find. Anything I can catch. Gives me a buzz, you know?'

'Oh yes, I know very well. There's a lot of that in my work. Hunting. Tracking. Like I've tracked you.'

Quizzically, Dinos looked at him.

'Tracked me? What for?'

'I had help, of course. From Sergeant Gazis. And the very worthy Constable Petridis. You know George Petridis socially, I gather?'

Dinos turned away and, putting his hand to his eyes to block the sun, scanned the beach again to find Mina.

'For God's sake,' he said under his breath, 'why doesn't the silly bitch get over here?'

He laid down the belt of weights, and began to walk away from the fat man towards the bar; but the fat man moved quickly to block him, and put a hand on Dinos's naked chest.

'You and I,' he said, 'have not finished talking.'

'What the hell are you doing?' Dinos pulled off the fat man's hand. 'Get out of my way!'

The fat man stepped aside.

'Go,' he said, 'and I will follow you. And as I follow you, I shall tell everyone what you have done. Everyone on this beach will know.'

'What do you mean, *what I have done*? You're a crazy man! Get out of my way!'

By the beach bar, the army conscripts had joined the three girls. Mina was laughing with them. Dinos cupped his hands at his mouth to amplify his voice, but as he was about to shout the fat man cautioned him.

'I wouldn't do that, if I were you,' he said. 'Don't call her over here unless you want her to hear what I have to say.'

Angrily, Dinos faced him.

'And what do you have to say, big guy?'

'That your opinion of yourself is very high, Dinos. You think you've got away with it, that the death of one old man is something you can sweep under the carpet, a minor inconvenience you've already overcome. And because your opinion of yourself is so high, your opinion of authority is correspondingly very low. But the constabulary would have got to you in the end, if I hadn't got to you first. Petridis has already put it all together. There's a reason Sergeant Gazis doesn't want him neutralised by you. Petridis has the makings of an excellent detective. In years to come, the boy will be a great asset to the CID.'

Dinos snorted with laughter.

'And, Christ knows, they need some assets! You seem to know little enough about the local constabulary if you don't share my opinion about the authorities. It's an opinion very commonly held, in these parts.'

'When I spoke of authority, I was not referring to them. I was speaking of myself.'

Sneering, Dinos looked him up and down.

'You? And on what authority do you act, friend?'

'A higher authority than Sergeant Gazis. My authority gives me access to facts the constabulary does not have.'

'Facts? What facts?'

'Facts you would prefer me not to know. Before I tell you, I would like you to answer me a question. Are you of the Orthodox faith?'

'What kind of question is that? Of course I'm Orthodox. Aren't we all Orthodox here?'

'Not all, no.'

The fat man bent down and, picking up the belt of lead weights, clicked the buckle fastened and flipped it open again. Dinos snatched the belt from him, and the fat man smiled.

Dinos fastened the belt around his waist.

'Just get out of my face,' he said.

'You killed my friend,' said the fat man quietly. 'You killed him, and didn't even have the decency to hold his hand as he died.'

Dinos gave a bark of laughter.

'You're crazy,' he said, screwing his index finger round at his temple. 'Crazy man.'

'Whilst your weakness is your high opinion of your own cleverness,' said the fat man, 'your boldness would have been your strength. Your escape plan was audacious, but it didn't work. I was on the scene too quickly. A day or two, and you would have been gone: a contract in another city, or just a simple, unexplained disappearance when the heat was off. You were smart enough not just to run; at least, you thought it smart. In fact, it was your only hope of getting away. And now it's too late.'

'I have no idea what you're talking about.'

'You have no idea how much I know. And you are desperate to find out, but you are good at appearing cool. So let me slake your curiosity, and tell you what I know.

'What caused the inattention that led to the collision? That I don't know. Were you talking on the phone? Changing the music you were listening to? Thinking of some girl? Were you tired from lack of sleep, or had you been drinking? It doesn't matter: you may keep that to yourself. The fact is, you hit him. You knocked him off the road. You stopped your car, braking hard; the skid-marks from your tyres were in the gravel, along with your footprints – running footprints. Did you go down to him? Yes, I think you did, because you were still hoping there was hope, that the old man would get up, brush himself off, no real harm done, that you'd drive him to a doctor's and be on your way.

'But you had hit him hard, and he was frail. You saw the case was hopeless. He wasn't dead, though, was he? Not *quite* dead.' Dinos looked away, as if to where Mina stood, but his eyes were focused elsewhere. 'No. I know he wasn't, because he had only just let go of life when I reached him, and I travelled a long, long way to get here. So far that I arrived too late, and I blame myself for that. So I suppose you said a prayer for him, and made your cross, and drove away. But not too far. I was far away; you were near to hand. It was no accident you came so promptly with the ambulance; all afternoon you waited, listening to the airwaves for the call. It didn't come, did it? But you wouldn't use your phone, because you knew it might be traced. And then, at last, the call did come, and you came close behind, your conscience pricking, anxious to be sure the body was found. If they hadn't found it, would you have guided them? I don't think so; I think that would have been too risky. But you felt better, of course, that he didn't spend the night out there, friendless, untended and alone. That would have been a dilemma, wouldn't it, for a good Orthodox boy; the old man's soul left out there for the devil to come and steal? Thank God it didn't come to that, eh, Dinos?

'So you followed the ambulance, and you were clever then, too. You parked your car so the damage wasn't visible to us. It didn't matter anyway, though the precaution was sensible; Gazis had me down for the crime, and their focus was on me and my Pony. And so you drove away, the body found, your conscience salved – what was one old man fewer in the world beside the rising star of your career? As for drawing attention to yourself with a radio appeal that might have closed the net on you – well, that would have been madness, wouldn't it? So you didn't run it. But other stations did. Of course they did. And so did the newspapers.'

'Your theory is intriguing,' interrupted Dinos, 'but you should know, as I told George Petridis, the damage on my car was caused in a traffic accident. So look elsewhere for your heartless hit-and-run.'

'I'm looking at you. Again, your best option was to run, leave town. But you, again, set too much store by your own cleverness. It was a very good idea, I grant you: involve yourself in a second accident to cover up the first. But it is possible to be too clever, you know. You have the cunning of a fox; but that has been your downfall. Do you know what the commonest colour of car is, Dinos?'

'I have no idea.'

'Silver. Statistically, you were far more likely to hit a silver car than any other colour. But the car you hit was black. And the way it was told to me, you waited at the junction you had chosen until a black car came along, and then pulled out.'

'My foot slipped. I wasn't thinking. I was on the phone, I admitted that.'

'You had your phone to your ear so it would look that way. But your attention was wholly on what you were doing. You were waiting for a black car to disguise the black-paint residue from Gabrilis's bike that was already there.'

'You're insane.' Dinos bent to pick up his flippers. 'It had absolutely nothing to do with me.'

'Unfortunately for you, forensics will prove my case. I've given Gazis the paint samples that will prove your guilt.'

'I believe I'll find another place to swim.'

'No, no.' The fat man raised his hands to object. 'Don't let me detain you any further. I'm glad we had this talk. It's proved to me my suspicion that there is no remorse in you. You are indeed a heartless hit-and-run, as you so aptly put it.'

'You've been too long in the sun, friend,' said Dinos.

He turned from the fat man, and, taking his kit, walked some distance away, across the shingle to the water's edge.

The fat man watched as Dinos pulled on his flippers.

'Be careful out there, Dinos!' he called. 'That undertow can catch out any man!'

But Dinos gave no sign that he had heard. Pulling his mask down over his face, he slipped into the sea smooth as a seal, and disappeared into the deep water around the rocks.

Along the beach, Mina was saying her goodbyes. Moving quickly, the fat man took Dinos's phone from his sportsbag and switched it off. Returning to his spot below the rocks, he zipped the phone into his own holdall, and folded up his towel.

Passing Mina, he wished her a *kali spera*. At the beach bar, he bought himself an ice-cold lemonade, and made his cheerful way along the track back to his car.

The water was cool, and Dinos's ears filled with its solid silence. Swimming easily, he stayed close to the shoreline rocks, scanning for prey. He waved his hand through a shoal of tiny fish, their bodies transparent and glistening like opals, lit within by electric-blue and red; in a swarm they surrounded him, and he wafted them impatiently away. The talk with the fat man had disturbed him. There were issues he must address.

Beyond the rocks, the clarity of the shallow water clouded into an infinity of petrol-blue, and there, for a second, something moved, the dark shape of a fish of excellent size; but when he turned his head to look full-on, nothing was there.

Before he rounded the headland – beyond which the beach would be out of sight – he stopped swimming and, treading water, raised his head above the waterline and pushed up his mask. Mina was there; he picked her out by the rocks, pedantically positioning her towel at the perfect angle to the sun.

Of the fat man, there was no sign.

Reimmersing himself in the water, he swam around the headland, where the water became cooler, and the cold currents running in from the open sea caused him to shiver. Away from the shoreline, the quality of the water was changed, its cheering, attractive blue deepening to the ultramarine of depths, which felt, today, intimidating. For the first time he could remember, the sea made him afraid.

He turned back towards the rocks, where the sun shone through the shallower water and the silvery light was bright. He peered down at a small octopus, wondering if it was worth his trouble, and as he did so he glimpsed that same dark shape ahead of him, to his right, towards the open sea. He turned again to face it, but it was gone, though its direction was clear. He kicked his flippers hard and moved faster in pursuit, and soon reached the weird formations of the Dragon's Teeth, where sharp pinnacles of ancient lava poked up from the sea bed, the cones of rock dividing the water into narrow channels between them.

He slowed, and looked about him. The splendid fish – a snapper, he thought, two kilos at least, maybe a little more – was in the open water to his right, but, as he considered strategy, some prey caught the fish's eye, and it changed course, swimming away from the deep water and in amongst the Dragon's Teeth.

In the shallows, the fish was a gift to him. Harpoon raised to take the shot, he drew closer; but the fish would not swim straight, darting instead one way, then another, drawing him into the Dragon's Teeth as though into a maze. The pinnacles rose around him like great stalagmites, and he swam with care amongst them, knowing the rocks were sharp as barnacles, and might grate the skin off him as easily as rind from a lemon. Always ahead, the fish's scales flashed silver, and he kicked strongly to close its lead on him, until he drew close enough to take a shot; but, as the trident flew, the fish darted downwards after some prey of its own, and disappeared into the black mouth of a sea-cave.

Hauling back the trident by its line, he forced it back inside the harpoon's barrel. The fish, he knew, was trapped; many of these caves had little depth, two or three metres at most. Above the cave's portal, he peered inside. All was darkness – except, he felt sure, for the silvery glint of his fish's flank.

The target now was an easy one. Filling his lungs through the snorkel, he dived, swimming forwards into the tunnel of rock. The water was cold, the light weak, but the fish moved like a shadow just ahead. He fired the harpoon; the trident pierced the fish through its side, and began to take it down to the cave floor. Quickly, he hauled on the trident's cable but, on his waist, something slipped and, suddenly too light, Dinos floated upwards, watching his belt of weights fall away below.

His head cracked on the cave roof, his back hit the cutting edges of the rock. For a moment, he was dazed, and disoriented; then, impelled by instinct, he tried to turn, to reach the light behind him at the portal. But, without weights, the cave roof drew his body like a magnet, and his head and back soon hit stone once again. He knew he must swim down, but he had not yet made the turn, and so his efforts took him deeper inside the cave.

His lungs were painful and, unable to resist, he took a breath. But no air came through his snorkel; instead, he swallowed the first mouthful of seawater. It choked him, and he coughed, but coughing was fatal, each cough drawing more salt water to his lungs.

The fish pierced by the trident was already dead, and, before too long, the hands fighting the cave's entombing walls were still.

The fat man phoned the lawyer's office again, and asked the secretary to put him through to Ilias.

Ilias was cheerful, and keen to share good news.

'It was quite straightforward,' he said. 'The paperwork's all done, and signed and stamped at their end. All that's required is a signature, with witnesses. I'm here all day tomorrow, at your convenience.'

The fat man thanked him.

'I'll buy you lunch,' he said. 'I've a yearning for stifado, if you know anywhere where they prepare it properly.'

Ilias laughed.

'I know a place,' he said, 'but I don't know if it's what you had in mind. My wife's an excellent cook, and her stifado's better than my mother's. Come and eat with us.'

The fat man smiled.

'It would be a pleasure,' he said.

Twenty

Another dawn. Its pinkness brought a blush to the temple's old stones; the first red light put a shine on the green-skinned watermelons, whose unwatered foliage was yellowing and crisp from neglect. On the sea, a fishing boat motored slowly out; from the hives, the industrious bees began their early forays.

A white van turned off the coast road, carrying the Paliakis men up the track to Gabrilis's land. In the driver's seat, Kylis was whistling; his eyes were bloodshot from lack of sleep, his breath unpleasant from last night's cigarettes and ouzo. Beside him, Pandelis sat uncomfortably, moving his knee from the gearstick each time Kylis changed gear. By the passenger window, their father sat in silence.

'Can't you shut up?' said Pandelis. 'Your whistling is getting on my nerves.'

'I'm feeling cheerful,' said Kylis. 'Or I would be if my head didn't ache so much. I met this girl last night, a knockout. You should come out with me sometime, brother. A girl like that'd put colour in your cheeks. In one or two other places as well.'

'For God's sake,' said Pandelis, 'spare us the details! The thought of you hard at it turns my stomach.'

'Shut up, both of you,' said Paliakis. 'Kylis, park it here. We'll get no closer in the van.'

Kylis switched off the engine, and Paliakis moved to open the door.

'Just a minute, Papa,' said Pandelis. 'I still think we should reconsider.'

'We've been through this,' said Paliakis. 'Let's get the job done, and go.'

'He's right, you know,' said Kylis. 'We won't get away with it. They'll know where to come.'

Paliakis faced them, his expression angry.

'And how would they know where to come?' he asked. 'Has either of you been blabbing?'

'The civil servants, Papa,' said Pandelis. 'We've been through this, too. We've gone along with you this far, but this whole idea is crazy. We'll find a better way, a legal way.'

'Hell,' said Kylis, 'why don't you just offer a fair price, and buy the land above board?'

Paliakis turned towards them, pointing with his finger.

'Now you two listen to me,' he said. 'The way things are – with compensation claims and drop-offs in trade – if we have to pay full price for this land, there'll be nothing left to fund your lifestyles, nor mine either. And we've already established – I thought we had already established – whilst we've got olives here, and archaeology, our new friends on the council won't be issuing building permits. So we're going to clear this land of its impediments, and we're going to do it, all three of us, together. This is a family business; we're going to work as a family, and get our hands a little dirty. Now, I know that you two don't have a pair of balls between you. But, just for once, for Christ's sake have some guts. We can be done and gone in twenty minutes, back in town in half an hour, and the land'll be ours for next to nothing. So get off your arses and let's do it, before the day gets too old.'

Paliakis climbed down from the van, and opened the rear doors; as he began untying the thin rope that secured the gallon containers, the morning air was filled with the stink of petrol. His sons stood behind him, watching and doubtful. Where the knots slowed him down, Paliakis cursed.

'Here.' He thrust one of the heavy containers at Pandelis, who clutched it to his chest, looking down on it with distaste. 'Remember what I've said. Spread it as far as it'll go, but work fast. Start with the house, then do the trees. If there's enough, do the orchard behind. Take two each. Come back for the rest.'

'For Christ's sake,' said Kylis. 'Four's enough. Everything's dry as bone.'

'And what will you be doing?' asked Pandelis.

'Keeping an eye out. If you hear me shout, you come running. With the containers, of course. If we have to leave fast, leave nothing behind. Now go. No. Wait. Kylis, fetch that barrow.'

The wheelbarrow Gabrilis used for harvesting watermelons stood by the fence. Ambling over to fetch it, Kylis rubbed at his temples; the fumes from the petrol had made his headache worse. His father waited, hands on hips and sighing with impatience.

Paliakis loaded up the barrow with six gallons of petrol.

'Save you the walk back down,' he said. 'Now go.'

Kylis picked up the barrow handles.

'Let's go, brother,' he said. 'I want to get back to bed.'

He led the way up the path towards Gabrilis's house, between the hives where the painted eyes watched the sky and the bees were hard at work. The load was heavy, and the muscles in Kylis's sun-browned arms swelled with effort, his calves the same; following behind, Pandelis glanced at his own pale arms, at the flabbiness of his legs and belly, and tried to push away his resentment.

At the house, by the verandah where the fat man had enjoyed so many hours with Gabrilis and Maria, Kylis lowered the barrow to the ground. The verandah was swept, the shutters on the windows had been closed, the plate of fish bones and the grapes Pandelis had cut were gone.

Kylis turned the door-handle. The door was locked.

'We should check inside,' he said, 'make sure there's nothing of value in there.'

Pandelis's face soured with disapproval.

'Are you thinking of committing an act of theft?' he asked.

'As a matter of fact, yes. There was something that took my eye. I meant to bring it away last time, but I left in a hurry in the end. What the hell does it matter anyway, steal it or burn it?'

'It matters, fool, because stolen property can be traced.'

Kylis laughed.

'You missed your vocation, brother,' he said. 'You should have been a policeman.'

'I might perhaps have been a policeman. If it had been allowed.'

Kylis raised his foot, brought his leg back, and kicked at the door just below the lock. The door resisted, but at the second kick burst open.

With reluctance, Pandelis followed Kylis inside.

'Breaking and entering,' he said. 'Criminal damage.'

'You're mad,' said his brother. 'There'll be nothing left of this place in a few minutes.'

The room had been cleaned and tidied; the stink of stale urine had dissipated, but the unmoving air was cloying with mustiness, with the stagnation of disuse. The broken glass and china had been removed, the damaged icons were gone. Maria's remaining knick-knacks and Gabrilis's collection of curios were dusted and arranged on the mantelpiece; the fireplace was free of ash and soot, and the chamber pot no longer sat beneath the bed, whose old mattress, stripped of its sheets, lay stained and faded on the springs. On the mattress lay Gabrilis's shotgun, and a box of cartridges, half full.

'See,' said Pandelis. 'Nothing for your trouble.'

But the shotgun was already in Kylis's hands.

'Just look at this,' he said. 'This is a good gun. A beauty.'

'You can't sell that. It'll be traced.'

'How can they trace what they don't know exists? Anyway, I might start shooting again myself. I used to be a pretty good shot.'

He led the way outside, and, leaning the shotgun against the barrow, dropping the cartridges by its wheel, handed a container of petrol to Pandelis.

'Here's what we'll do,' he said. 'I'll do round the house. We'll start it here, so it'll look more natural.'

'There's nothing natural about fires started by accelerants. The fire department aren't as stupid as you think.'

'They're stupid enough for our purposes. It's a long step from finding accelerants, as you call them, to pinning their use on us. You make a trail from here to the trees. If we can get those trees going, the rest will take care of itself.'

'You sound like an expert in arson.'

'Common sense, brother mine. Wood burns.'

'Not green wood.'

'Anything will burn, if it's hot enough. For Christ's sake. Just do it.'

'Since you're such an expert in arson, you probably know already that the more that burns, the more time we'll serve. Small fire, short sentence. Big fire, years and years and years.'

Kylis ignored him, and unscrewed the cap from a container. Fumes rose shimmering above it; the stink of petrol intensified. Pandelis watched him splash petrol on the wooden verandah. Kylis worked until he noticed Pandelis was doing nothing.

'Are you helping me, or just standing there?'

'Just standing here.'

Kylis said no more, but splattered fuel all over the front of the house. With a second container, he moved along the house side, dousing the wooden shutters, soaking the shrubs that grew under the windows. Soon, he moved out of sight.

Quickly, Pandelis unsealed a container. Pacing out what he judged an adequate firebreak, beyond the clean ground he splashed a trail of petrol in the direction of the trees and hives, so Kylis, returning for more fuel, saw Pandelis working hard beneath the pine trees. When Kylis was gone again to the rear of the house, Pandelis emptied the fifth container on the verandah that Kylis had already covered, then hurried with it empty to the trees. When Kylis reappeared, he saw Pandelis emptying the last drops amongst the hives.

'I've done the trees,' Pandelis said, joining his brother. He placed his container in the barrow. 'We've done enough. Let's go.'

Kylis looked at the last container.

'No point in not using this,' he said, unscrewing its cap. 'You take the empties down to the van. I'll be there in a minute. And don't forget this.' He laid the shotgun across the empty containers, and dropped in the box of cartridges.

Pandelis, glad to be leaving, picked up the barrow as Kylis carried the last petrol towards the house.

Passing the verandah, Kylis patted his pockets, and stopped.

'Crap,' he said. 'I left my lighter in the van. Go and get it, there's a good brother.'

Pandelis gave a short laugh.

'What an expert arsonist you are!' he said. 'Come out without your lighter!'

But Kylis had walked on, out of sight.

The morning was already growing warm; the track down the hillside was steep, and Pandelis was reluctant to make the trip there and back. A few paces down the path, he turned the barrow around and wheeled it back to the house. By the stove, surely there would be matches.

Inside the house, the smell of petrol was intense. He looked about him; then, drawn by curiosity, he crossed to the mantelpiece. Gabrilis's curios were as intriguing as they were tempting; as Kylis had said, what difference, stolen or burned? He pocketed the little terracotta horse, and a small tortoise carved in jade. Clearly, the objects were antiques; it was his duty, he told himself, to preserve them.

There were matches, as he expected, by the stove; they lay alongside the pistol tinderbox Gabrilis had never received. Intrigued by this curio, too, Pandelis took the flintlock in his hand, admiring the fine engraving on its silver-encased stock and examining the strange workings in place of the barrel. He wondered at the object's use. He tried its weight, cocked it without difficulty and pointed it at the wall; and, thinking of robbers and pirates, expecting nothing but a click as the hammer fell, he pulled the trigger.

There was a whoomph of air, and a force of pressure against him which struck his face as warm, and so powerful, it blew him back into the centre of the room. Dazed, he looked out on an inferno, on high-burning flames that filled the doorway. The burning created noise, a kind of muted roaring; but above the roar, he heard his brother shout.

'Kylis!'

His own shout was loud, pitched by panic and with no restraint on volume. Beyond the flames, he saw the world he'd left – the pine trees and the sky, the cool blue sea, the path down to his father – but not Kylis. His lungs were filling with smoke, and he coughed; when the coughing passed, he looked again through the burning doorway, and Kylis was there.

It was hot beyond belief; already, sweat was running down his back. His face was stinging; again, he coughed.

'Kylis!'

But his brother responded strangely to his shout. He didn't rush forward to fetch him out; instead, he very slowly raised his hand, as if in farewell to one already distant.

Kylis could see terror in his brother's face, a face already changed: the skin was raw and pink, his eyebrows and the hair across his forehead were burnt away. Despairing, Kylis began to shake his head, and Pandelis, reading the implication, began to yell at him: *Papa, fetch Papa, fetch Papa.* But seconds passed with Kylis still unmoving, and Pandelis's yelling turned to screams.

Pandelis didn't see what Kylis saw: fierce burning barring every exit, the dreadful, fatal hopelessness of his situation.

In Kylis's eyes, tears welled. Snatching up the shotgun, he broke it and, with unsteady hands, loaded two cartridges. Snapping the barrel back in place, he clicked off the safety. In these last moments, the truth of his feelings was quite clear to him – he loved his brother deeply – and from that would come the strength to do this kindness, to perform the act of love that must be done.

He took his aim – through the door, an easy shot at a standing target – but could not meet his brother's eyes, knowing the fear and horror he would see there.

He squeezed the trigger, blasting a bloody hole in Pandelis's chest.

The second shot was not required. Pandelis was dead before he hit the smoking floorboards.

By the van, Paliakis saw smoke, and waited for his boys. He expected them running; instead, there was shouting.

And a gunshot.

Panting, cursing their incompetence, he made his way up the winding path.

The house was well alight; before it, on his knees, Kylis hugged himself, crying like a man out of his mind. The shotgun lay beside him on the ground.

Grabbing Kylis's hair, Paliakis pulled him round to face him, looking into eyes demented with remorse.

'Where's Pandelis?' yelled Paliakis. 'Your brother, for Christ's sake, where is he?'

But Kylis could not speak; he only shook his head, and pointed a trembling finger towards his brother's funeral pyre.

Twenty-One

At the village *kafenion*, the quiet of siesta was breaking. A small boy, barefoot and wearing only shorts, pedalled a battered bicycle to the grocer's, a shopping list wrapped in a banknote poked in his handlebars. A cat high on a wall licked at its tail, pausing to watch a youth in waiter's black-and-white buzz by on a rattling moped, heading for town. An old man clattered dice on a backgammon board; when the numbers came up against him, his opponent hid a smile behind his hand.

As the fat man took a seat inside, the *patron* wished him *kali spera*. With the tables outside for the season, only two remained in front of the counter, and the fat man was crowded by cases of water, by crates of beer and boxes of Sprite. Above his head, a linnet in a bamboo cage sat lonely on its perch.

'*Kali spera*,' said the fat man. 'Iced coffee, if you please, no sugar, plenty of milk. And would you be kind enough to turn on the television? I have an interest in this evening's news.'

The ancient TV stood precariously on a shelf behind the counter; the pictures it showed were unstable, moving slowly upwards towards the top of the screen, then reappearing at the bottom to travel up again. The *patron* thumped the set on its side, and the picture settled, but the images were grainy and blurred. As compensation for the shortcomings in its visuals, the *patron* turned the volume up too loud.

The fat man sipped his coffee through a straw, watching with mild interest the lead story on state politics. A journalist in a flak jacket reported on a foreign war, his right eye twitching nervously as smoke billowed from the ruins behind him.

And then, the scene shown was familiar: the police station, and two men hustled inside by uniformed police. As the cameras flashed, the fat man saw a red-faced Petridis in the background, and heard Gazis's voice command the press to move back, and let them through.

On the police station steps, a suave, suited young man held up a microphone carrying the TV station's logo, and made his report.

'The men are likely to be charged with both murder and arson,' he said. 'Early information suggests Aris Paliakis and his son Kylis shot Paliakis's eldest son dead, then set fire to the building he died in to destroy the evidence. The motive for this shocking killing is unclear, though sources close to the family suggest a dispute over money. Paliakis is a well-known entrepreneur in this area; his son, Pandelis, was a well-respected lawyer. The question being asked this evening is, *What would drive a father to kill his own son?*'

The fat man frowned, and finished his coffee. Behind the counter, the *patron* whistled a love song; in its cage, as if responding to a distant memory, the linnet stretched its throat and began to trill. Outside, a small audience had been drawn to the game of backgammon, and a cheer went up as the dice fell in one man's favour.

The fat man called out to the *patron*.

'A beer, if you please,' he said, 'a small glass of the draught. I'll take it outside, if I may.'

Leaving the linnet to its song, he found a chair close to the backgammon players. Inside the *kafenion*, the *patron* turned off the TV, and in the quiet whistled as he poured the fat man's beer.

Two days had passed since Dinos was reported missing, and two hours since Sostis put to sea. His catch, in the first hour, was respectable; but now the late-afternoon meltemi had picked up, whipping the waves into whitecaps, rocking the boat and tangling the line as he hauled it in.

Sitting at the tiller, he steered towards the Dragon's Teeth, where the steeply rising land gave shelter, and anchored the boat in water deep enough to make the rocks no threat to *Agatha*'s hull.

But the wind worked against him, and his luck stayed poor. Winding in the last cast of the day, he glanced up at the sun to judge the time: 3:30, 4. Tying up the bag of bait, he dropped it in the basket with the line; then, making his way up to the prow, he roped the basket to the handrails, knowing the wind on the homeward leg would take it if it weren't secured.

Back in the stern, he turned the magneto key and pressed the starter to fire the engine. Under the engine cover, there was a light click, but nothing more.

'*Yiamo to.*' In frustration, he cursed aloud, surprised at his voice sounding loud as a shout. Raising his head from the engine, he listened. The wind had dropped; the canvas canopy which gave him shade was no longer flapping, the boat was almost still on a gently moving sea. Baffled, he climbed up on the bench that ran around the inner stern, and looked out across the water. All the way to the horizon, the sea was settled and calm.

In puzzlement, he frowned; then the frown deepened. Close by, a ship was passing, cutting in close to the coastline – as he had done – to avoid the wind. The strong waves of the ship's wake were moving in his direction, the rolling water innocuous at this distance, but the upset to *Agatha* would be significant if she were not faced head-on into the swell.

A memory stirred, a sense of déjà vu; he recalled the day he mistook the bloated goat's corpse for an apparition, the coldness of the water that day, the stillness, that irrational dread. Some of that dread was with him now.

The rolling swell came on, and slowly, from her anchor point, *Agatha* turned, until, by happy chance, her prow faced into the waves. From prow to stern, she bucked, and bucked again; and then the swell was gone, breaking white on the shoreline, spray leaping over the pinnacles of the Dragon's Teeth, breaking again in backwash where the rocks were hidden beneath the surface.

In a minute or two, *Agatha* settled, and soon, at the shoreline, the sea had settled too. Above Sostis's head, the canopy edges flapped, and the wind – rising again – put ripples on the surface of the water.

By the control panel, he touched the icon of St Nicholas that was his talisman, and said a prayer for luck. Switching on the magneto, he pushed the starter. The engine fired, rattling and roaring, expelling clouds of diesel smoke from the exhaust. Relieved, he went back to the prow to raise the anchor. Rope in hand, he took the strain; but as he was ready to haul, his eye was caught by an object at the shoreline, rising and falling with the swell amongst the rocks.

A breath of wind sent a coldness down his back.

He steered the boat in slow and close, until he could reach the body with the boat-hook. Its skin, pale as milk, was waterlogged and peeling, with small fish nibbling at its frond-like edges. The corpse's face was in the water, and Sostis was grateful, even though avoiding the face meant looking at the back, where little was left but bone, as if the flesh had been scoured away by pumice. Around the body's waist, the net bag for holding the snorkeller's catch was empty. Sostis caught the bag with the boat-hook, but never considered bringing the body aboard. Let those who were paid for it take the bad luck. With hook and pole, he dragged the body from prow to stern and, holding it steady with his right hand, put in the VHF call to the coastguard.

Twenty-Two

At the public enquiries desk, the officer was filling out a claim for overtime. For a short while, the fat man waited patiently for him to finish but, when the policeman's concentration on his paperwork didn't waver, he put his hand to his mouth and lightly coughed. The officer counted eight on his fingers, and pencilled in a figure in Tuesday's box, then, laying down the pencil with a sigh, he stood and crossed to the desk.

The fat man smiled.

'*Kali mera sas*,' he said.

'You should ring the bell if you want service,' said the policeman. A few fibres of cotton wool stuck to a razor-cut on his jaw.

'I have all the service I need, without the bell,' said the fat man reasonably. 'I'd like to speak with Sergeant Gazis, if he's in the building.'

The officer regarded him. Without speaking, he pointed to a bench against the wall. As the fat man sat down, the policeman was speaking into a phone.

The fat man looked at his feet, where the toecap of his right shoe had acquired a scuff mark. Unzipping his holdall, he took out a bottle of shoe-whitener, and dabbed it on the blemish. Finding no more, he replaced the bottle in the bag, and zipped it closed.

Gazis approached smiling along the corridor, Petridis a pace behind. The creases in Gazis's uniform shirt were crisp, his handsome face seemed shaved especially close.

The fat man rose from the bench.

'Sergeant Gazis,' he said. 'I've come to wish you goodbye.'

With warmth, the men shook hands.

'It's been a pleasure,' said Gazis, 'though the circumstances of our meeting were unfortunate. You've forgiven, I trust, my initial suspicions of you? It's a hazard of the job; it becomes second nature to suspect everyone.'

The fat man smiled.

'There is nothing to forgive. I was the only suspect at the time, though I think we agree, now, who our man was. The paint samples from Dinos Karayannis's car – I presume there was a match for Gabrilis's tricycle in there somewhere?'

'There was indeed. It would have been a small step from there to an arrest, though how the case would have gone in court we'll never know. Sentences these days can be unduly lenient. It seems, in this instance, the gods took matters into their own hands.'

The fat man nodded thoughtfully.

'Perhaps,' he said. 'I believe, by the way, I saw you and Constable Petridis on the television news. What a shocking case that is! For a father and brother to commit such a crime seems unthinkable. I met Mr Paliakis, once. He struck me as a man obsessed by money. No doubt it will transpire money's at the root of it.'

'It's a fascinating case,' said Gazis, 'and not so cut and dried as you might think. The father's claiming all the guilt, but it's the son's prints we've found all over the gun. Both tell the same story – a mercy killing – that the brother was trapped inside the burning house. As to why the house was burning, or why the place was awash with petrol, they've no good answer. Someone shot that poor man like a dog, and there's not enough left of him to tell his own story, forensically. Whether he inhaled smoke before he died, no one can say. My guess is, the father's willing to do the time for murder, manslaughter, whatever the verdict is, on the son's behalf, if the court will let him. They'll both do time for arson, regardless. I'd throw the book at them for that.'

'One wonders at the motive for arson.'

'The family has interests in property development, and arson's almost a tool of that trade, these days – by firing the land, they render it virtually worthless. Then they either buy it at a knock-down price, or simply move the bulldozers in, and start building. The landowner on this occasion, at least, had a lucky break. Paliakis called the emergency services whilst the fire could still be controlled; in fact, the fire investigator believes he and his son made some efforts to extinguish the fire with well-water. The house is nothing but ash, but, apart from a little singeing, the land round about escaped.'

'Which makes one wonder, doesn't it?' said the fat man. 'Why set the fire, and then throw water on it? I'm sure you're pondering that question already; perhaps it is some mitigation for one, or both, of them. I am going away for a while, but I shall certainly watch the press to see how the case develops. Keep up the good work, Sergeant. Your zeal and commitment are not unnoticed, you know.'

Gazis laughed.

'That's truer than you know,' he said, 'though not everyone views my commitment in a positive light. But I have George here now to follow in my footsteps.' He placed a hand on Petridis's shoulder. 'A like mind to train as my successor, and soon to join me, too, in the ranks of respectable married men. Somehow, he's persuaded that lovely girl of his to take him on. She'll keep him on the straight and narrow.'

Petridis, colouring, smiled as the fat man offered his hand.

'Does the lady have a name, Constable?' asked the fat man.

'Yorgia. Her name's Yorgia.'

'Well, my congratulations. Take good care of her, won't you?' The fat man turned back to Gazis. 'I mustn't keep you. You're busy, I know.'

'As a matter of fact,' said Gazis, 'we're on our way to a little job that'll really get us noticed, aren't we, George? It doesn't matter to me: two more years and I'll be hanging up my hat. And George has enough talent to get away with it, or youth enough to start a new career, if they boot him out. For the moment, we're on our own little crusade. Equality in justice. Come outside, and enjoy the show.'

In the street, the fat man watched from the shade cast by the police station's wall. Across the road, outside the town hall, a group of people waited: a camera crew with a dark-haired woman presenter, two photographers with long-lensed cameras, a young man with a stenographer's notebook. The national flag hung limp from its rooftop pole; red-legged pigeons pecked in the unswept gutter. A little apart, in the shade of a plane tree, Gazis and Petridis stood silently together.

The stately doors of the town hall swung open, and the mayoral party – three men in French-tailored trousers and pastel shirts – ran down to the black Mercedes parked in the *No Parking* zone. The driver folded his paper and tucked it beneath his seat, then jumped out to open the car door for the Mayor.

But Gazis and Petridis were there first. Gazis blocked the doors on the near side, leaving the three men facing the members of the press; Petridis moved round to speak to the driver. As Gazis took out his ticket book and pen, the cameras flashed; as he began to write the ticket, the Mayor threw up his hands. One of the aides began to shout objections, until the TV camera pulled focus on his face; as the Mayor concocted a good-humoured speech for the reporter, the aides remained silent, their eyes hidden behind dark glasses.

'I applaud the actions of these officers,' said the Mayor into the microphone. 'The law is made for all, not just for some. I shall pay my fine promptly, of course.'

Completing the ticket, Gazis held it up for the press to photograph. Then, with a practised action, he lifted the Mercedes's windscreen wiper and deftly slipped the ticket beneath it, snapping the wiper back into place.

The dark-haired presenter patted her hair, preparing for her piece to camera. The Mayor glanced up at the upper-floor windows of the police station, where the Chief Constable stepped back, out of sight. Across the street, the fat man smiled, and slipped away to find a baker who would supply his morning pastry.

At Paliakis's house, little – to the fat man's eyes – seemed changed, though at the windows of the *salone* where he and Ourania Paliakis had talked the shutters were now closed, and fastened with iron bars. Beneath the gracious portico, the fat man applied the lion's-head knocker, its banging echoing through the house as in the high halls of museums.

Father Babis opened the door only a few centimetres, and put his eye to the crack to see who was calling.

'I'm sorry,' he said. 'She's not receiving visitors.'

'That's understandable,' said the fat man, 'but I didn't want to leave without offering my most sincere condolences. Please tell her that; please tell her I am deeply, deeply sorry.'

'I'll tell her,' said the priest. He moved to close the door, but the fat man raised a hand to stop him.

'Father Babis,' he said. 'Before you go, I have a gift for you.'

The priest opened the door a little wider.

'For me?'

From his pocket, the fat man took a bottle of brown glass filled with a pale and viscous liquid.

'Forgive my impertinence,' he said, 'but I brought you something to ease the condition of your skin, a natural remedy based on clay minerals from the north. My cousin suffers a similar complaint, and swears by this to bring relief. If you apply it at night, you'll find your skin improved by morning. Will you try it?'

The priest took the bottle, and held it up to the light.

'It has a lot of sediment,' he said.

'You must shake it well before use. Otherwise the cure stays in the bottle.'

'Thank you,' said the priest. 'I shall be glad to try it.'

Again, he moved to close the door, but before he did so the fat man spoke.

'How is she?' he asked. 'She has taken his death very badly, I assume.'

The priest sighed.

'How else should a mother take the death of a favourite son?' he said. 'And yet, some good may still come from it. She blames her husband, of course, and has already filed the papers for a divorce. There is a lesson to be learned, she says, from poor Pandelis's death. He was a good man, you know.'

'I suspected so,' said the fat man, 'though I didn't know him.'

'She feels she must compensate for the waste of his life, and that wasting her own life in this mausoleum – I think you used that word, and it stayed with her – is not acceptable now.

263

She's thinking of establishing some charity, whether here or abroad she doesn't yet know.'

'And where will that leave you?' asked the fat man.

Father Babis gave the smallest of smiles.

'Once she's divorced, perhaps she'll consider me,' he said. 'Our interests are the same. As husband and wife, we could work together very well, I feel. Africa, perhaps. There's so much of God's work to be done there.'

The fat man smiled.

'Indeed,' he said. 'I've never been there myself, though I'm sure it would be quite an adventure. A little different from the tea and chess you enjoy here.'

'Very different,' agreed the priest. 'But I think the time has come for me – and Ourania – to forget our chessboard, and embark – together – on a more useful kind of life.'

'Good luck to you, then,' said the fat man. 'It's early days, of course, but perhaps I may hope that, before too long, I might be offering congratulations in place of today's condolences.'

'I brought you a gift.'

In the shade of *Agatha*'s canopy, the fat man drew a small confectioner's box from his holdall: white, with writing in curling pink script, tied round with pink ribbon, and at the corners, cherubs teasing flying bluebirds. The boat rocked languidly on the light wake of a yacht.

Sostis looked at the romantic images on the box, and askance at the fat man.

The fat man laughed.

'Not for you,' he said. 'For your wife. Turkish delight, but of a rather special kind. The rose water used in its manufacture is unique. It has the gift, they say, of sweetening bad temper, and I've known it be effective in many cases. Encourage her to eat a piece each day. Within a week, you'll see a difference. You'll go home to a content and kinder woman.'

Sostis took the box and laid it on the bench beside him, where flies crawled on a bait knife and buzzed frustrated around a closed pot of chopped shrimp. The grey imprint of his dirty thumb was on a cherub's face.

'If it works,' he said, 'if a few sweets are all it takes to change the sourness of fifteen years, then I'm indebted to you. Better live with the devil than a mean woman. I know the truth of that.'

Feeling the light touch of a bite, he jerked the line suspended in the clear water, and swiftly started to haul it in; but there was no weight there, and so he brought the rest of the line in slower, hand over hand.

'Bastard,' he said. 'I had him, and he's taken my bait, and gone. Your luck's much better than mine today.' In the bucket between their feet, two good-sized bream stared bright-eyed, as if in surprise at their unexpected surroundings. 'You know, I'm pleased to have the water as a friend again. I'm not afraid of it today. Perhaps it's your company.'

The fat man finished winding his line around its holder, and put it aside. Taking a cigarette from his box, he lit it with his gold lighter, inhaled deeply and exhaled, blowing the smoke out over the calm sea.

'The mind,' he said, 'is willing, but the flesh is weak. I have had a long debate with myself over my smoking, and I find I enjoy cigarettes too much to give them up. I suppose you'd have to call it lack of willpower.'

Sostis pulled up the end of his line. The bait was gone from all three hooks.

'Bastards,' he said.

He took the lid from the shrimp pot and dextrously rebaited the hooks. He cast the line far from the boat; as

265

bait, hooks and lead weight hit the surface, ripples spread across the water. The line ran through his fingers until he felt it touch the rocks on the sea bed.

'Forgive me for saying this,' he said, 'but you don't strike me as one who lacks willpower.'

The fat man smiled.

'Perhaps not,' he said. 'Perhaps I'm nothing more than a hedonist.'

He drew again on his cigarette. Around the resealed bait pot, agitated flies still buzzed. The fat man watched them, until a honey bee, dull-brown and marked with black, landed on the hem of his yellow bathing shorts, and settled there, quite still, seeming to rest.

The fat man touched the bee with a fingertip.

'You're a long way from home, friend,' he said, 'and too far from land for your own good. Better take a long rest, before you attempt the homeward journey.'

'We'll give him a ride,' said Sostis, 'if he can pay the fare.'

'There's a legend of bees in Arcadia,' said the fat man. 'Do you know of Aristaeus?'

'I was a dunce at school. I never paid attention.'

'The legend stems, I think, from what the ancients observed – that bees will sometimes use decaying carcasses as hives, though I have never seen a case of it myself. The story goes that Aristaeus – a shepherd and a bee-keeper – took a fancy to a woman who ran away from him, and in doing so, she stepped on a snake, was bitten and died. In anger, the nymphs killed Aristaeus's bees, and he – showing behaviour still typical of men today – went running to his mother for advice. She told him to make a sacrifice of bullocks to the gods, to bury them and, after three days, to see what had transpired. And Aristaeus was amazed to find, in the bellies of the rotting cattle, swarms of bees, and a harvest of honey. Sweetness from corruption. Blood sacrifice yielding gifts. Are such things possible, barber?'

'All things under heaven are possible. This Turkish delight you've given me may sweeten my wife's temper. But the possible isn't the likely.'

The fat man laughed.

'Have faith, barber, have faith. An attitude of mind can change an outlook, and a future.'

He drew on the end of the cigarette and leaned over the side to douse it in the water, laying the wet stub on the bench for careful disposal on dry land.

Sostis felt again the nibbling on the hooks, and once again jerked hard and fast and began hauling up the line. This time, the line stayed heavy.

'Hah!' he said. 'Got you this time, you bastard! It's a good one, I can feel it! Here he is – let's have a look.'

He pulled the twisting fish from the sea, its wet skin metallic and beautiful, like platinum in the sunlight. Droplets flew, from the fish and from the line, and one landed on the bee, so it flew off, heading unswervingly back to the shore. Sostis grabbed the fish's slippery body in his hand, holding it firm whilst he unhooked the barb from its gasping mouth, its tail flapping at the other end of his fist. The hook came cleanly from the bony roof of the mouth; the bait was still intact. He dropped the fish into the bucket, and peered in after it.

'Another bream,' he said. 'Not quite so good as yours, but not bad nonetheless. Not bad at all.'

He wiped his slimy hands on his shorts, looked up at the sun to judge the time, and began to wind up his line.

'Time's up,' he said. 'My wretched duty calls.'

'Your wretched duty,' echoed the fat man. 'How would you feel, barber, about a change of career?'

'I'd welcome it with open arms,' he said. 'Never to cut another head of hair would be like heaven.'

'I'm looking for a steward for my land,' said the fat man. 'To take care of my bees and olives, and to look after my vines.'

Sostis's face fell.

'Regretfully,' he said, 'I have no knowledge of agriculture.'

'That is a problem I am finding everywhere,' said the fat man. 'The new crop of foreigners is obliterating our old knowledge. On the coast, a generation's growing up knowing nothing of the land. I want to do my part to redress the balance. You may know nothing now, but there are men I know who can mentor you – and, as importantly, your son. He'd grow up to be a farmer. Would that suit you?'

'Would it suit him?' asked Sostis doubtfully.

'I believe he'd come to love it.'

'Where is your land?'

'I have a holding at Palea Chora. And land you know – the land at the Temple of Apollo.'

'That's yours?'

'In the absence of natural heirs, Gabrilis named me. The land was my gift to him, some years ago, and he saw it as the natural thing, I think, to give it back. The house there is gone, as you'll have heard, but the land survived the fire with little damage, and I plan – with the right permissions – to build a family home. There'd be no rent to pay: the house would be part of your salary. I'd take a cut of what's produced, of course. The honey and the wine from my land cannot be bettered.'

Still Sostis hesitated.

'There's my fishing,' he said. 'It's a poor farmer who spends half his time fishing.'

'Perhaps you'll find,' said the fat man, 'that, as your interest in the land grows, your need to escape to sea diminishes. But whether it does or not, it's not my intention to chain you to the hives. It's a poor Greek, after all, who spends no time at sea. So what do you say, barber? Does the title of farmer sound better than your present job? Do we have a deal?'

He held out his hand.

Sostis smiled. He slapped his salt-dried hand into the fat man's and shook it vigorously.

'Deal,' he said. He pumped the fat man's hand. 'We certainly have a deal. I shall think of you as my liberator – the one who freed me from service to other men's hair.'

The fat man chose a wine of the millennium year, of which only a few bottles remained. Blowing the dust and sandy dirt from its neck as he lifted it from the rack, he noticed a little fall on his freshly whitened shoes, and a small frown of irritation crossed his face. At the cellar steps, he paused for a moment, looking at the empty spaces where the vintage of the past two years should be, but as he climbed the steps his mood was light. Before too long – not this year, but perhaps the next – with his vines in the care of Sostis, he'd be drinking from his own vineyards once again.

The cellar was cool, but on the verandah the contrast in temperature was not so marked as it had been just a few days ago. The evenings were growing cooler, and the season was, unmistakably, shifting. Summer's ending had arrived.

The table was laid for one. By his wine glass lay a corkscrew, and the fat man peeled the lead foil from the bottle, then smoothly pulled the cork and half-filled his glass. Carrying his wine to the verandah railing, he looked out into the night, towards the village lights and, beyond them, to the dark mountains and the starlit sky. Far off, a goat's bell rattled; on the new road, a distant motorbike roared.

The fat man raised his glass to the stars, and drank. The wine was excellent, lush with fruit, pleasingly dry. At his back, Kokkona laid warm dishes on the table: his favourite courgette fritters, flavoured with mint and fried till crisply golden, thick tzatziki pungent with dill and garlic, and the sea bream he had caught grilled over wood and sprinkled with lemon.

The fat man turned to her, and smiled.

'Food fit for the gods,' he said.

He took his place to eat; she sat down in her wicker chair, and took up her lace-making.

Breaking into a fritter with his fork, he dipped the mouthful into tzatziki before tasting it.

'You've taken the best care of me, as always,' he said.

'What time will you be leaving in the morning?' She didn't look at him; her attention seemed all focused on her work.

'When the time is right,' he said. 'Not too early, not too late.'

'You should stay longer. We need you here. We miss you.'

'I'll be back before you know it.'

'Every time you say the same.'

He laid down his fork and, leaning across, placed a hand on top of hers. The hand was changed from what he remembered; the veins were prominent across the bones, and the brown marks of ageing had covered the thinning skin. Gently, he squeezed her hand.

'I'd love to stay,' he said. 'You know that. But matters elsewhere demand my attention.'

In the morning, she intended to be there early and give him breakfast; but the baker had overslept, and the wait for the pastries was half an hour. Still, when she slipped into the kitchen, the sun had barely risen, and only the keenest bees buzzed in the roses. Moving quietly so as not to disturb him, she made his coffee just the way he liked it and carried it down the hallway to his room.

The door was ajar, and his room was empty. The bed was made; the clothes he'd left behind were folded, ready to put away. On the dresser, a vellum envelope held her wages. Beneath the bed, forgotten or lost, was a half-used bottle of shoe-whitener. She crossed to the window, and looked out on the shady place beneath the garden trees, but of the red Namco Pony there was no sign.

Read on for the enthralling opening of *The Doctor of Thessaly*, the third Mystery of the Greek Detective – a gripping tale of revenge, jealousy and desire . . .

One by one, peal by peal, the joyful church bells all fell silent. First, word reached the chapel of St Anna's; from there, the message passed to St Sotiris's, where the ringer looped the bell-rope on its hook, and set off to her daughter's for more news. Long before the time agreed, the bells stopped at St George's on the coast road, and at Holy Trinity in the foothills, though for a while, the bell at distant St Fotini's still rang out, its elderly ringer not noticing, in her enthusiasm and her deafness, that all the others were quiet. So they found a bicycle, and told the oldest boy to travel quickly; and, mid-way through a celebratory peal, that bell too faltered in its rhythm, and was still.

Across the fields, the buff slopes of the mountains were growing dim. Small waves broke harmless on the town beach, and the dark sea stretched towards a sky already pale with evening. The mildness of the afternoon was gone, and a cold breeze raised ripples which ran like shivers across the water.

From the beach-head, a woman headed down to the sea. The heels of her satin shoes caught between the stones, turning her ankles; but she went determinedly on, carrying the hem of her white gown above her feet, whilst behind, the long train of her dress dragged like a trawl-net, hooking debris left by the high spring tides: brittle kelp and the cap of a beer bottle, the bleached, ovoid bone of a squid, liquorice smears of marine oil.

Close to the sea, the stones were small, becoming shingle at the water's edge, and, beneath the water, sand. As she followed the water-line, her satin heels sank deep into the shingle, discolouring the shoes with damp. Where three flat rocks stood out from the shallows, she stopped, and looked back up the beach, along the road.

No-one was there. No-one followed.

She turned back to the empty sea. The last good light of day lit her face, picking out the crow's feet where powdered foundation had set in lines; the trails of mascara-dirtied tears marked her cheeks. In her hands – where raised veins and slender bones stood prominent, and the first brown stains of liver-spots were established – she held two garlands of fake flowers: pretty orange blossoms twisted around paper-covered wire, and joined by a length of pure white ribbon – *i stefani*, the head-dresses of a bride and groom.

As hard as she could throw, she cast the garlands away from her onto the sea, expecting them to float on the deep water, and drift away to the horizon; but her throw was weak, and the *stefani* landed in the shallows, where the water quickly turned the flowers ash-grey. The garlands sank; the ribbon flickered briefly on the surface. Settling on the sea-bottom, their shape was lost, shifting and distorted by the water.

Along the road, the street-lamps were lit. Still no-one came. Sinking down on the shingle, she kicked off the satin shoes; and, pulling her knees up to her chest, burying her face in the soft skirts of her wedding dress, she wept.

* * *

The women gathered at the house (nieces and aunts, cousins, second cousins, neighbours and acquaintances) were reluctant to leave. It was not the care they had taken over clothes and coiffure, the time and money they had wasted; much more than that, the aborted wedding was a drama to which they were witnesses, and it seemed harsh, to them, to ask them to leave the scene. They went slowly, muttering to each other behind diamond-ringed hands, carrying their gifts – still wrapped – beneath their arms. To Noula, they said nothing; there was no form of words for this occasion.

Noula shut them out, forcing home the bolt on the apartment door. On the *salone* floor, by the cane-bottomed chairs where they had sat, were the musicians' empty glasses and the whisky bottle they had drained before they left. The plates for the walnut cookies held nothing but crumbs; the roasted peanuts and the pumpkin seeds were all gone, their cracked shells scattered by the children across the rugs and into the room's far corners. A silver tray was still half-filled with long-stemmed glasses of unwanted liqueurs; the tall, ribbon-trimmed candles the page-boys should have carried were abandoned in the window alcove. After the chatter, the laughter and the music, the silence of the room seemed profound.

The room must be put back to how it was before. Chrissa had taken liberties, moving the sofa, changing the tablecloths, rearranging the coffee service in the cabinet.

But all could be quite easily restored. Noula surveyed the work to be done, and smiled.

In the doorway, Aunt Yorgia pulled on a jacket over her black dress. The loose flesh of her upper arms trembled; on the skin of her bony chest, a gold crucifix glittered. With each year, Noula was growing into her likeness; in both her and Chrissa, the legacy of that generation's women was manifesting: lines and loose jowls, thread veins and thin lips. The make-up Chrissa had lent Noula had worked no magic, and Chrissa had been right about the greyness in her hair. Perhaps, as Chrissa said, she should have coloured it. But what did it matter, now? Dyeing out the grey had not, in the end, saved Chrissa.

'I paid the musicians,' said Aunt Yorgia. 'I gave them half.'

'I'll give you the money.' Noula's purse lay on the dresser, beneath the mirror; pulling out banknotes, she turned from her reflection in the glass. 'There's enough there for a taxi. You'll find Panayiotis in the square.'

'If there's a blessing in this, it's that your mother didn't live to see it, God rest her.' With three fingertips, Yorgia made the triple cross over her breast, then took the money Noula held out to her. 'The shame of it would have finished her, for sure. You should get those good clothes off now, and go and find your sister.'

Noula spread her arms to take in the room.

'How can I leave this mess? There's a week's work to be done here, and I'll get no help from Chrissa. She doesn't need me running after her. She'll come home, when she's ready.'

'With things as they've turned out, she'll never want to come home,' said Yorgia, sharply, 'and in her place, neither would you. You go and find her, as your mother would want. Fetch her home, and take good care of her. Be a sister to her, until all this blows over.'

'But where's her home to be, aunt? Up here alone, or back downstairs in the old place, with me?'

Yorgia picked a length of cotton from the shoulder of her jacket.

'If you can manage to be civil with each other, I should say downstairs, with you,' she said. 'Your father paid for this apartment as a dowry.'

'As my dowry.'

'As your dowry, because he expected you to be first to marry. As there's still been no marriage, we'll keep the dowry ready until there is. Now go and fetch her. There're only a few minutes left before dark. Take her something warm to put on over that dress. It's cold, now the sun's gone down. And you be kind to her, Noula. Your sister's been dealt a hard blow, and we'll all be made to feel it. Things will be difficult for us all, but we'll keep our heads high. Ach, *Panayia!*' She put her hand to her face, remembering. 'No-one's told the taverna we won't be coming! I'll go; I'll tell the taxi to go round by there. They'll have to be paid, of course. I'll tell them you'll call in, in due course.'

'Me? Why should I go?'

'Because,' said Aunt Yorgia, 'it would be cruel to make your sister suffer the embarrassment of paying for a wedding breakfast she never got to eat. Don't let them charge you anything for wine. They won't have opened any yet, no matter what they say.'

She stepped across to Noula, and placing her hands on her shoulders, kissed her on both cheeks. Noula smelled the sweetness of old cosmetics, of lipstick and loose powder, the sharp, lemon scent of eau-de-cologne. 'Now go and fetch you sister. Bring her straight home and put her to bed. And make her some camomile tea; it'll help her sleep. Be kind, Noula. I'll come and see how she is tomorrow. Your uncle will bring me over in the morning.'

The apartment door banged shut, and Aunt Yorgia's court shoes clattered down the outside stairs and away down the side-street, fading into the dusk.

Noula moved to the *salone* window. The outlook was commonplace, onto a street she had known a lifetime, yet this elevated angle gave it novelty. From here, she could see over the neighbour's wall, into Dmitra's kitchen, and even to the upper windows of the buildings around the square. Downstairs, where they had always lived, the view was dull, of high walls and their own garden.

She switched on a table-lamp she had chosen, years ago, and in its light, gazed round the objects that had so long been hers: the soft-cushioned sofa with its matching armchair, the unused china displayed in the cabinet, the Turkish rug woven in burgundy and cream, the lace cloths and doilies relatives had made for her. As the oldest, all this was intended for her – except no suitor had ever come. So when the doctor had asked for Chrissa, Noula was expected to step back and hand her sister everything.

But not now.

In the bedroom, the bed – her bed – was made with white satin sheets, and on the coverlet, the local girls had made a heart in sugared almonds. Noula took the almond from the heart's tip and, putting it in her mouth, bit down on the hard, pink coating. No-one had listened to her view that, at Chrissa's age, fertility rites were pointless. The girls had gone through all the rites regardless, scattering handfuls of un-cooked rice between the sheets; the grains they had let fall cracked beneath Noula's feet.

Opening the wardrobe, she ran a hand through Chrissa's clothes, hung where her own should be: Chrissa's best dress, Chrissa's skirts and blouses, Chrissa's two pairs of shoes placed carefully together, as if Chrissa had been playing house arranging them. On the shelves, she found a cardigan of black wool, and put it aside to take to her sister.

There was nothing of his in the wardrobe, but by the bed

was a suitcase battered with use. Pricked by curiosity, she crouched beside it: what had the faithless doctor left behind? A guilty glance to window and door confirmed no-one would see, and so she slipped the catches, and raised the suitcase lid.

A scent she didn't know came off his clothes, a man's scent, earthy but intriguing. One by one, she lifted out the shirts, the sweaters and the ties, and beneath the trousers found his underpants, large sizes in white cotton. Then there were vests, and a wash-bag with a razor, soap, cologne and ointment used for rheumatism; and, at the very bottom, concealed by everything else, a large, manila envelope, unsealed and un-addressed.

With careful fingers, she took the envelope from his be-longings. She didn't hesitate; withdrawing the papers it con-tained, she opened up the folded sheets of paper.

They were letters of some length, whose opening pages bore the coats of arms of official offices. But the language and the alphabet were foreign, and Noula could make out nothing but the years of writing: last year, and the year before.

Outside, a motorbike roared past, its rider calling a greeting to someone walking by.

Replacing the letters in the envelope, she repacked the suitcase as best she could, fastening its latches as she closed it.

The envelope, she kept.

Switching off the lamp which had been hers, she pulled the *salone* door closed behind her, locked it and pocketed the key. Downstairs, she hid the envelope in a kitchen drawer, and set off to look for Chrissa.

But the suitcase in the bedroom stayed in her mind; for why would the doctor, disappearing, leave most of what he owned behind him?